Tink's Neverland:
Cosmos' Gateway Book 1

By S.E. Smith

Acknowledgments

I would like to thank my husband Steve for believing in me and being proud enough of me to give me the courage to follow my dream. I would also like to give a special thank-you to my sister and best friend Linda, who not only encouraged me to write but who also read the manuscript.

—S.E. Smith

Montana Publishing
Science Fiction Romance
TINK'S NEVERLAND
Copyright © 2010 by Susan E. Smith
First E-Book Published December 2010
Cover Design by Melody Simmons

Summary: Tink connects with an alien man when she goes through a portal to another world.

ISBN: 978-1-942562-43-6 (paperback)
ISBN: 978-1-942562-07-8 (eBook)

Published in the United States by Montana Publishing.

{1. Science Fiction Romance – Fiction. 2. Science Fiction – Fiction. 3. Paranormal – Fiction. 4. Romance – Fiction.}

www.montanapublishinghouse.com

Synopsis

Jasmine "Tinker" Bell has always had a love for life, looking forward to any new adventure that happens to come along. When a friend's experiment creates a portal to another world, she finds herself swept into a faraway star system she thought only existed in the movies.

J'kar 'Tag Krell Manok had given up hope of ever finding his bond mate. He is surprised when a pint-size female unlike anything he has ever seen suddenly appears on his spaceship to save the life of his brother during an attack. When she is suddenly taken from him, he will do anything to get her back and claim her.

Two different worlds collide when Tink, a mechanic in a small college town, meets J'kar, a Prime warrior from a far-off galaxy. When Tink's life is in danger, only J'kar can save her. Now Tink has to decide if she is willing to give up everything she has ever known and loved to stay with the alien she has fallen in love with.

Will their worlds survive the collision or will they be torn apart?

Contents

Chapter 1

"Hey, Tink, you were great tonight," yelled one of the guys who had been trying to get Jasmine "Tinker" Bell's attention all night.

There was a full house tonight at the local brewery called Purple Haze, where they made and sold all types of homemade beers and specialty dishes. It was a well-known college hangout and a great place to get picked up if that was what you were looking for.

The two guys walking away had been the two most aggressive in trying to get Tink's attention. Tink made it a rule not to pick up anyone from the bar. She had bad enough luck with guys without having to add any other liabilities to her choices.

Tink raised her hand and gave an offhanded thanks before turning the opposite way. She and her band mates closed the brewery down tonight. At two o'clock in the morning, the only lights shining were the streetlights and occasional headlights from a car leaving the place, but she wasn't worried.

The small college town of Calais, Maine was one of the safest in the country. Even if it wasn't, anyone who had heard of Jasmine "Tinker" Bell knew better than to mess with the pint-size spitfire if they didn't want a wrench upside their head. At five feet, four inches and one hundred ten pounds of toned muscle, Tink was known for her sense of humor and easy personality.

But when riled, she could take down even the toughest of mechanics in the town thanks to her mom's determination that all her girls learn to defend themselves, even if it meant fighting dirty—which Tink had been known to do on occasion. Besides, if she wasn't able to do it, then one of her two sisters or eleven fellow mechanics around town would do the job, and there wouldn't be much left for the cops to pick up. Life was good as far as Tink was concerned, and she enjoyed it to the fullest.

Softly humming one of the songs she had played, she hung the guitar case over her shoulder and tightened the tool belt around her small waist. She'd promised her best friend, Cosmos, she would stop by the lab in the warehouse where they lived to look at a generator he needed her to work on. She'd picked up her tool belt from work to bring home with her earlier since she needed some of the special tools she had machined for the job. She loved working on some of the things Cosmos created, almost as much as she loved the big guy himself.

Cosmos might have been born with a silver spoon in his mouth, but it didn't show. Cosmos' parents made a mint off different patents they developed, and Cosmos was just like them. He'd had his doctorate by the time he was twenty-two and had bought the old warehouse near the river as a lab and house.

While many considered him a nerd, Cosmos didn't follow the typical description of one. He was six foot two with wide shoulders, long light-brown hair, and hazel eyes. The kind of eyes a girl could drown in—any girl except Tink, that was. She and Cosmos had developed a kinship more like siblings. So, when Tink's family passed through the town, she'd decided it was time to try out her wings and moved into the top floor of the warehouse while Cosmos took the first and second floors as his own.

Tink's family was as different as Cosmos', which was probably why they gravitated to each other. Tink grew up traveling the country in a forty-foot motor home. Her parents, Angus and Tilly Bell, were the best parents any girl could have, and they had three children all living, learning, and growing in a mobile home with ten wheels that took them all over the country.

Tink's father, Angus, was a well-known science fiction writer. He was one of the few authors who was not only very talented, but also very prolific and profitable. They could have lived on his income alone. He often stated his ideas came from his family and all the mischief they got into.

Her mom, a petite spitfire like her three daughters, was hell on wheels—literally. An accomplished mechanic who grew up working in her grandfather's garage in a small town in Oklahoma, she loved to tinker on any type of engine. She was constantly upgrading the RV to greater power. She was also a computer geek who loved to design and develop software that engineering firms around the world used in developing power for all types of buildings. This skill provided a comfortable living, and she shared all her wonderful knowledge and skills with her daughters.

While all the traveling was great, when the family had pulled into the local campground for the summer when Tink was eighteen, Tink knew she was ready to stop moving. Tink met a group of boys camping nearby and fell in love with the quiet one out of the bunch, in a totally platonic way. The awkward boy had been Cosmos, and they had become best pals. When her parents determined it was time to head to the next great adventure, Tink decided to stay.

Her parents were sad to see their youngest and last child make the decision but were totally supportive. So monthly phone calls became Tink's connection to a family that lived all over the country. Life was great then, and it still was four years later. At twenty-two, Tink couldn't think how life could get any better. She had a great job at the local garage that did customized work, worked part-time for the college on all their miscellaneous equipment, helped Cosmos with the equipment he used for his experiments, and played with a small group of musicians a couple times a month at the brewery. Yep, life was great.

Turning right down Main Street and heading east two blocks, the river came into view. *Over the small two-lane bridge and I'll be home,* she thought with a contented sigh.

The warehouse was dark except for a couple of soft lights shining out over the dark water from the first and third floors. Walking over the bridge, Tink stopped to listen to the soft sounds of the water flowing under it. She loved the sounds and smells of the town.

Sighing, she turned and headed over the bridge, thinking about the generator Cosmos wanted her to work on. Even if she didn't know what half the stuff Cosmos talked about was or what he was working on, she did know the equipment and how it worked, and loved doing it.

She already had an idea of how to get more amps out of the generator and wanted to see if it would work. She didn't know why Cosmos needed so much power. She would hate to have to pay the electric bill each month.

Cosmos insisted her electric was included as part of her monthly rent, when he let her pay it. She protested, but Cosmos stated it was too much hassle to try to determine the little she used from the large amount that he did. So, in exchange for her help with the equipment and the little she occasionally was able to slip to him, she had a huge living space at almost no cost.

Stepping up to the softly lit entrance, Tink punched the code into the electronic locking system on the heavy metal door. Tink installed it after Cosmos kept losing the keys to the door and locking himself out. The locking mechanism made a clicking noise, and the lock slid quietly open.

Pushing the door open, Tink closed the door and reset the lock. While Calais might be one of the safest cities in the country, Tink wasn't a fool and didn't take unnecessary risks.

"Better safe than sorry" was one of her parents' favorite sayings. "Think of all possibilities before making a decision" was another saying, but Tink didn't always follow that one, and it sometimes got her into trouble. Like the date she went on last week with the "Professor" from the engineering department at the college.

All he wanted was a quick tip in bed and a chance to see what Cosmos was up to. She figured that out about thirty minutes into the date when he kept trying to get her out of the restaurant and his hands down her pants. Forty-five minutes after the date had started, Tink was nursing bruised knuckles on her right hand where she punched the jerk after he didn't listen to the word "stop" for the third time when he grabbed her ass. Enough was enough, and she didn't appreciate getting groped in public by some pompous ass.

The lights came on automatically as she moved through the hallway leading to the lab, shaking Tink out of her musings of that disastrous date. Placing her hand on the palm-print scanner, Tink waited for the scan to finish and for the outer door to the lab to open. Moving to the second security scanner she sang the first verse of "Twinkle, Twinkle Little Star."

The voice-recognition program called out a greeting in a soft husky voice that sounded a lot like Tink's mom, Tilly. "Welcome, Tinker Bell. I hope you had a nice night. Cosmos wanted me to give you a message. He had to fly out to Chicago to see his parents and will be gone for a couple of weeks. He hopes this doesn't cause you any problems. He left his charge card if you need to get any parts or need anything. He can be reached at the following number." Tink sighed again. She missed the big guy when he was gone. Oh, well. It would be her and RITA for a lonely couple of weeks.

"Thanks, RITA."

RITA—Tink's mom's latest software program that Tink had modified—was an acronym for Really Intelligent Technical Assistant. Tink used her mom's voice simply because it made her feel like she had family with her whenever she was at home.

RITA used an artificial intelligence program that Tink's mom, Tilly, developed a couple of years ago to help with some engineering project for the government. Tink copied the basic program last year when she was visiting and was developing it during her spare time. RITA was now a very advanced and sophisticated program that learned and developed every day. She had become a substitute mother to Tink, often giving her advice, like "Do you really think you should go out with that professor?" or "You really should eat better."

"How was your gig tonight, dear?" RITA asked. Her voice came through the audio system that was wired throughout the warehouse, which the software could access at will.

"It was awesome! Oh, RITA, I wish you could have heard it. Doug played better than he ever had on the drums, and Mike was smoking on the piano. Gloria didn't show, so I didn't have to risk her being pissed that I was playing the bass tonight."

Tink spun around in a circle, her rainbow-colored high-top sneakers squeaking as she turned on the waxed concrete flooring. Her baby blue below-the-knee skirt swirled out around her like one of the dancing tulips from a movie, showing off her long legs encased in a pair of calf-length dark blue spandex tights. Her white peasant top slipped a little farther down one shoulder as she danced across the floor singing one of the sultry pop songs that were currently all the rage.

She slid the guitar strap from her shoulder and held held the instrument in front of her like she was dancing with a man, her tool belt making soft, metallic clicks and clacks as she moved. As she danced around the room, her soft, short curls of golden-brown hair bobbed up and down with the motion. Tink's hair and eyes were just two of her wonderful features that often gave her the appearance of a pixie or fairy.

Her wavy hair was light and flirty, matching her personality. It was the color of fall leaves with natural highlights of gold and amber. Her almond-shaped eyes were the color of melted dark chocolate, so dark, it felt like a person could drown in the depths.

Her figure showed her love of dancing and hard work. She moved with a natural grace she'd inherited from her mother, with long legs, long waist, and high firm breasts that were on the slightly plump side, making them seem a little large for her small frame. This used to be a problem until Tink learned to take advantage of her larger assets. Another wonderful lesson from her parents—"If you've got it, flaunt it, then knock the shit out of the problem."

Yep, her parents were wise and wonderful people. She did just that when Mister Professor grabbed her that last time. He hadn't known what hit him until it was too late because he had been looking at her breasts instead of her fists.

"That's wonderful, dear. You know, I could short-circuit Gloria's car the next time she takes it in for repair or hack into her computer and put a nice little virus in it," RITA said with a hint of amusement.

"Thanks, RITA, but I don't think that's necessary...at least, not yet. If she keeps giving me a hard time I'll let you have a go at her," Tink replied with a slight laugh and a mischievous lift to her lips.

"Did you get a chance to run the configuration I sent to you this morning on the changes I wanted to make to the generator to get more amps out of it?" Tink asked as she walked over to the steps leading down to the lower section of the lab.

The lab took up most of the lower section of the warehouse and housed a split-level with the upper half for computers and the lower for the generators and power sources. The top level was filled with computer equipment and some type of console that controlled Cosmos' latest experiment.

Tink ignored the console as she walked by, more interested in the lower level. The lower half was where the generator and electrical cabinets were located. Those were her babies. It also contained a strange metal framing that looked almost like a huge doorway. There were cables from the electrical panels and generator attached to metal cabinets that contained the necessary circuit breakers in case of a problem.

"Of course, dear. I sent some additional changes I made to your iPad. You should be able to pull it up. The changes you made were brilliant, and you should be able to pull an additional 11.52368 amps from the generator."

"Cool!" Tink said as she skipped down the metal steps.

Leaning her guitar and oversize purse against the bottom step, Tink ran her hand through her hair and adjusted her tool belt. Moving over to the large generator located under the upper platform, Tink pulled out the tools she was going to need to open that bad boy up, and started to work. Luckily, tomorrow was Sunday, so it didn't matter that it was going to be a long night. She could sleep in, and she was off Monday for the holiday weekend. Humming softly, she slowly slid under the generator to pull open the panel she needed to get into first.

She spent the next three hours working on the different modifications she had drawn out on the schematic. Finishing up the last modifications, she slid the panel back into place and tightened the screws down. Making sure she had all of her tools put back into her tool belt, she rose stiffly off the floor.

"Ugh, I think I'm getting too old for this!" Tink muttered under her breath as she slowly stretched out her tired muscles. "RITA, can you fire up Cosmos' new program, and let's test the generator out to see if I got everything?"

"Sure thing, dear. You sound beat. Do you want to wait until later?" RITA commented, even as she started the programming that would fire up the console.

RITA knew Tink enough to know she wouldn't stop until she confirmed that the changes she'd made worked. If they didn't test it now, Tink would go upstairs and worry that she should have changed this or done that.

Laughing, Tink let out a tired breath. "You know me better than that. Let me know when you get a power reading."

Tink walked over to the metal stairs slowly, twisting this way and that to relieve her aching muscles from all the sitting, bending, and awkward leaning over she had done for over three hours. Glancing at her watch, she noticed it was almost five thirty in the morning.

Well, no coffee for me this morning if I plan on sleeping the day away, she thought tiredly.

As she moved past one of the panels on the wall next to the stairs Tink noticed some strange lanyards hanging next to it. Moving closer, she picked one up, turning it over and over in her palm. She glanced up again. There were four of them with small cylinder devices hanging from them. They were absolutely beautiful! The cylinders had carvings on them that matched the carving Cosmos put on the metal frame of the "doorway" thing. Tink could tell they were some type of electronic device. Tink placed the lanyard in the pocket of her skirt. She wanted to take a closer look at it when she wasn't so tired. She would have plenty of time to replace it before Cosmos came back.

Bending over, Tink picked up her guitar and her oversize purse. Sliding the purse over one shoulder so it draped across her and sliding the guitar case strap over the other, Tink moved to climb the stairs leading to the upper floor and her long-awaited bed.

Chapter 2

Tink was just putting her foot on the first step when out of the corner of her eye, she noticed a strange light emitted from the metal "doorway." The entire thing seemed to shimmer, and then it cleared up, opening to another room. The room was a soft gray with low lights emanating from the floor and ceiling. Tink blinked a couple of times, thinking she was hallucinating from being overtired.

What the...? She thought as she shook her head again to try to clear her eyesight.

No matter how much she shook her head or rubbed her eyes, the room was still there. Hesitating, she slowly put her foot back down onto the concrete floor of the lab. Turning, she walked toward the metal "doorway." Glancing up, she looked at the metal surrounding the door, noticing there were a series of lights running faster and faster around it.

Shaking her head from the dizziness of watching the lights going around, she gently stretched her hand out to touch what should have been solid concrete where the wall of the lab should have been. She felt a slight tingling as her hand passed through the doorway but nothing that felt dangerous or disturbing. Tink pulled her hand back and glanced up toward where the console was with a frown.

"RITA, what do you make of this?" Tink asked in a slightly husky voice.

"I'm not sure, dear, but I don't think it would hurt you. Why don't you take a look and see what it is!" RITA replied, sounding almost eager.

Take a look? Was RITA nuts? Could a computer be nuts? Was Tink going nuts? Hooray, now all she was doing was thinking about nuts!

"What do the readings say?" Tink asked curiously.

"You were able to pull over 12.8695 amps out of the generator! What a wonderful increase, dear. It seems to be just what Cosmos needed to get his project running," RITA said, sounding excited.

"Well, maybe you should power it down now that we know it worked. I'm not sure what Cosmos is doing, but if he can create a room that wasn't there before, maybe I don't want to mess with it," Tink said, starting to turn around.

Tink hadn't taken more than a step when she heard something coming from the other side of the "doorway."

"What was that? RITA, did you pick up anything?" Turning back toward the doorway, Tink looked closer.

A tall, dark-haired man was fighting with… Tink shook her head again. A… *What the hell is that?* Tink moved closer as the man raised his sword. Holy crap, the guy had a huge sword! The man looked like he was fighting a big iguana! The other creature was hissing, its tongue moving in and out as it swung what looked like a double-edged sword toward the tall, dark-haired man. The dark-haired man moved backward trying to stay out of the iguana dude's reach. He was holding his right arm close to his body like he was hurt, and he was dragging his left leg.

Tink glanced down at it as he moved by and saw blood flowing from a deep gash that had to hurt like hell. As he moved by, Tink saw the dark-haired man's face for the first time. The man's features caused Tink to gasp. He looked more like a kid! Not more than sixteen or seventeen! The iguana dude raised his double-edged sword over his head and struck a particularly brutal blow on the sword arm of the dark-haired boy. The power of the blow caused the boy to fall backward where he lay sprawled on the floor of the hallway. The iguana dude roared with triumph and raised his sword over his head in order to deal a death blow.

* * *

Derik knew his time had come. He knew death would come quickly now. When their ship was attacked, he gripped his battle-sword, ready to defend his shipmates and his brothers. A feeling of regret surged through him as he thought of his parents' and brothers' reaction to his death.

He was only seventeen planet cycles old and had begged and pestered his father and older brothers to let him join them on this trade mission to a nearby star system. Everything was fine until they'd received a distress call from a starship two clicks ago. They were the closest ship and offered to help. The signals coming from the ship identified it as a class-five passenger starship on on course to Caldara Four to drop off its passengers. The distress signal also identified multiple system failures, including environmental.

Responding to the distress signal, they encountered the Juangans instead. The Juangans had obviously hijacked the starship. They used it as a decoy in an effort to get unsuspecting ships to come to its rescue. They were a fierce species that preyed on anything that moved and were known for their brutal treatment not only of each other, but of any species they encountered. They were not picky about who or what they ate. They were known to even sacrifice members of their own crew to fulfill their grisly appetites.

Derik was a member of the Prime, a proud warrior people who lived in a galaxy that had several habitable planets. There were three planets in the Prime system that supplied a wide variety of materials the Prime used for trading with other nearby galaxies, though only one was fully inhabited. Baade was the home world of the Prime.

Two smaller planets, Lacertae and Carafe, had only small, isolated cargo ports, mining facilities, and military sites. Their most important resource was the crystals that helped to power their world and their ships. Mined on the smallest of the three planets, Carafe, the crystals were heavily protected. Their ship on this trip had not contained a cargo of the crystal, but of fruits and other natural products the nearby galaxy of Grus used for their space stations and planetary needs.

While this ship was a military warship, they used it sometimes to transport products to nearby galaxies as a cover to gather and observe data on the neighboring inhabitants. They had already dropped the shipment off and were returning with a variety of materials that could not be found on their home planet.

One of the things they would have liked to have found were females from the other galaxy that were a match for their men. Women on their home planet were held in very high regard. Unfortunately, there were not very many women available. Most of the women on Prime were already spoken for through the mating rites which were performed as soon as the female came of age. The problem was the birth rate of females remained low, making it difficult for the unmated males to find mates.

Prime males were matched to their mates though a mating rite ceremony, and if no match was made, life for the unattached males meant a solitary existence. The mating rites were a chemical reaction that occurred when a Prime male had a physical and emotional chemical reaction bonding them to a female. The males become overwhelmed with feelings of possessiveness, protectiveness, and sexual desire. A mating mark, a series of intricate circles denoting the unbreakable bond between mates, appeared on the palm of the male and the matching female when they come into contact with each other. Each mark was as individualized as the bonded pair. It would not appear until the male and female reached the age of mating.

Due to the decline in the birthrate of females, fewer and fewer males were finding mates. This decline had reached an almost critical level. The Prime males were desperately looking for an alternative solution.

One of the main reasons for the trips to other galaxies was the hope of finding a compatible species that could procreate with the Prime males. A mating rite had never been done outside their species before, even though some of their males had tried to bond with other species from nearby galaxies. All had failed. Procreation was impossible without the mating rite and with the fact the species found so far were either incompatible or downright unappealing to the males. It was hard to get turned on to a green, scaly creature with six arms and four legs, or one who had more hair on her body than a Prime Tookey, a long-haired, long-limbed creature found in the thick forest of the mountainous region of Prime.

I'll never have the chance to find my bond mate, Derik thought, disheartened as he stared into the cold, dead eyes of the Juangan standing over him.

He stared defiantly at the Juangan, determined to end his life with honor. The Juangan took one step toward Derik, then suddenly stopped. Its mouth opened slowly, and a green slime slowly trickled down its chin. It slowly dropped to its knees before pitching face-first toward Derik. Derik scooted back, looking down at the dead Juangan with wonder before glancing up to see which of his fellow warriors came to his rescue.

"*Ja tasn meszk talkock,*" he muttered. "I must be dreaming."

Derik stared at the vision in front of him. It was a goddess! It could only be that as he had never in his life seen anything so beautiful. Behind the vision, a shimmering wall of color swirled in the narrow corridor. The vision of the goddess before him appeared out of it. Light danced around her, and she looked like she was—furious. All he could do was look at the tiny figure standing before him. She truly was the most beautiful creature he had ever seen, and she had just saved his life!

Chapter 3

Tink didn't know what else to do. When she saw the boy fall and the iguana intent on cutting him in half, she moved without thinking. Grabbing her hammer out of her tool belt, she stepped through the doorway and up behind the iguana dude when he moved by the opening of the doorway.

When he raised his sword, she knew she couldn't let the boy die, so she did what any self-respecting girl would do in the same situation, she popped Iguana Dude in the back of the head with her hammer. She had no idea his head would crack like a walnut, spilling green goop all down his back.

"Gross!" Tink cried out, lowering her hammer coated in the green slime and bent over to wipe it clean on the back of the creature's clothing.

Glancing at the boy on the floor, Tink gingerly stepped over the dead iguana dude's body so she could see how badly he was hurt. From the amount of blood, it looked pretty bad. Tink slowly put her hammer in her tool belt and shrugged the straps of the guitar and her oversize purse off her shoulders. She set them down next to the wall and held out her hands, palms up. The last thing she wanted to do was frighten the poor kid and have him attack her.

"It's okay. I'm not going to hurt you." Tink spoke softly. "I just want to see if we can stop some of that bleeding." Tink smiled a reassuring smile and took another hesitant step toward the boy.

Derik looked at the beautiful creature moving toward him. He couldn't understand what she was saying, but could tell she was trying to reassure him.

I must have died and gone to the world of the gods and goddesses. That's what happened, he thought to himself.

He didn't think the next plane of life would have hurt the way he did, but it was the only explanation. How else could a goddess appear suddenly to save his life?

Derik watched as she pulled her smaller bag toward her. She seemed to be looking for something in it. When she found what she was looking for, she turned to him with a triumphant smile. Derik caught his breath at how her face became even more beautiful as she smiled. She was saying something, but he didn't understand what it was. He only knew she could do whatever she wanted with him. He was happy just looking at her.

Tink pulled her oversize purse toward her. She always carried a small first-aid kit with her. When you were a mechanic and worked on machinery, you were always getting cuts and scrapes. She pulled the small plastic case containing bandages and antibiotic creams out with a triumphant smile.

"And the guys say I'm paranoid!" She muttered under her breath.

Turning toward the boy, who continued to stare at her like he had never seen a woman before, Tink smiled softly and tried to explain what she was doing. *He really is adorable,* Tink thought as she watched his eyes following her every movement.

"I'm going to see if I can stop some of this bleeding. It might hurt a little while I'm doing this, but everything will be okay once we get you patched up enough to get to a hospital. Although I don't have a clue how I'm going to explain Mr. Iguana Dude to the police." Tink pulled on a pair of blue latex-free gloves and pulled out the butterfly bandages, gauze, larger bandages, and antibiotic cream.

"Let's look at your leg first," Tink said softly as she scooted forward on her knees until she was next to Derik's leg.

Pulling out her razor knife, she cut his pant leg from the knee to the top of his thigh. Tink drew in a sharp breath when she saw how deep the wound was. It had to be at least four inches long and half an inch deep.

Taking a clean piece of gauze, she cleaned the wound as best she could and slowly pulled the edges together, running a small amount of antibiotic cream along the cut, then using most of her butterfly bandages to hold it together. Once she was done with that, she pulled out some gauze patches and laid them carefully over the wound and followed it up by taking a roll of gauze and winding it around the boy's leg, slowly reaching up and under to make sure it held the butterfly bandages in place.

Tink glanced up a couple of times to make sure she wasn't hurting the dark-haired boy too much. She smiled gently at him as she continued to work on patching up his leg. He really was adorable with his dark hair falling down over his forehead and his silver — silver? — eyes gazing at her with a look of pure adoration. He reminded her of a lost puppy looking at someone who had decided to take him home.

"Okay, your leg is done as best I can fix it right here and now. Let me take a look at your arm. You know, you really shouldn't have pissed off someone bigger than you without someone to cover your back," Tink said in a teasing voice, trying to distract the boy. His staring was beginning to make her feel self-conscious.

Pointing to his arm, Tink smiled gently again. "I need to take a look at your arm," she said.

Derik looked down at his arm. Realizing she was pointing to it, he held it out for her to mend. He watched as she pulled a sharp knife from her strange-looking belt and cut his shirtsleeve from his elbow to his shoulder.

She smiled again at him and reached for the same type of materials that she used for his leg. He realized his leg didn't hurt as much as it had. The beautiful goddess smiled at him again as she began cleaning and bandaging his arm. When she was done, she leaned over, pushing a tuft of hair from his forehead with a gentle hand. Derik's breath caught in his throat as he felt her lay her palm against his cheek.

"All done. I think we should try to get you out of here in case any more of those things come looking for their friend," Tink said as she nodded her head toward the dead Juangan.

She quickly cleaned up all the leftover first-aid materials, packing them back into the case and putting it back in her purse. Sliding her purse over her shoulder so it crossed over the front of her, Tink moved over to the boy's unhurt side. Bending her knees, she leaned over and helped him stand slowly. He wobbled a little, but then straightened up.

Grabbing her guitar with her other hand, she wrapped her arm around his waist, and they slowly began a shuffling walk down the corridor with Derik's arm around Tink's shoulder on one side and holding onto his sword and the wall with the other.

In all the confusion of what had happened, Tink didn't even realize the "doorway" that brought her to this strange hallway was no longer there. Tink stopped at the spot she came through earlier. Blinking rapidly, she looked around, glancing back and forth as much as she could while trapped under the weight of the boy's arm.

She studied both sides of the corridor for a good ten feet on either side. There was no opening! She couldn't see Cosmos' lab or even a glimmer of the doorway she came through.

Beginning to feel a sense of panic, Tink took a deep breath. The boy holding onto her said something and pointed toward the end of the corridor. Tink didn't understand a word of what he said, but figured he knew where she needed to take him. She would come back after she got him some help and find the doorway. Nodding to the boy to show she understood what he was trying to tell her, Tink took one last look before moving toward what looked to be a door.

Chapter 4

Derik glanced down at the woman holding him around his waist. He noticed she seemed to be looking for something as she kept glancing around the corridor as they walked down it. She had a funny expression on her face as they walked toward the elevator. He knew his brothers had defeated the remaining Juangans who boarded the warship. He was listening carefully to the communicator he had in his ear to see what was going on.

It was a relief as J'kar, his older brother and commander of the warship, had ordered them not to use the communicators during the battle for fear the Juangans might use it against them. They hadn't had much contact with that species and didn't know what level their technology development was. Their current files on the Juangans just documented how dangerous and deadly they were.

J'kar was giving the all clear to use the communicators again. Derik wanted to head to the bridge to see what damage was done to the warship. He wanted to know how many brave warriors were hurt or killed during the battle.

"J'kar," Derik said into the communicator. "What is your location?"

Listening to the response, Derik looked down at the woman who stopped to look up at him, and nodded toward the end of the corridor.

"*Takq waga*," he said, nodding his head again toward the door at the end of the corridor. "This way."

Moving slowly toward the door, Tink held tight onto the boy's waist so he wouldn't fall. She knew his leg had to be killing him. She had seen enough cuts to know this one had to hurt like hell.

She glanced up in surprise when the door opened automatically to reveal a type of elevator. Walking through the opened door Tink glanced one last time down the corridor, hoping against hope to see a glimmer of a doorway to Cosmos' lab. Where had it taken her? Would she be able to get back? Holy hell, she couldn't wait to tell Cosmos, her parents, and her sisters about this place!

Tink took a deep breath and released it, letting the questions melt away as the doors closed soundlessly before her. There would be time to answer them after she got the kid to a real doctor. As the elevator moved, Tink gripped the dark-haired boy a little tighter to prevent the motion from causing him to lose his balance as he swayed.

She knew he had lost a lot of blood, and the last thing she wanted was for him to fall down unconscious and go into shock. No, all she wanted to do was find someone or somewhere to lay him down so he could get the rest and medical care he needed, and she could do a little exploring, then find her way home.

Yep, that sounds like a great plan, she thought to herself.

The elevator lights flickered as it passed each level, finally slowing to a stop. The doors opened to another long corridor. Only this corridor wasn't deserted. There were two huge black-haired men standing in the corridor which opened to another room at the end.

Tink stood frozen, totally forgetting the boy next to her or the men in the corridor. In front of her the corridor opened into another room that looked like one of Cosmos' control centers or something out of *Star Trek*. She could see a variety of lights flashing and more men in that room. Even that didn't seem to have much of an impact. No, what caught and held Tink's attention was what was at the very front of the room. A huge A huge clear window looked out into deep space. Tink could feel her mouth dropping open as she moved slowly forward down the corridor toward the window that seemed to look into the very heavens themselves.

* * *

J'kar looked over a screen showing damage reports from around the ship. He was furious that the Juangans not only had the nerve to attack one of their warships but that they had the nerve to attack *his* warship. He barked out orders to a young warrior, who immediately turned and left.

"J'kar," another tall warrior called out quietly as he came to stand next to him. "Have you heard from Derik?"

His quiet voice did not reflect the worry he felt. He knew his younger brother had gotten separated from the group of warriors he was fighting with, and he had most likely not survived the fighting. He felt the weight of guilt upon his shoulders.

His younger brother was not experienced in battle, and Borj had been the one to assure his parents he would watch over him on this voyage. They'd lost four warriors during the siege, and he feared his little brother would be the fifth.

"Yes, Borj," J'kar said as he turned to his brother who was two planet cycles younger than his own thirty. "He checked in a few minutes ago and said he would be here shortly."

Borj let out a silent sigh of relief as he looked at his older brother. He could tell by his stance that his brother was furious with not only the Juangans but with himself for having walked into the trap they set. J'kar was tall even by Prime standards, a full three inches taller than himself. At six feet six, he towered over most of the warriors. He had wide, muscular shoulders developed from years of training. His black hair was cut short, and his dark silver eyes flashed, reflecting his current rage. Dressed in all black from his form-fitting shirt to his black boots, he made an impressive obstacle not even the Juangans could ignore.

For the past five hundred planet cycles, the 'Tag Krell Manok had ruled the Prime galaxy, bringing technology and prosperity to its people. No one would dare to challenge their rule… at least no one who wanted to live. The one thing they hadn't been able to do, though, was bring more females to the population. Now, things were getting critical.

"You should get that cut on your arm looked at," Borj said, knowing full well his brother wouldn't until everything was back to normal as much as it could be.

"It can wait," J'kar replied impatiently. "Have you sent the security team to make sure all Juangans have been killed? I also want to make sure a team has been sent to the other ship. It is ours now."

"Lan has his security doing a thorough search of the ship. He has also dispatched a team which has already taken control of the other starship. The Juangans had been overconfident and left only two behind to maintain it. They are dead," Borj said in a calm voice.

Out of the four brothers, he was known for his ability to never be ruffled. His calm, quiet manner was in direct contrast to his older brother's assertive directness and his youngest brother's eager, cheerful personality. His third brother, Mak, was a combination of himself and his older brother. He was currently commanding one of their other warships in search of women from yet another galaxy they had only briefly traded with over the past two planet cycles.

Borj inhaled a deep breath when he saw two men helping his bloodied, white-faced younger brother onto the bridge. Borj and J'kar started forward moving quickly toward the group, concern etched on their faces. J'kar muttered into the communicator for the healer to meet them on the bridge as he took in the bloodied bandages on Derik's leg and arm and his pale complexion.

Chapter 5

Tink hadn't known what to expect when the doors of the elevator opened, but it sure never entered her mind she would find herself in outer space! As she stepped out of the elevator, the men in the corridor rushed forward. At first, Tink thought she was going to be roadkill from the looks on their faces, but the boy said something that changed their expression from murder to curiosity.

The two men instead came forward to help him, casting wondering looks at Tink. Tink was glad. Her shoulder was killing her from helping take as much weight as she could, and the boy was fading fast. She didn't think she would have been able to go much farther!

The two men took the boy, wrapping their arms under his. They carefully lifted him off the floor and moved in quick, sure steps toward the room at the end of the corridor. This left Tink with no option but to follow.

Besides, she shrugged, she wanted a closer look at what the window up front contained because she decided she was either in some weird sci-fi adventure, dead, unconscious, on a movie set, or totally out of her frigging mind! Whatever the answer was, she wanted to enjoy it as long as she could, so when she either returned home, met her family in the afterlife, woke up, or saw it on the big screen, she could tell everyone back home about it. Life was full of adventures, according to her parents, and she was never one to turn away from the wild rides it sometimes offered.

Tink followed the men into the room. She stopped and gazed in total amazement as she entered, her eyes widening as she took in everything. The room was circular and was maybe thirty feet in diameter. Each side of the circular room had computer panels with all types of lights and monitors on them before stopping about five feet away from the huge front view-screen showing the darkness of space. On the left side, about halfway down the curved wall, there was a door that led to another room, from the looks of it. Two steps in the front led down to a center console area with a chair positioned in the center of the room by itself.

"Well, wake me up, Captain Kirk! I think Scotty's transported me to the Enterprise!" Tink whispered under her breath as a huge smile started to curve her lips.

"Hot damn!" Tink said loud enough to be heard by everyone in the room. Grinning, she moved down the steps and toward the front view-screen. Before she got halfway to the front, another tall, dark-haired man stepped in front of her.

What on earth did they do, clone the guys and give them steroids? Tink thought to herself before ducking under his outstretched arm and doing a graceful twist around the center chair, leaving the man grabbing empty space.

Tink was an expert at flag football and learned quickly how to avoid getting caught. That was a necessity of life when you were as tiny as she was and played with a bunch of Neanderthals, better known as mechanics. Tink was determined to look out the window, to see if it was real or not. *No clone-man is going to stop me either,* she thought with determination as she headed for the huge front panel.

* * *

J'kar caught his breath when he saw the vision following his younger brother onto the bridge. He hadn't seen the female at first. She was hidden behind his brother and the two men helping him. When the men moved aside to seat his brother in a nearby chair, she stood there, a vision of pure beauty. Speechless, all he could do was grunt into the communicator in response to the reply from medical saying the healer was on his way.

J'kar was barely aware of his brother Borj's response to her. He vaguely heard his breath catch and noticed him stiffen beside him. Others in the room began to notice as well.

Each of the men in the room, six not counting him and his brother, turned to watch as the vision in white and blue stood looking around at all of them. He watched as her eyes widened and a beautiful smile lit up her face. J'kar could have sworn his heart stuttered before beating out a fast *thump thump*.

He ran his eyes over her. She was so tiny compared to the women of his world! He watched as she turned her head from side to side, taking in everything in the room, then returning to the front to look out the front view-screen. He turned to see what she was looking at, but all he saw was the darkness of space that was always there.

"What... who...?" stuttered the normally calm Borj.

Borj cleared his throat and tried again. "J'kar, who is that? Where did she come from?" He followed her with his eyes as she slowly moved down the steps leading to the center of the room.

"I don't know, but I intend to find out," J'kar said roughly.

He couldn't have taken his eyes off the vision if he'd wanted to. He watched her as she slowly moved down the steps. There was a soft sway to her hips as she moved almost like water flowing.

As she moved, he noticed the highlights in her hair as the lights captured the hints of gold and amber. When she tilted her head slightly to the right, then to the left, he sucked in a breath, noticing the curve of her jawline and how her hair seemed to dance around her face. The smile on her face seemed to keep growing, showing off small white teeth and pouty full lips.

She was different in her build and coloring than Prime females, who were much taller and darker. While she was small in stature, she moved with a natural grace that caused him to suddenly become very aroused. Her color was much lighter than Primes. Her skin had a soft, pale peach color compared to their darker tan. Her eyes were so dark he felt like he could drown in them. He had seen dark eyes on other species they encountered before, but nothing that was so warm and seemed to glow with an internal light.

As his eyes continued downward, he could feel his body reacting to her even from a distance. He scanned her face and body, from her small nose and perky little mouth with plump, rose-colored lips to her full breasts, small waist, and slim hips. Never before had he felt this type of reaction, even with the women who were trained to please the men on their planet.

He had not felt for any women of their race before what he was feeling right now for this creature. He was always able to control his sexual reactions to females before, and this reaction to one he had not even been close to took him by surprise. He felt confused, off-balance.

His gaze moved over her white top that slid alluringly down one shoulder, showing a small expanse of creamy peach-colored skin. He wanted to slide it further down and run his lips along her shoulder where it was exposed. He could almost taste how sweet her skin would be.

Her slim hips were covered in a flowing, blue material that seemed to float around her as she walked across the floor. Wrapped snugly around her slim waist was what appeared to be a tool belt of some type. While puzzling, he couldn't stop as his eyes finally traveled farther down, widening when he noticed her feet.

He had never seen such covering before. Her feet were encased in a multicolored fabric that reached up to her delicate ankles. She looked so fragile, he was afraid if he touched her, she would either break or disappear. It didn't matter, all he knew was he had to touch her, taste her. He had to have her. He had never felt this feeling of possessiveness in his life. He was compelled to see if she was real, and make her his.

Moving forward to intercept the female as she moved across the center of the room, J'kar reached out and gripped—empty air! The female moved so quickly it caught him by surprise. J'kar frowned.

She didn't even appear to have been looking at him. When he reached out, she ducked and twisted with such speed and agility, he was left gripping empty air. J'kar let his hand fall to his side and muttered a dark curse as he turned to watch the female move out of his reach.

He watched as she twirled around the console, putting it between them, and continued moving toward the front view-screen. He frowned, watching in puzzled silence as she reached out tentatively and touched it. Then, she leaned over the front railing to look up, down, and side to side.

He couldn't help but wonder what she was looking for. In the back of his mind, he wondered why he wasn't more concerned as she could be looking for a ship poised to attack them. At the moment, he vaguely wondered if he would even notice if someone or something did. He was so focused on the vision in front of him that for once in his life, he was oblivious to everything else.

* * *

Tink was distantly aware of the silence that fell over the room, but she ignored it. Her focus was entirely on the front view-screen. Oh, she knew how many men were in the room: eleven, counting the boy and the two men who came in with her. She was aware they were all watching her, but now was not the time to become self-conscious. She would worry about being the only female in the room after her curiosity was satisfied.

Sucking in her breath as she glanced at the man trying to grab her, Tink couldn't resist thinking he was the hottest thing she'd ever seen. God, talk about died and gone to heaven! Her sisters would be having a shit fit if they could see him. He was the classic prince charming—tall, dark, and handsome!

With her luck, he would be all that until he opened his mouth and inserted his big foot! Or, he would prefer guys to gals. She had rotten luck when it came to men! She decided to cut her losses after the last disaster with "Mr. Professor" and just be friends with all the guys she knew, met, or fantasized about. There were some things in life she decided weren't worth the adventure, and heartache was one of them. Although, glancing at the huge hunk next to her, she debated on cheating on her plans. Tink sighed in self-reproach.

I never did have very good self-discipline, she thought to herself.

He was well over six feet, even taller than Cosmos! He had hair the color of the deep space she saw when she first looked out the front view-screen. His strong, square jaw made her want to run her fingers over it as she guided his luscious lips down to hers.

Could guys have luscious lips? She wondered absently.

He also had the cutest nose. It was strong and almost straight, containing a small bump on it like it had been broken once before. Shrugging her shoulders, Tink decided it was her dream adventure, and the guys could have anything she wanted them to have. If she wanted luscious lips and sexy jawlines she could have it.

His broad shoulders were almost as wide as her arms spread wide open. She could get lost in those arms! If the rest of him looked as good as what she could see through his dark, form-fitting clothing, she knew she was going to be in big trouble. *Scratch that!* He was going to be in big trouble! That was… as long as he, one: wasn't already taken, two: didn't prefer males only, three: wasn't a momma's boy, or four: all the things she hated about all the pricks she had dated before, which was a list too long to think about at this time.

Oh, yeah. If he doesn't fall into any of the above categories, he's going to be in big *trouble,* Tink decided with a sigh of delight.

Chapter 6

"This is so totally wicked!" Tink exclaimed excitedly as she moved to the railing running under the giant view-screen.

As far as she could see, there was nothing but the darkness of space. She leaned over, raising one leg up in the air behind her to help give her more balance, unaware it showed off more of her long legs, and looked to the left side.

"Oh!" She exclaimed. Tink turned around and looked at the dark-haired man who'd tried to grab her on her way to the front view-screen and who now stood slightly behind her watching every move she made. "There's a spaceship!" she said in awe, looking up into his dark silver eyes. "Do you see that?" Tink whispered in excitement as she grabbed his hand without thinking and pointed out the front window.

"Oh. My. God! My dad is going to have a shit fit when I tell him about this!" Tink said excitedly as she squeezed the hand she was holding and put her other hand on the view screen.

"It is so beautiful!" she said in a whispered voice.

Realizing she was leaving a perfect palm print on the glass-like material in front of her, she muttered softly, "This is just so cool. I can't believe this is real."

Tink glanced down and turned a little pink when she realized she was still holding the dark-haired man's hand. She made to let go, but he tightened his grip on her hand, refusing to release it. Tink blinked up at him in surprise. What she saw made her catch her breath.

He looked like he had no plans to let her hand—or the rest of her—go anywhere! It was a look of pure possession, one she had never encountered before. Tink stared into his dark silver eyes, giving him a small questioning smile before tugging her hand again until it was free. Turning back to the view-screen, she looked out the window and watched as a small shuttle moved slowly out from under the ship she was on to the one off the left side.

"Wow!" Tink couldn't believe how beautiful it was.

She continued watching the shuttle grow smaller as it approached the other starship. Fumbling with the guitar strap on her shoulder, she lowered it against the front railing before pulling her purse around to the front of her. She had to get a picture of this to show her family! They were never going to believe her. Just wait until she showed her dad this. He was going to be totally jealous of her... but in a good way.

My folks would love this, Tink thought wistfully.

* * *

J'kar watched as the female lowered the black case down off her shoulder, laying it up against the wall by her before reaching for another bag lying crisscross across her body. He was still trying to comprehend what happened to his body when she turned and grabbed his hand. He was surprised when she touched him. He hadn't known what to expect, certainly not a kaleidoscope of emotions. He felt a jolt of electricity run from his hand down his body, overwhelming his senses both physically and emotionally.

Stepping closer, he drew in a deep breath, breathing in her scent. A wave of dizziness engulfed him as the scent of her skin and hair assailed his sensory system. Grabbing hold of the railing next to her, he tried to control the emotions cascading through him. He felt a heated rush through his body and a pleasure so intense, it was painful as it coursed through him.

Physically, his body responded to her by wanting to grab her and take her right then and there. He felt his groin tightening, his heartbeat increasing, and even his canines wanting to explode out of his mouth as the need to claim her washed through him! It was the emotional feelings he needed to control.

Gritting his teeth together, J'kar fought the feelings rushing through him. He had never felt so possessive, so protective, so… afraid? J'kar shook as this response flooded through him. He needed to get control of himself and figure out what was going on.

* * *

"This is so beautiful," Tink whispered softly to the man next to her.

She knew he couldn't understand her from the looks she was getting so far. She pulled out her cell phone and aimed the camera on it toward the shuttle docking with the other spaceship. She took several pictures of it before turning around to the man standing next to her.

Tink turned to take a picture of the man standing beside her. Tink drew in a swift breath, drawing in his scent. Pure male fragrance swirled through her. He had a wonderful musky scent with a hint of sweat, almost like a combination of sage, leather, and mountain air.

Normally, she thought, guys had more of a tendency to smell, well, like an old car, or after flag football, a sewer. This man's scent was doing some really weird things to her thought processes! She felt more like jumping his bones. This was not something she normally thought about. Aiming her camera at him, she noticed he was gripping the railing so tightly his knuckles had turned white. He was leaning forward slightly with his eyes closed and his head tilted down like he was contemplating some major decision. Tink took a quick picture before moving away.

Distance is good when your self-control is doing the Indy 500 in the opposite direction, Tink thought with a silent chuckle.

Moving up the left side of the circular room, Tink walked up to the next closest man in the room. He was sitting by a row of computers, but was watching her intently as she approached. Tink put on her most "customer-friendly" smile. It was the one she used when she had to either work on a particularly difficult client's car at the garage or when her parents dragged her to some author's convention.

"How do you do? My name's Jasmine Bell," she said, sticking her hand out.

When all the man did was stare at her hand blankly, Tink reached down and grabbed his hand, shaking it. *Boy, lack of communication is the pits sometimes,* Tink thought as she moved to the next guy, who gave her the same curious "What the fuck?" look. She continued up around the room, coming to a halt in front of another tall man.

"Hi, Jasmine Bell, but everyone calls me Tink," she repeated as she pointed to herself.

Tink studied the guy standing in front of her with a frown. He looked familiar. Like a combination of the boy she helped earlier and the man whose hand she'd grabbed near the front window. Turning to look into the deep silver eyes now staring at her intently from the front of the room, she turned back again to look into the lighter silver eyes staring at her now. A light bulb clicked on.

"Brothers?" Tink asked, pointing to the man watching her and the man in front of her, trying to convey her meaning.

She pointed between the two of them again and put two fingers together, repeating slowly, "Brothers?"

The man standing in front of her looked at J'kar, then back down at Tink and smiled. *"Ta, mankko."* The man's eyes widened as he realized what she was trying to say.

"Brothers," he repeated.

Pointing to himself, he said, "Borj 'Tag Krell Manok."

Tink smiled even bigger. Finally, someone who was willing to communicate!

Pointing to herself, she said, "Jasmine 'Tinker' Bell." Then she pointed to herself again and said, "Tink!"

Holding out her hand, she grabbed the hand of the man named Borj and shook it firmly. *Man, they really do only come in one size so far on this ship! Huge,* Tink thought as she watched his hand swallow her smaller one.

"Tink," Borj repeated slowly. Borj turned his head to look at his brother J'kar in amazement and said in their native language, "The female is called Tink."

J'kar was so shaken by the reaction he was having to the female, he hadn't even heard her move away from the railing next to him. When he opened his eyes and realized he had a death grip on the railing, he released it with difficulty. As he released the railing, he noticed the hand the female had gripped was burning.

Turning his palm upward, he stared in disbelief. A series of intricate circles were forming on his palm. Touching his fingers to the palm of his left hand, he slowly traced the circles. The mating mark! He'd found his bond mate.

Turning, he stared as the female moved from one male to another along the left side of the bridge before she stepped up to his brother. As she touched first one, then another of the males, a low growl started in his throat. She was his! She should not touch other males. He would kill any male who touched her! The growl became louder as she reached out and grabbed his brother's hand the way she grabbed his. He barely heard his brother say the name of the female to him. All he could see was a haze as he became totally focused on the female who was to be his bonded mate.

Borj looked with concern at J'kar. His brother's face had turned to a dark mask of fury. "J'kar, what is it? Did the female do something?"

Borj looked down at the small female gripping his hand and smiling up at him. He couldn't see that she had done anything to his brother, but he didn't know what species she was. Could she have done something harmful during the time she touched J'kar?

Borj glanced at the other three men the female touched. They seemed fine. They watched her with open desire, but nothing else appeared wrong. Borj glanced down at the female and could feel a stirring of desire himself.

She was very attractive to him visually, and her scent was unusually appealing, but was nothing that would cause the fierce look that was on his brother's face. Looking up again, he barely had time to release the female before his brother was upon him.

J'kar didn't even realize he'd moved until he was holding his brother by the throat. A deep growl rolled through his clenched teeth.

"Mine!" J'kar snarled in a low voice. His grip tightened around Borj's throat. "Do not touch her!"

Tink let out a startled squeak as she stumbled backward away from the two huge men. She hadn't even seen the man down front move, until the one named Borj let her go suddenly, thrusting her to one side. Tink held on to the railing briefly for support as she watched the huge man from down front wrap his hand around his brother's neck.

"Now wait a minute, fellow. Let the nice man go," Tink said, rushing forward and grabbing the dark-haired man by the arm.

"What *is* your problem?" Tink asked in frustration as she ducked under the angry, dark-haired man's arm to get between the two.

She knew that wasn't the smartest place to be, but she had finally gotten one of the men to understand her. The last thing she needed was the one person who was trying to communicate with her getting killed. So, she did the first thing one should never do in a fight situation—she put herself in the middle of it.

Raising her hands to press against the stone wall that was the dark-haired man's chest, she pushed with all her strength. He didn't even move. She doubted he even knew she was there. Tink rose up on her tiptoes to place the palms of her hands on each side of his face, tugging until she had his attention. Slowly he looked down at her.

I really need to find out his name, so I can quit calling him "the dark-haired man." Especially since it looks like all the men are dark-haired! Tink thought in exasperation.

Tink stared into his eyes and smiled shakily. "That's right, darling. Release your brother before you hurt him."

Letting her hands slide down to his chest again, Tink said in a soft, husky voice. "Come on, you can do it. Just let the nice man go before I have to do something we'll both regret, like bean you upside the head with my nice little wrench. Come on, it would be a shame to mess up a perfectly good wrench on your gorgeous head," Tink added with a mischievous little smile. It wasn't like she would do anything to mess up the big guy's face – his hair, maybe, his clothes – definitely, but never that gorgeous face.

Tink kept up the pressure of her hands on his chest while she talked calmly. Slowly, the dark silver eyes lowered to meet hers again. Tink knew she had his full attention when she saw his eyelids droop with desire as he gazed down at her.

Smiling again, she nodded her head up and down and pushed again. This time, he backed up a step, then two. Tink kept the pace until she was a good five steps from the man named Borj. Patting the chest she was pushing against, she let out a loud sigh. One disaster averted.

Now to figure out what just happened, without getting ravished, she thought with another silent chuckle.

How did she always seem to get herself into these situations? Tink wondered as she ran her hand through her short curls, causing them to bounce all over the place in disarray.

"Well, that was interesting," Tink said as she put her hands on her hips, still standing between the two men. She didn't know what was happening, but she was suddenly very conscious of the fact she was away from home and her left hand was burning like hell. Rubbing her left hand on her thigh, she looked back and forth between the two men with a raised eyebrow.

Blowing a strand of hair out of her face, Tink asked in a suddenly leery voice. "So, can anyone tell me what that was about in English or mime, or whatever in the hell I might be able to understand?" At this point, she would even take stick-figure drawings.

Borj looked at J'kar. He didn't understand what had happened. Why would his brother suddenly attack him? Why was he claiming the female?

"J'kar, what is happening?" Borj looked shaken at his brother's behavior. "Why are you claiming the female as if she was bonded to you?"

"She *is* mine. She is my bond mate," J'kar was suddenly ashamed at having attacked his brother.

He ran his hand through his short hair before looking at Borj. He had never done anything so out of control before, especially not to one of his brothers. Looking at his left palm again, he slowly raised it for Borj to see the intricate circles now clearly visible.

Borj's eyes widened at the sight of the circles normally found only during the mating rites indicating bonding between two mates. He glanced at the female through new eyes. If what his brother was showing him was true, they had finally found a species they were compatible with as bond mates.

Physically, the female was very attractive, and the knowledge a Prime male would be able to bond with her through the mating rites was life-altering for their entire planet. The only problem Borj saw was there was just the one female. They had no idea where she came from, and there was no way of communicating with her. Their translators were unable to translate anything the female had said so far.

Tink didn't like the look going back and forth between the two brothers. They, and the other men in the room, were suddenly looking at her like she was their favorite new toy or something. Even the new guys who came into the room to look after the boy she brought in stopped what they were doing to stare at her. The boy, who was looking decidedly pale earlier, now had a huge grin on his face. What the hell was going on?

Tink looked back to the two men who had been about to kill each other and found them both staring at her. Taking first one step back and then another and another until the railing was pressed tight against her back, Tink decided she really didn't like the look in their eyes, especially the one named J'kar. He was looking at her like she was edible!

Tink was deciding whether to make a break for the entrance to the room when she felt her cell phone vibrate in her pocket. Startled, she patted the sides of her skirt. She forgot she put it in the pocket of her skirt after taking a few pictures to show her family. She highly doubted she had cell service this far! Pulling her phone out, she saw a text message written across it from RITA. Stunned, she re-read it twice before it dawned on her what it said.

Portal set to open behind you in twenty-eight seconds. Time to go home, sweetheart, RITA's message stated in bold letters.

Looking up again, Tink took one last look around her before gazing at the man named J'kar. She wondered why she felt dismayed at the idea of leaving him.

Maybe it's for the best, Tink thought vaguely as she gazed into the burning flames of desire in his eyes.

The image of the two of them entwined in a burning mass of naked skin flashed through Tink's mind as she imagined what would happen if they were ever alone in the same room for more than a couple of minutes.

No, Tink thought with regret, *a relationship with tall, dark, and delicious would never work. We are literally worlds apart.*

* * *

J'kar let a slight curve lift his lips as the impact of what was happening began to sink in. *I have a bond mate,* he thought with a feeling of disbelief. He had all but given up on the idea of ever finding one as he had attended all the mating rite ceremonies since he turned of age and never found his bond mate. That he found one in such an unusual way could only mean she was sent by the gods and goddesses.

His gaze drifted around the room to the other men. He saw hope and amazement in their eyes as what he said and showed to Borj sank in. If he found his bond mate, then they had a chance to find theirs.

His gazed moved possessively to the female. *Tink,* he reminded himself.

He watched as she reached into her pocket and pulled out the small square disk again. His eyes took in the slight frown between her eyes, then watched as they widened a little.

As he watched her look around the room, then back at him, he began to get an uneasy feeling in the pit of his stomach. As if something bad were about to happen. A low growl started deep in his chest, then burst forth as he made a lunge for her.

All hell broke out in a matter of seconds. J'kar let out a roar of pure outrage as behind Tink a shimmering doorway appeared and a huge male suddenly stepped out of it behind her. J'kar vaguely heard Tink gasp and heard her let out a small scream before she was grabbed and pulled up and over the railing by the large male.

J'kar raced to the railing, bracing one hand on it as he cleared it in an attempt to get to his bond mate before the male had a chance to reach the shimmering doorway. At the same time, his brother Borj and two other men rushed to stop the male. The male pulled Tink through the doorway, releasing a small smoking device as he went, and then there was nothing but empty space.

Chapter 7

Tink gasped and screamed as she was grabbed from behind and lifted over the railing like she weighed no more than a ten-pound sack of potatoes. A strong arm gripped her tight around the waist and held her snug against a huge chest. Tink was about to fight when she heard a familiar oath escape from the massive form holding her.

Tink's eyes widened even further when the familiar voice whispered in her ear, "Hang on."

One minute she was on a spaceship God-knew-where, and the next she was in Cosmos' lab. She watched as he tossed a small smoking device onto the spaceship's bridge. Her breath caught in her throat as she watched J'kar lunge for her a moment too late.

He leaped over the railing using one hand to give him momentum, but the doorway was already closing before his feet hit the other side of the railing. The last thing she saw was a look of pure rage — she had never seen anyone look like they had pure death in their eyes before. It was not directed at her, but at the man holding her. It was a look that said painful restitution would be paid for taking her. Then, everything went mercifully black.

* * *

Tink slowly stretched her arms over her head, tilting her head back and arching her back like a cat. "Mm, what a dream," she mused as she tried to get her brain working.

Moving like she had weights tied to her arms, Tink rolled over to look at the clock. Her eyes flew open when she realized it was four in the afternoon. Groaning, she pushed herself into a sitting position.

"Well, it's about time you came back to the world of the living," Cosmos' deep voice said from the doorway. "I thought I was going to have to call in reinforcements if you didn't wake up soon."

Tink let out a little yelp before flopping backward on the bed. Raising a hand to her chest, she gave the man standing in the doorway her best "evil eye." The last thing she needed was a scare before caffeine, especially after the weird dream she just had.

"You scared the holy crap out of me, Cosmos!" Tink said as she let out the huge breath she was holding. "What are you doing here? You weren't supposed to be home for a couple of weeks, according to the message you left with RITA."

"The trip turned out to be a bust. Mom and Dad had another invitation to present in Japan and called at the last minute to cancel my heading to Chicago. It's just as well. What the hell do you think you were doing? Do you have any idea how dangerous what you did was? Have you lost your mind! You scared the shit out of me. If I hadn't come back when I did there is no telling what could have happened to you!" Cosmos' face darkened the more he spoke, and the level of his voice rose higher than Tink had ever heard him speak before.

Normally when Cosmos got mad he got really, really quiet. Tink couldn't ever remember hearing him actually raise his voice before. Not even when she took his favorite motorcycle, Harvey, for a spin and crashed it into a tree. It took her three months to rebuild it, and he had hardly talked to her until she presented it to him. Even now, he kept it locked up so she couldn't get to it.

"What the hell are you talking about? What did *I* do?" Tink couldn't think. Her head felt like it was full of cotton. "God, I need some caffeine. Can you wait to tell me what I did after I've had a cup or two of coffee?" Pushing herself off the bed, she started to walk across the room when she caught her reflection in the mirror.

"Oh, God," she said as she took in her appearance. She was still dressed in the outfit she wore to the Purple Haze the other night.

Turning to look around the room for any evidence of a hopefully nonexistent one-night stand, Tink let out a breath when she realized only one side of the bed was messed up.

"I don't remember drinking anything. Please tell me you didn't rescue my virtue or I let that bonehead of a professor into your lab." Tink ran her hand through her hair again and tried to smooth out some of the wrinkles in her clothes. Sighing loudly, she shook her head.

"Forget it," Tink said, raising her hand to silence Cosmos before he could even utter a word. "I don't think I could deal with it yet if I did such an asinine thing. Give me fifteen minutes to get a shower. If you could get the coffee and maybe some toast for me, I'll be out in a few minutes," Tink begged a very disgruntled-looking Cosmos with pleading eyes.

"Fifteen minutes," Cosmos said as he turned to leave the room.

Pausing, he turned back around. The look in his eyes made Tink's breath catch again. She had never seen Cosmos look so shaken.

"Tink, I'm glad you're okay." Cosmos turned again and left before Tink could reply.

Shaking, Tink moved into her bathroom, slowly undressing. Raising a shaking hand to her mouth, she wondered what she had done that was so bad it could affect Cosmos this way. Pulling her hand away, she looked at it. There, in the palm of her left hand, was a series of intricate circles.

Frowning, Tink rubbed the fingers of her right hand over it. It looked sort of like a tattoo, but was so finely drawn she couldn't image how anyone could have created it. It wasn't raised up or red like it had just been done. She had seen new tattoos on some of the mechanics after they got them done, and they were always red for a couple of days afterward. This didn't make sense either. As sensitive as the palm of your hand was, there was no way she could have been so drunk as to not remember getting it. Hell, she didn't even drink, so that left being drunk out. Could someone have slipped something into her water? No, she remembered leaving the bar just fine. In fact, she remembered everything from the time she left the bar until... the dream.

It had been a dream, hadn't it? There was no way she could have gone through a magical doorway and landed on a spaceship, could she? Turning the water to the shower on, she adjusted the temperature to be a little cooler than she liked it in the hope it would help clear her mind.

God, she felt like Alice in Wonderland falling through the rabbit hole. She remembered working on the generator and planning on sleeping in late. Leaning forward, Tink rested her forehead and arms against the side of the shower and let the water run over her.

Shaking her head from side to side over and over, she tried to remember when she went to bed, but all she could remember was being on the spaceship staring into the most amazing silver eyes she had ever seen. Then, being pulled over the railing and hearing a roar of rage, so intense she shook out of fear.

J'kar. The man with the dark silver eyes was called J'kar.

Sliding her hand down, Tink turned off the water and reached for the towel on the towel rack. Drying herself off and wrapping the towel around her hair, she slowly dressed. What if it hadn't been a dream? What if it was real?

Pulling a pair of white lace panties on, Tink slid her legs into a pair of black jeans. Slowly pulling on a matching lacy bra, she tugged the towel off her head and pulled on a white T-shirt. Tink hung the towel back on the towel rack and grabbed her dirty clothes off the floor, stuffing them into the dirty-clothes hamper. At the last minute she remembered the lanyard with the odd metal device hanging from it. She could ask Cosmos what it was.

She pulled her skirt out of the hamper to retrieve it. She remembered putting it in her pocket. Patting each side, she frowned when she didn't feel anything. Pulling the other clothes out, she looked through them… nothing. Where could it be? Shrugging her shoulders, she wondered if maybe it had fallen out when Cosmos grabbed her, and he had it. Grabbing her hairbrush off the counter, Tink left the bathroom and headed for the little kitchenette.

* * *

Cosmos looked up from placing two slices of whole wheat toast on a plate next to two eggs over easy. He watched as Tink came into the room. She was brushing out her short hair which was drying into a wild swirl of curls around her head.

Dressed in a tight white, V-neck T-shirt, black jeans, and barefoot she was beautiful. He felt his chest tighten when he thought of what could have happened to her if he hadn't come home when he did. He closed his eyes when he remembered the look on the other men's faces.

He knew the one man would kill him without a second thought. The way he came after him and Tink was enough to make him glad he hadn't had to fight him. But it was the way the man looked at Tink, as if she belonged to him, and the look he gave Cosmos that left him in little doubt he would never have willingly let Tink leave.

Pouring a cup of coffee, he pushed it next to the plate he set out on the breakfast bar. "Feeling better?"

"Yeah. What about you?" Tink set the hairbrush on the stool next to her and climbed up onto the one in front of the food. Leaning over, she took a deep sniff. Her stomach let out a growl. "Mm, caffeine and food. I could get used to this," she said appreciatively.

Cosmos' lips curved up at the corners. "Yeah, well don't plan on it. That's about the extent of my culinary skills." Taking a sip of his coffee, he leaned against the counter. "Tink, I have to ask you about what happened last night."

Tink's hand paused in the act of taking a bite out of her eggs. Setting the fork back down on her plate, she picked up her coffee cup instead. She needed to feel the warmth of the cup between her hands and the smell to calm her suddenly racing pulse.

"What do you want to know?" Tink asked hesitantly.

"Tell me what happened. All of it," Cosmos asked quietly.

Tink took a sip of her coffee to give herself time to get her thoughts in order. Setting the cup in front of her, but not letting it go, she took a deep breath and began telling Cosmos everything that happened the night before. When she finished, she took another sip of her coffee. It wasn't as hot as it had been, and she realized she wasn't hungry any more.

"So, what happened after I passed out? What did you throw onto the ship? The men didn't hurt me or anything. Hell, we didn't even talk to each other, really. We couldn't understand each other," Tink said defensively.

"It was a smoke bomb from Halloween. I had a couple of them left over, and it was handy. After I grabbed you, you passed out. Scared the shit out of me at first! Then, I realized you were breathing okay and your color looked good. I figured your body was just saying enough was enough. I carried you up to your room and let you sleep it off. I kept an eye on you all day and had RITA monitoring your respiration." Cosmos reached for the coffee pot and filled his and Tink's cup back up.

"How did RITA know the portal was about to open?" Tink asked as she picked at the toast on her plate.

"I set a default on the portal to open two hours after the initial opening. It is set to find the DNA signature of the person who goes through. From what I could gather from RITA, when you opened your cell phone to take pictures—which by the way I want to analyze—she was able to connect with the computer system on the ship via their "wireless/Bluetooth" connection. It isn't quite that simple or easy, but gives you an idea. Anyway, she was able to contact you," Cosmos explained.

"Are you saying RITA is still on the spaceship I was on?" Tink asked faintly in disbelief.

"A part of me is, dear. It's like my twin is there now," RITA said in a cheerful voice. "I was able to load my basic programming to the ship's computer. By now, my 'twin' should be analyzing and adapting to their system. It will take a little while, a couple days at least, for my 'twin' to fully acclimate herself."

"RITA, can you give me it in basic terms?" Tink pleaded her head beginning to ache again.

"I'm taking over their ship and giving them a taste of Earth etiquette. How does that sound?" RITA replied.

"Like trouble with a capital T." Tink groaned as she laid her head on her arms which she had resting on the countertop.

Cosmos tried to cover his laugh with a cough. "You can say that again. God, your mother has taken over the spaceship. They won't know what hit them!"

Barely raising her head to glare at Cosmos, Tink muttered darkly. "You think this is so funny, don't you?" Raising her left hand to stop his sarcastic reply, Tink lowered her head back down to rest her chin on her right forearm.

"What the hell is that?" Cosmos asked as he grabbed her hand, yanking it toward him so he could see it better.

"I don't know. It suddenly appeared after J'kar touched me." Tink tugged on her hand, trying to pull it away from Cosmos.

For some reason she wasn't sure she wanted to talk to him about it. God, she was so confused. It felt like someone was tearing her apart on the inside. She felt itchy and achy and having a major PMS attack all at once. All she wanted to do was cry. She never cried! Not even when she was PMSing. All she wanted to do then was beat the crap out of someone. What was going on? She felt like she was falling apart all of a sudden. Fighting back tears, she pulled on her hand again.

Cosmos looked at the intricate circles, then at Tink. His eyes widened when he saw she was on the verge of tears. Letting her hand go, he walked around the breakfast bar and slowly pulled her into his arms.

"It's okay, baby," Cosmos said gently as he rocked Tink back and forth against his huge chest.

Tink suddenly couldn't hold the tears back anymore. She began sobbing uncontrollably. Wrapping her arms tightly around Cosmos' waist, she pressed her face into his chest and cried like her heart was breaking. It felt like it was. She hurt so much, and she didn't understand why.

All Cosmos could do was hold Tink tightly against him as she cried. When the sobs finally calmed to hiccups, he picked her up in his arms and carried her back to her bedroom. Laying her gently down on the bed, he pulled the covers over her. He brushed the hair away from her face before leaning down and giving her a kiss on the forehead.

"Let me get you some aspirin. You need to lie down for a little while longer. You haven't had near enough sleep," Cosmos said softly.

Letting Tink's hand slide from his, he walked into the bathroom. In the medicine cabinet, he found some aspirin. He shook out two and filled a cup with some water. Walking back to the bed, he helped Tink into a semi-sitting position and held out the aspirin. Tink took the aspirin and water before slowly sinking back down into the comfort of her bed.

"Thanks, Cosmos. I don't know what happened. I'm just so confused. Maybe after I get some sleep everything will seem better." Tink turned onto her side and wrapped her arms around a section of the comforter, almost like she was trying to snuggle up to someone and hold tight to them.

"No problem, baby. I'll be down in the lab if you need me. Just call out to RITA, and she will let me know." Leaning down again, Cosmos brushed another kiss across Tink's forehead before getting up and heading out the door.

He paused briefly at the door, watching as Tink's eyes closed and her breath evened out as she slipped into a light sleep. His eyes were full of worry as he studied her one last time before he walked out to go downstairs to his lab. He needed to review everything that happened. Including what the intricate circles on Tink's hand were and what they had to do with the man who had murder in his eyes.

Chapter 8

J'kar let out another loud roar before his fists hit the wall behind the conference table. Nothing! They had found nothing. He was breathing heavily and shaking.

At the table, four men watched him with concern. His brothers, Borj and Derik, sat near the head of the table in the conference room right off the bridge. Lan, his head of security and childhood friend, and Brock, his head engineer and another childhood friend, sat across the table near the windows facing the black darkness of space. J'kar felt that black darkness all the way to his soul. For a Prime male to find his bond mate, then lose her was devastating. The male was very protective of the female and would fight to the death to protect her if necessary.

"What do you know?" J'kar asked harshly. He was trying to control his breathing and the desire to destroy anything he could put his hands on.

Lan cleared his throat before responding. "The video of the corridor where the female appeared does not show much. All we can see is once she steps up behind the Juangan. The video from the bridge isn't much more helpful. Out of nowhere there is an energy disruption. There does not appear to be any reason for it except the female. The energy output is impressive. The device the male tossed seems to be harmless. There were no poisonous chemicals or explosive qualities to it. It appears to merely produce a harmless colored smoke. There is also the black case she left near the front. It contained a strange device for making sounds. In addition, there were numerous images of the female along with other females and males," Lan reluctantly added the last part.

After viewing the images, he didn't think J'kar was going to be very pleased with the finding. Many of the images were of the female with other males. Most of the images showed the female in the arms of the other males, usually in a passionate embrace.

"What images? Where are they?" J'kar demanded, holding out his hand.

Lan handed the images over to J'kar reluctantly. J'kar's face became darker and darker as he viewed the collection of images Lan handed him. A nerve twitched on the side his jaw as he stared down into the smiling face and twinkling eyes of his bond mate. She appeared to know a great many males! Many showed her in some type of embrace with them and her face alight with laughter.

"J'kar, we did find a device on the floor near the railing. It appears the female dropped it when she was taken," Borj said quietly as he studied his brother.

He had never seen his brother this upset, and worried at his control. He wondered what the images contained that would cause his brother's face to become even darker with fury than it had been before.

J'kar seemed to realize his brother was staring at him intently. He turned, his face set. He looked coldly at Brock. "What have you discovered about it?"

Brock leaned forward, holding the device and turning it over and over in the palm of his hand. "It appears to be some type of signaling or location device possibly. I am analyzing the information, but have not been able to decipher it yet."

"Derik, what can you tell me about the...about Tink," J'kar asked his youngest brother. He purposely used her name. He had to talk as if he would have her with him again.

"Just what I've told you so far and what you have seen on the video capture. She was unbelievable! She attacked the Juangan, patched me up, and helped me to the bridge. Everything else you know," Derik said with a hint of worship in his voice.

J'kar sank slowly into the seat at the head of the table. "We do not know who she is, where she came from, how she came to be on the ship, or who took her. Is there anything that we do know?" he asked quietly.

He felt an overwhelming feeling of hopelessness. He had never felt out of control. For once in his life, he felt like he had no control over what was going on. At this moment, he did not know what to do.

All they had was some useless video and a device that told them nothing. J'kar looked at the men seated at the table. They were his most trusted, valued friends and warriors. They had never been defeated by anything. Now it seemed the appearance of a single female and her disappearance were going to be their first defeat.

"Testing one, two, three... testing. Mm, is this thing working? Do you understand what I am saying?" a husky, feminine voice said.

The four men sitting at the table, each deep in thought, jumped when the female voice came on over the com. Moving quickly, the men assumed a defensive position looking around the room for the voice.

"Hello, can you understand me? Oh, dear. I wonder if I got the programming right. Damn, I thought it was working," the voice said with an amused sigh.

"Who's there?" J'kar demanded. He looked around at the other men in the room. The voice was coming from the com center attached to the wall. He glanced at Lan and nodded. Lan murmured into the com attached to his lapel. He glanced back at J'kar and nodded.

"What? Oh, hello! You can understand me. I tell you, your language is quite complex. If FRED hadn't been so cooperative I don't know if I would have ever figured it out. You know..." the voice said with building enthusiasm.

"Who in the name of all the gods and goddesses is this?" J'kar demanded. His fists tightened into tight balls as he fought the urge to put one through the com panel.

"Oh. Sorry, dear. I'm RITA. I'm Tink's guardian angel of sorts. Well, a combination of that and her mom," RITA said cheerfully. "Do you realize this is an absolutely amazing piece of engineering? I've never been on a spaceship before, and the programming running it is... well, positively decadent!"

"What are you doing on my ship, and where is the female... Tink?" J'kar asked in a strained voice.

"Oh, Tink is back on Earth. I uploaded myself to your computer when Tink was taking pictures. I figured you were going to need my help if you wanted to get her back. You know I saw, well, not really saw, but I could tell from your respiration you were attracted to her. She is such a joy and—" RITA was just getting going when J'kar interrupted her again.

"Earth. What are the coordinates? What do you mean get her back? You can get her back?" For the first time since Tink disappeared, J'kar felt a small hope.

"Well, it is a little too far to go if what I've been able to gather from FRED is our current coordinates. Using the portal is the only reasonable form of transportation to get back and forth from what I can tell. Although, I really do need to learn a little more before I can be one hundred percent sure," RITA mused.

"Will this portal take me to Tink? To the man who took her from me?" J'kar asked through gritted teeth. He wanted to find the man who took Tink and kill him. Then he was going to get Tink and make sure nothing ever took her away from him again.

"Oh, you mean Cosmos? You know, you should be thanking him. If you hurt Cosmos, Tink would never forgive you! She's loved him for years. Cosmos is the one who invented the portal," RITA said sternly. She could tell from the different pitches in J'kar's voice he wasn't feeling too friendly toward Cosmos. It would never do if she got them together just to have J'kar kill Cosmos. Why, he was like her son! No, that would never do.

"If you want my help, you have to promise not to hurt anyone when you go to get Tink, especially Cosmos. Tink is very protective of him," RITA said in her most no-nonsense voice.

"What is this portal you mentioned?" Borj asked. He thought it would be best to steer the conversation toward more useful information. "And who is this FRED you talk about?"

"FRED? Oh, well, since I've been in your computer system I knew I needed to learn and adapt to the information available. The best way was to modify your system to interact with mine. I couldn't go around calling it computer this or that, so I named it FRED for Foreign Relations Entity Dignitary, FRED for short. I was able to upload my basic artificial intelligence, adaptive program Tink's mom developed. Now I have a better understanding of your language and programming. The portal is a time-space transportation portal Cosmos has been working on. It bends space and time using a complex formula allowing a dimensional doorway to open. As the traveler passes through, a scan of their DNA is locked into the system allowing the portal to find them when it is activated. The device you have in your hand is a remote portal, but we haven't been able to get it to work right yet. It can be used in cases of emergency to open a portal if the main portal is unable to locate a person's DNA."

"Do you have the schematic for the portal in your programming?" Brock asked. His hand tightened on the metal device. Brock turned toward J'kar, speaking quickly. "If we can get a copy of the schematics, I might be able to replicate the portal device, and we can use the coordinates to find the female."

"We could find females for all of us," Derik said with a grin. He couldn't wait. He looked at some of the images Lan showed his brother, and there were a few females in the images he wouldn't mind meeting.

"RITA? Do you have the schematics?" J'kar asked, not realizing he was holding his breath waiting for the computer to respond.

"Of course, dear. Well, most of it anyway. There will need to be modifications done, but since I helped with some of the development of the project, I should be able to help you—with FRED's help, of course," RITA responded brightly.

"Download the program to our computers and assist Brock in the building of the device. I want it done as soon as possible," J'kar ordered briskly.

He turned to Brock. "Assign whatever extra help you need to engineering. I want this portal operational as soon as possible." Brock nodded his head in affirmation before hurrying out of the room.

"Derik, I want you to work with RITA on developing a translation program of the Earth's language to work with our translators. It is imperative we be able to communicate with those we meet."

Derik stood up. He felt proud his brother recognized his expertise with language translation and programming. He felt for the first time he was a true member of the crew. Nodding to his brother, Derik replied, "I'll get right on it."

"Lan, did you get anything on RITA?" J'kar asked.

"A scan of the computer shows no malicious viruses or other anomalies. In fact, the software seems to be learning and adapting at a rapid rate. It has already implemented some minor changes to our translation programming already which should help Derik," Lan responded with a slight frown. "I would like to study the changes more in depth. I am assuming I will also need more information on the inhabitants of Earth if we are going to retrieve the female. I need to know what security measures will be best when dealing with them."

"Very well, I want a report in four hours on your progress," J'kar said.

He stood and walked over to the windows, staring out at the rich blackness of space. Lost in thought, he did not hear Lan leave the room or his brother, Borj, move to stand next to him. He started when he felt the hand on his shoulder.

Turning his head, he glanced at Borj. Borj let his hand drop. "We will find her."

"Yes," J'kar said, nodding his head toward the images on the table. "There are other possible bond mates to our men. We must be successful."

Borj looked at the image on top. It was an image with three females in it, all of them smiling. The one named Tink was in the middle.

The other two females were similar in appearance to Tink, but the one on the left caught and held Borj's attention. She was slightly taller than the other two and had twin golden-brown braids on each side of her head hanging to her waist. She was wearing very short, tan pants ending mid-thigh, two small triangular pieces of fabric barely covered her breasts, and boots.

All three were standing on a rock outcropping with what appeared to be a wide expanse of water behind them. It was very bright around them, and the sky and water were a brilliant combination of light and dark blues. Small plants of green, yellow, and pink were scattered in the rocks around the females.

Borj couldn't take his eyes off the taller female. He picked up the image as he walked by, slipping it into the pocket of his uniform top. Yes, they would be successful. He had a feeling his brother's future was not the only one that might depend on it.

Chapter 9

Cosmos spent the last two hours poring over everything he could download from RITA from before Tink walked through the portal to what little he was able to get from her time on the ship. The portal opened into an unknown galaxy. He'd had RITA search all known star clusters and galaxies, and she hadn't found anything yet. In addition, he was reviewing the technology he saw during his brief glimpse.

RITA hadn't been of very much help as she had been in the process of uploading herself to the alien spacecraft and had not been fully functional. He had a little bit of what she was able to analyze, but the cell phone memory was limited and RITA was basically trying to decipher her own shorthand. He found nothing on the markings on Tink's left hand and that worried him.

Grimacing as he took a sip of cold coffee, Cosmos stood up and stretched. He ran a hand through his hair and picked up his coffee cup. Walking to the small kitchen area in the lab, he poured his cold coffee down the sink and filled it up with two-hour fresh coffee from the carafe. Leaning back against the counter, Cosmos closed his eyes and pinched the bridge of his nose, trying to relieve some of the strain he felt.

"Hey, you okay?" Tink's soft voice asked.

Dropping his hand, Cosmos opened his eyes to see Tink standing in front of him. She was still wearing the white T-shirt, black jeans, and no shoes. Cosmos set his cup on the counter next to him and held his arms open.

A smile danced around Tink's lips as she moved into the comfort of Cosmos's strong arms and broad chest. The smile faded when she thought of another set of arms and even broader chest. She had the weirdest feeling she should be wrapped in another man's arms.

"I could ask you the same thing. Are you feeling any better?" Cosmos asked as he held Tink tightly in his arms.

He loved her so much. He felt if he ever had a chance to have a little sister, it would have been Tink. He couldn't shake the feeling his experiment had somehow put her in danger. He would never forgive himself if something happened to her. Tilting her chin up to look up at him, he pressed a kiss to her forehead.

"You look better," he teased.

Laughing, Tink ran her fingers over Cosmos' sides, tickling him. Tink laughed even harder when he yelped and tried to get away from her. "Did you save me any coffee?" Tink reached for Cosmos' coffee cup, pulling it toward her and taking a sip.

"Hey, get your own!" Cosmos said, acting outraged. He smiled again, glad to have Tink safe.

"So, what did you figure out while I was acting out Sleeping Beauty's hundred-year sleep upstairs?" Tink sat in one of the rolling chairs. She tucked one foot under her and used the other one to turn back and forth.

"Not much I'm afraid. The extra power you were able to produce from the generator gave the portal just enough power to activate it. The power company is going to love me this month!" Cosmos said with a small chuckle. The electric company loved him every month.

"Yeah, if the cops don't bust you first, thinking you are a major grow house or meth lab!" Tink teased.

Since the sheriff and half the force were friends with her and Cosmos, that wasn't a real possibility. It was always nice to have friends in the right places. Especially when some of your experiments took up enough electricity to power a small city block—you needed to make sure you didn't get busted in the middle of one. Known for some really cool Halloween, Christmas, and New Year's get-togethers, they often hosted parties for the community. Of course, those parties often had ample special effects with a wiz like Cosmos at the helm and Tink's expertise with power grids.

"Do you remember anything about the mark on your hand?" Cosmos asked, noticing Tink was rubbing her left hand up and down her jeans.

"Not really. I remember grabbing his hand... What?" Tink asked when she noticed Cosmos' eyebrow lift. "Give me a break! I had never been on a spaceship in outer space before, and I didn't think! I grabbed the guy's hand, for crying out loud! I didn't jump his bones and make mad passionate love to him on the bridge of the frigging ship." Tink turned a bright shade of pink as she was talking.

"From the look on your face, that might have been a possibility," Cosmos commented dryly.

Twirling around in the chair and standing, Tink walked over to the railing overlooking the portal. "You're right, it was a possibility," Tink said as she stared down at her hand, remembering J'kar's dark features.

Turning back around to face Cosmos, Tink blinked up at him as if coming out of a daze. "I felt a jolt. Like electricity running up my arm and moving throughout my body. It was like I had suddenly come alive for the first time. I think he felt the same thing. It was like looking at everything through new eyes, and all I could see was him. I tried to ignore it. I had never felt that way about anyone before, and I had just met the man. For heaven's sake," Tink said with a small, self-conscious laugh. "He's an alien! We were just trying to figure out each other's names. You know—a *you Tarzan, me Jane* type of communication! How could I feel anything for someone I just met, who I just touched one time? Anyway, my palm started burning and itching. When I looked down, these circles started showing up. What was I supposed to do? Ask him if he gave me some kind of alien cooties or something? 'Oh, and by the way, have you been practicing safe sex, because I have circles showing up on my hand?'" Tink added sarcastically.

"God, I feel like I'm going crazy!" Tink said, slamming the coffee cup down so hard some of it spilled over the side onto the console top.

Running both hands through her hair, she pulled her left hand down to study it. "Cosmos, what am I going to do?" Tink whispered, looking at Cosmos for help and reassurance.

Tink looked so confused and frightened. Whatever happened when the alien man had touched Tink, it had some type of psycho-emotional effect on her. It was tearing him up seeing her look so vulnerable.

"Maybe it will disappear after a few days," Cosmos replied.

Cosmos didn't know what else to say. Maybe being away from the alien environment would cause whatever happened between Tink and the man to simply disappear. Cosmos hoped the marks on Tink would vanish after a few days. He just hoped the markings weren't caused by something parasitic. Just the thought some parasitic creature could be inside Tink made Cosmos feel physically ill. He would see if he could get a tissue sample and test it. For right now, Tink looked so hopeful he didn't have the heart to suggest it. Maybe he would wait until she was asleep again to get it.

"Why don't we go out and get a bite to eat down at Helena's? I could go for a nice juicy steak, and you haven't eaten anything all day," Cosmos suggested as he wrapped his arm around Tink.

"Sounds good. Give me a minute to get my shoes and purse, and I'll meet you downstairs," Tink replied with a small smile. She needed the distraction and getting out of the warehouse for a little while might help clear her brain.

Dinner at Helena's was always a good time. An old-fashioned eatery, Helena's had simple food, but lots of it. An old jukebox stood in the corner playing oldies from the '50s and '60s. Red-and-white checkered table tops with matching red booth seats made from fake leather helped add to the feeling of being in a 1950s-era diner. Helena's was now owned by Ralph Barker. He was the perfect man for the job as he thought of himself as the reincarnation of one of the guys from the movie *Grease*. He wore a tight white shirt over his thin frame, high-water jeans, a black leather jacket, and had his thin hair dyed black and greased back. At almost seventy years old, Ralph loved to remind people he had actually lived the time period. It didn't hurt that he also loved socializing with all the customers, especially the ladies.

"Tink, Cosmos, welcome!" Ralph said loudly with a heavy New Jersey accent. "Welcome. Marge, table for two of my best customers!" Marge rolled her heavily made-up eyes before mouthing word for word everything Ralph said. "We have the best steaks in town, and you are going to love the special tonight."

Tink and Cosmos had a hard time not laughing at the way Marge rolled her eyes and waved her arms in the air mimicking every move Ralph made. When Ralph turned to look at Marge, she acted like she was adjusting her cap before giving them a wink and turning to get some menus.

Sitting in a window seat, Tink let out a sigh. She loved this town and the people who lived here. They all seemed to have a story to tell. Tink wondered what life was like where the men on the spaceship came from. Did they have blue skies and water? Was their landscape lush or barren? What were the plants and animals like? What were the women like? She thought the last thought with a tinge of jealousy. She knew what the men were like: tall, dark, and delicious. Tink started when Marge put the menus and two glasses of water on the table.

"So, my folks headed to Japan to present their ideas on solar energy cells," Cosmos said.

He was determined to distract Tink. He knew she loved hearing about some of the places and people his folks often went to and met. He didn't hear from them often, and like the cancelled trip to Chicago, he saw them even less.

"Seems there are some people there thinking of building a major resort using mostly solar energy." Cosmos went on to tell her about some of the places his parents had been to recently and some of the big names they met. Tink listened halfheartedly, her thoughts wandering back to the last night—or was it just this morning?

After a delicious meal of steak, a baked potato, and a salad, Tink sat back and smiled at Cosmos. She knew what he had been doing for the past hour and a half. He seemed to know her better than she knew herself sometimes. Stifling a yawn with the back of her hand, she stretched her legs out under the table.

"You ready to call it a night? I know I slept most of the day, but I feel like I could crash again after that meal," Tink said as she yawned again.

"Yeah, I didn't get much sleep either since I flew to Chicago just to turn around and come back on the red-eye. I'd like to go over everything again tomorrow and review what RITA has when my brain isn't so fried," Cosmos said as he let out a big yawn. "Besides, your yawning is contagious!"

The walk back to the warehouse was quiet, both of them deep in thought. They walked arm in arm up to the second floor, which was Cosmos' living area. As they came to the section leading up to the third-floor living area where Tink lived, she reached up and wound her arms around Cosmos' neck, giving him a light kiss on his lips.

"Thanks for everything, Cosmos. See you in the morning," Tink whispered sleepily.

Cosmos watched as Tink walked the rest of the way up the stairs to her living area. He didn't care what it took, he would always make sure Tink was safe and happy. With a sigh, he made plans in his head for the next morning to solve some of the questions he had about where Tink had gone and what those circles on her palm meant.

Chapter 10

The engineering level was full of activity as clean-up from the attack was still under way, repairs to different areas of the ship that were damaged were taken care of, and the female was excitedly discussed. Only one man seemed to be oblivious to everything going on. He had total confidence in the men under him. Brock had handpicked every one of the men in his section for their assignment. He walked quickly across the room, heading for a small office/work area.

Brock wasn't as tall as some of the other Prime males at six feet one, but he more than made up for it in his stocker build. Pure muscle across a broad chest made him seem taller than he really was. He had the same black hair common to his people, but, unlike many aboard the ship, he preferred to wear it longer, letting it hang down to his shoulders.

His eyes were a deep, molten silver with a hint of purple. He had the strong jaw and short, broader nose of his kind as well. His family had been friends and supporters of the 'Tag Krell Manok family for as long as they had been in power. His grandfather and his father before that fought alongside them during the great wars.

He always had a knack for technology and building devices. When he was chosen to be the chief engineer on the *Prime Destiny* as it was being built ten years before, he made some changes to the power grid, power modules, weapons systems, and outer hull structure. He took pride in his work and enjoyed the challenges of designing a superior ship. He had over the past ten years made modifications to the ship, making it one of the most feared vessels in the known galaxies. It had been some of those modifications that prevented the Juangans from taking over the ship.

Standing in the small workroom of engineering, he had designed specifically for working on some of his more creative projects, Brock contemplated his next step. He had been reviewing the schematics RITA downloaded over the past four hours. While the design was so simple and innovative he was amazed his own people—hell, amazed he hadn't thought about it before—there were still too many questions unanswered.

He was still trying to decipher some of the components and the energy grid on the design this Cosmos used to materials he was familiar with. In addition, not all of the design was there. There were still too many missing pieces of the puzzle to figure out how to build it so it could safely be used. The main concept was there—just not enough of the details.

Picking up the small metal device the female had dropped, Brock gave a deep sigh, stood up, and stretched. He needed to take a break and get something hot to drink. Walking over to the replicator, he gave the command for his favorite Nitearan tea. Made from the bark of a plant on one of the small planets from their solar system, it contained a slightly nutty flavor with a hint of black root. Calming and rejuvenating.

Rolling the device around in his hand while he waited for the replicator to finish producing his tea, he moved some of the cylindrical dials to match the numbers on the coordinates RITA gave him for Earth. When the final cylinder clicked into place, the device began to glow, and a knob popped up on the top of it. Curious, Brock pushed the knob down. One minute he was standing in the darkened engineering office, the next, the room was lit with a shimmering swirl of colors, and a doorway appeared.

"*Hockta balmas!*" Brock muttered in disbelief as he almost dropped the device when he realized what it was.

It was a portable portal! As he stared at the device, the shimmering lights flickered, then disappeared as the power grid supporting it faded. He now knew what the device was; what he needed was a power source that would last long enough to let someone through.

This he could do much quicker than trying to recreate the larger device from the incomplete schematics RITA had given him. Forgetting his tea, Brock picked up a device scanner from the table. The scanner would create a three-dimensional image of the device and create a detailed schematic for replication.

If he could modify the power source to use the base crystals, it would provide more than enough power for the device! More excited than he had been in years, Brock felt all the fatigue from the past days' events fade away as his mind began contemplating what needed to be done.

Chapter 11

The rest of the week seemed to drag by for Tink. She was off on Monday, so it threw the rest of the week off by one day. She thought the weekend would never come! One would have thought having one less work day would have made it go faster, but it didn't.

She had to work Saturday morning and was playing at Purple Haze starting at eight o'clock that night. She worked on several projects over the week at the garage and had some minor repairs at the College of Engineering to do. She ran into the "Professor Jerk" the night before at the college and had to put up with his shit for an hour before she was able to get away. Now, she was rushing to put all her tools back in order so she could be ready for Monday morning.

She admitted being busy helped to keep her mind off the silver-eyed man she'd met. God, had it only been a week ago? The nights were the worst.

Cosmos did his best to keep her busy once she got home at night, but he couldn't keep her mind off what happened after the lights went out. The circles on her palm continued to burn and itch with regular intensity. It didn't actually hurt—it was just a constant reminder of her adventure.

"Tink, do you think you can take a look at the '63 Corvette over in Bay 2 on Monday? I can't figure out why it's still running a little rough," Mike, one of the mechanics, asked.

Mike was a cute guy. He started a little over a year ago. He was in his mid-twenties, had dark brown hair and eyes, and an easy personality. He'd asked Tink out a couple of times. They enjoyed each other's company, but agreed they made better friends, and now just hung out when the mechanics around town got together.

"Sure," Tink replied as she put the rest of the tools back in the tall tool drawer. She wheeled it back against the wall and took a quick glance around before heading for the door.

"Can you make sure everything is locked up before you leave? I gotta get going if I'm going to get everything done before I play tonight. If you get a chance, come on down to Purple Haze. Some of the other guys are going to be there. It's Pete's birthday, and I was going to play him a special song," Tink called out.

"Sounds great, see you later," Mike answered with a grin.

Pete owned the garage. He had been married to Peggy for the past twenty-five years. He was a grizzled man who spoke his mind. He never finished school, but he was a wiz at tearing an engine apart and putting it back together.

He met Peggy shortly after she moved into town, and they fell in love. Peggy ran the office. Pete was popular for all his surliness, and everyone loved Peggy. She planned a surprise birthday party at Purple Haze and asked if Tink could do a country music night. Tink talked to the owner who thought it was a great idea.

Tink grabbed her oversize purse out of the cabinet and headed for the door. She had a lot to get done before she got ready to play. She drove her car so she wouldn't have to backtrack before heading home.

Pulling her list out, she headed for the grocery store. If she didn't buy some food for her and Cosmos, they were going to be spending a lot more time at Helena's. She also needed to get some new jeans and boots for tonight.

Three hours later Tink was pulling the last bag out of the back of her Prius. Cosmos loved to tease her about her choice of vehicles. He seemed to think she would have been a big truck or SUV person.

Tink never liked driving something she had trouble seeing over the dashboard in. Plus, with global warming, energy conservation and gas prices constantly going up, she thought she made a smart move. Clutching the last bag to her chest, she slammed the back trunk down.

"Cosmos! Groceries!" Tink yelled.

"He's in the lab, honey. I'll let him know. Your sister called and wants you to call her back," RITA answered.

"Thanks. Which one?" Tink huffed as she moved up the stairs to the second level.

"Hannah," RITA replied.

"Hannah? Wow, I thought she was still in Africa doing a shoot on lions." Tink sounded muffled as she reached under the counter to put some of the can goods away. "Did she leave a message?"

"She just said to call her. She says she is worried about you. She has the satellite phone with her and don't worry about the time. She is in a village stocking up right now, so you won't disturb her."

Tink straightened with a groan. Hannah had a knack for knowing something was wrong before anyone else. She hoped she hadn't talked to their mom yet. If she had, Tink was in for company, soon!

Hannah was the oldest out of the three girls and the most like their father. She was a freelance photographer for several nature magazines and did documentary work on some of the more endangered species around the world. Her skills with a camera were known internationally, and she was always being asked to do one project or another.

She received her first camera at the age of six and had a natural talent for knowing when the lighting was just right for a shot. All the traveling the family did was the perfect opportunity for her to develop her hobby, and at the age of ten she received several awards for her photographs. By the time she was thirteen, she was doing articles and photo shoots for a variety of magazines.

She attended college on a photography scholarship and immediately was offered jobs with some of the most illustrious companies in the world. She turned them down, not wanting to have to be told where to go or what to do by anyone.

Glancing at the clock, Tink saw she still had time to finish a few of her chores upstairs, get a shower, and call Hannah before she had to leave. The phone call would be the last on her list so she would have an excuse to cut it short if Hannah started asking too many questions Tink didn't want to answer. Turning to see Cosmos coming up the stairs, she put her hands on her hips.

"Perfect timing, I just finished lugging everything up here and putting it away," Tink said trying to look stern.

She could never be angry with Cosmos. She looked at him and fought the curve of the smile threatening to sneak through. His hair was everywhere, like he had been running his hands through it over and over in aggravation. His shirt was buttoned wrong, and he was muttering to himself.

Yep, he was having one of his "brain-days," as Tink liked to call it. Cosmos' brain-days consisted of him being totally absorbed in whatever new concept or problem was running through his brain. He was totally oblivious to everything else on those days, and there would be no communicating with him, at least, not in anything that made sense to anyone else.

"What? Sorry," Cosmos replied with a sheepish smile. "Guess I wasn't paying attention. I haven't found out anything about..." He trailed off with a distant look in his eyes.

Tink cleared her throat and raised one eyebrow, waiting for him to finish his sentence. "About...?" she prompted.

"Nothing. Do you mind if I stay in tonight? I'm working on another theory and don't want to lose focus," Cosmos asked distractedly.

Cosmos liked to come down to the bar and listen if he was in town. Tink thought he did it so the rowdier college boys wouldn't hit on her. He was so protective. It was worse than having her parents and her two sisters watching over her.

Shaking her head, she grinned. "No, I won't mind. I'm going to go do some housekeeping upstairs before I call Hannah, then get ready." Walking up to Cosmos, she re-buttoned his shirt and patted him on the chest. "Just don't forget to eat something. I bought some chicken you can warm up, and there are some microwavable veggies in the freezer." Giving him a quick kiss, Tink headed upstairs to finish what needed to be done.

Two hours later, Tink was stepping out of the shower when her cell phone rang. Quickly wrapping a towel around her hair and another one around her body, she hurried into her room to grab it. Glancing at the screen, she grimaced. Hannah.

Sliding her finger across the screen, she answered, "Hi, Hannah."

"Why didn't you call me back? What is going on?" Hannah demanded. Yep, just like dad—to the point.

"I'm fine, thanks for asking!" Tink bit back a grin. She knew what buttons to push, and she loved to push Hannah's buttons. "I had to work today and had a bunch of errands. I was just about to call you ," Tink said as she crossed her fingers, hoping Hannah would drop whatever bone she had to chew on.

"Okay." Tink could hear Hannah's impatient sigh. "Hi, Tink. How are you? I'm glad you're fine. Now, tell me what is going on. I had one of my feelings, and you know they always come true."

Tink undid her fingers, nope—no luck. Letting out her breath, she turned and sat on the edge of her bed. "Okay, but you aren't going to believe me," Tink said softly.

Tink never held anything back from her family, at least not if they asked. It was an unspoken rule: be true and as a family, they could overcome any obstacle. Taking a deep breath, Tink explained everything that happened over the last week, including how she felt at night when she was alone. When dead silence came from the other end of the phone, Tink wasn't sure if Hannah was still there or just too stunned to speak.

"Hannah?" Tink asked hesitantly.

"I'm trying to decide whether I should kill Cosmos or give him a kiss for saving you," Hannah replied softly.

Hannah believed everything Tink told her. Their father might be a science fiction writer, but Tink wasn't and she wouldn't make something like this up. If Tink said she was on a spaceship in another galaxy through a portal Cosmos built, then she was.

"I'm coming home. I'll be there as soon as I can make the arrangements," Hannah said in a voice that meant there would be no arguments.

"You aren't going to tell mom, dad, or Tansy are you?" Tink asked quietly.

The last thing she wanted was to be invaded by her whole family. Tansy was the middle daughter and was nothing like their mom and dad. She worked for Homeland Security or the CIA or something. No one really knew.

She didn't talk to anyone about what she did for a living. She was the most reserved of them all. She kept an apartment in Washington, D. C., but was never there. She seemed to have a different hairstyle and color every time they saw her. She always said she liked to change her appearance.

She could look like a supermodel one minute or a homeless person the next. She was definitely the chameleon of the family. If she got wind of something like this, if she suspected Tink might be in danger, she would have the whole government involved! It would be an *X-Files* episode on a grand scale.

"No, at least not until I see you and determine if I need to involve them," Hannah replied. "I'll make the arrangements now and email them to you later this afternoon. Oh, it's night there, isn't it? I love you, kid. Stay safe until I get there."

They talked for a few more minutes, then hung up. Tink tried to feel guilty about Hannah coming, but it was hard to do. She loved her sisters and missed having their companionship. They had always been close. Even with the work Tansy was doing, she would drop whatever was going on and come if one of them said they needed help.

Heading for the bathroom to finish getting ready, Tink dried and styled her hair until flirty waves hung around her head. Putting on minimal makeup since anything heavy would sweat off on stage, she pulled on her favorite black lacy bra and panty set. Pulling on low-rise, hip-hugger black jeans and her "Goddess of Wrenches" T-shirt that stopped just below her breasts, leaving her firm stomach uncovered, she added a small gold chain around her neck with teardrop-shaped diamonds hanging down and put small diamond studs in her ears.

Picking up the new gold belly chain she purchased during her shopping trip earlier, she slid her feet into soft black ankle boots. She didn't have her favorite guitar as it was left behind on the spaceship the previous Saturday, so she would just have to borrow one from the back room. Maybe she could grab the bass guitar again before Gloria got there, she thought wickedly. Grabbing her jacket, she turned and headed down the stairs to the lab to remind Cosmos not to forget to eat.

Palming her way into the lab, she saw Cosmos sitting at the computer typing in numbers. Walking up behind him, she wrapped her arms around his neck from behind and rested her chin on his shoulder.

"How's it going?" she said cheerfully.

She didn't want Cosmos to know she was still having problems with her emotions. Moving to lean on the console, she faced him and made sure she had his attention. Otherwise, she had learned from experience, he wouldn't even remember she had been there.

"Hannah's coming for a visit next week," she told him with a nudge.

"What?" Cosmos' eyes slowly focused on Tink. "Hannah? Oh, that's great. When will she be here?"

"Not sure. She is going to email me her itinerary later this evening, and I'll let you know. I have to head out to the bar if I'm going to make it there in time to help set up some of the party stuff. Don't forget to eat." Tink leaned forward and gave Cosmos a quick kiss. "Don't forget to take a break every now and then."

"'Kay," Cosmos responded absently.

He was already focused on the screen in front of him again. Shaking her head, Tink walked out of the lab with a quiet laugh, feeling sorry for whoever ended up marrying him. Whoever fell for Cosmos needed to be as smart as he was and have the patience of a saint when he was working on one of his projects.

Purple Haze was buzzing with excitement by the time Tink got there. Besides the regular crowd, there were almost two dozen mechanics from the surrounding area there to celebrate Pete's birthday. Tink got there an hour early to help set everything up.

She chatted shoptalk with some of the mechanics from the surrounding towns and got filled in on Pete and Peggy's two kids and their grandkids. They couldn't make it there tonight, but Pete and Peggy were flying out tomorrow for Florida to meet up with them for a cruise.

"Hey, beautiful. I missed you this past week," a low voice said as hands came around her waist, and she was pulled into a set of unfamiliar arms.

Grabbing the hands that were wandering over her bare stomach, Tink tried to pull away. Putting enough room between them so she could turn around to face the person who grabbed her, Tink looked up into the face of one of the guys from the week before who'd tried to get her attention. Frowning, she put her hands on his chest and pushed.

"Let. Me. Go," Tink said through gritted teeth. "You don't know me well enough to be grabbing me."

"I think we can remedy that," the arrogant bastard said with a smile. "The name is Scott Bachman. Senator Bachman's son."

Obviously he thought dropping his father's name would impress Tink, she thought vaguely. Tink had been around enough famous people that name-dropping had just the opposite effect.

"Well, good for you. Now, get your hands off me," Tink said again, pushing even harder than before.

For a Senator's son, he was firmer than she expected. She doubted he had done a day's labor in his life so he must be a health club junky. Whatever he was, she was not impressed. She didn't like anyone pawing her, and he was giving off some really negative vibes she wasn't about to ignore.

Smiling, he slowly released her almost as if saying he was the one in control over when she could be released or not. "I'll meet up with you later," He said, turning and nodding to a guy behind him.

Tink watched him walk away with a look of disbelief on her face. Where did the guy get his ego? Egos-R-Us?

Tink placed "The Senator's Boy"—as she named him—in the drop-dead file in her mind. She shook her head once more before heading for the storage room the band used to put excess equipment in. She really had to change the neon sign on her forehead that attracted losers.

Chapter 12

J'kar waited impatiently for Brock in the transporter section of the *Prime Destiny*. The rest of the team had finished gathering the equipment they would need. Derik updated each of their translators to include the English language J'kar's bond mate spoke. He also had clothing more recognizable to the Earth inhabitants replicated based on information he received from RITA.

Lan was finishing up his preparations for nonlethal weapons. They would only be using stunners since RITA said killing anyone was heavily frowned upon, no matter how much someone might deserve it. It also would attract unwanted attention from the local authorities. The stunners could be passed off as someone being drunk or on drugs and caused no permanent side effects.

His brother, Borj, would remain behind to command the warship and make sure the ship did not move from its current coordinates. Brock emphasized the importance of making sure the warship did not deviate from its current position, otherwise they could find themselves opening the portal into space.

It was seven sleep cycles since the female had appeared aboard their ship. There were no visible signs of the fight with the Juangans left as everything had been repaired. The second ship was sent ahead with a skeleton crew and was being met by the *Prime Challenge,* his brother Mak's ship. He had slept little since then, and it was beginning to show. He was at the end of what little patience he had. He growled low in his throat when Brock entered the transporter room.

"What took you so long?" J'kar growled again as Brock approached him.

Brock smiled, "I wanted to test it once more before we actually used it. The last thing I want to do is walk through a doorway over thin air. I double-checked the coordinates against what RITA had. We should appear in this lab which is where the female lives with the male."

J'kar's eyes narrowed as the last words left Brock's mouth. He felt another growl vibrate in his chest as he thought of the man touching his bond mate. He closed his eyes briefly and took a deep breath. Reaching for one of the portable portal devices Brock held out, he gripped it tightly, wishing it was the male's neck.

Brock was explaining how the device would work to take them there and back. Lan would go through first, followed by the rest of them within milliseconds of each other. This would give them the advantage of surprise.

They were not sure what type of defenses the human male might have in place. They did not know if he would be there, or even be alone if he was. If he was, they would neutralize him and force the whereabouts of the female from him. They would then grab her and get out as quickly as possible. Future trips would depend on how quickly they could get in and out without being detected.

Borj watched as each man checked his equipment to make sure everything was in order. Borj looked at his brother. "May the gods and goddesses be with you."

J'kar returned his steady gaze. With a tilt of his head, he acknowledged Borj's support. "*Dulu mata ki.*" As faith guides. Turning to look from one man to another to see if they were ready, he looked at Lan and nodded.

Lan pressed the switch to activate the portal, staring as the device glowed and a shimmering doorway appeared. He looked through it quickly before disappearing totally. Within a fraction of a second, three other shimmering doorways appeared, and the other men walked through.

Borj stood alone in the transporter room, hoping for the success of the warriors in their quest. If they were successful, it could mean the survival of his people. Speaking into the communication link attached to his lapel, he ordered two men to stand guard in the transporter room until the return of the warriors. He still had a ship to run and wanted to make sure there were no more surprises waiting for them.

* * *

Cosmos forgot all about eating. It was pushing eleven o'clock when he finally felt the uncomfortable rumbling of his stomach. He was analyzing the data from the portal and still didn't have a clue how it could have bent time and space to such a degree.

Pushing his chair back from the computer console, he stood and stretched. He needed some coffee and maybe he would grab some of the chicken Tink bought. He walked up to his second-floor living area and made a pot of coffee.

While it was brewing he decided he needed a shower. Maybe he would take a break and go see Tink at the bar. He could listen to her and the band for a while and walk home with her.

After a quick shower Cosmos pulled on a T-shirt and jeans. Grabbing a piece of cold chicken out of the refrigerator, he poured himself a cup of coffee. Sipping the coffee and taking a bite out of the chicken, he headed down the stairs to the lab. He wanted to set up one more analysis before he left.

Palming his way into the lab, he had just taken a couple of steps into the room when right in front of the console a shimmering doorway appeared, and a tall, dark-haired man emerged, holding what appeared to be a gun. Freezing, Cosmos barely had time to let out a yell before an electric shock hit him, and he collapsed into darkness.

Lan drew his stunner before he walked through the doorway, ready for the worst. When he stepped through and saw the man walking toward him, he squeezed the trigger out of reflex. He was a little disoriented by the portal, but it passed quickly.

Turning as the other men appeared, he silently motioned for them to search the room. Brock pulled a slim computer module from his waist and aimed it at the computer equipment the moment he walked through the shimmering doorway. RITA2 uploaded the translator program into the system while Lan walked over to an unconscious Cosmos and inserted a translator device in his left ear. J'kar and Derik scanned the area for any other life forms.

"Oh dear. You didn't hurt him did you?" RITA asked anxiously. "You know, he wouldn't have hurt you if you had just walked in."

"RITA?" J'kar asked, looking around the room. It was filled with primitive equipment compared to what he was used to.

"Yes, and you are?" RITA inquired.

"Captain J'kar 'Tag Krell Manok. Are there others in the building?" J'kar demanded.

"Well, Captain, I'm not sure I should share such information with you. Can you give me a reason as to why you would want to harm my Cosmos?" RITA demanded right back with a stern tone.

Clearing his throat, Derik replied. "J'kar, perhaps I should respond to RITA." He walked over to stand next to Lan. Lan was monitoring Cosmos, who was slowly coming around. Derik spoke loud enough for RITA to hear him. "RITA, we have come for the female who traveled to our warship. She is my brother J'kar's bond mate. You are a part of our warship as well. We do not mean any harm to the male or the female. My brother would give his life to protect the female."

Derik spoke to J'kar in their native language. "The females on this planet are very romantic and are more likely to help if they believe love is involved."

J'kar looked at his brother, then nodded his understanding. "I mean no harm to the male or the female, to Tink. I only wish to find my bond mate, my..." J'kar looked inquiringly at Derik. In their native language he asked, "What do they call them here?"

"Wife," Derik responded with a grin.

"My wife," J'kar said.

"Tink's your wife?" RITA squeaked as much as a computer could squeak. "When did that happen?"

"Seven sleep cycles ago," J'kar responded.

"Mm. Does Tink know she is your wife?" RITA inquired.

J'kar was interrupted from answering by a groan coming from the male on the floor. J'kar walked over to stand over the male who had taken his bond mate. Narrowing his eyes, he watched as the male slowly regained consciousness.

Cosmos groaned as he shook off the effects of the stun he received. Slowly opening his eyes, he recognized the man standing over him as the son of a bitch who'd looked like he wanted to kill him a week ago.

Lunging at the man, Cosmos was quickly grabbed by both arms. Cosmos struggled to kneel on one knee, trying to break the hold the two men had on him. He glared at J'kar with a look of pure fury.

"You son of a bitch! Let me go," Cosmos snarled at J'kar.

"Where is the female you took?" J'kar demanded in a harsh voice. He could smell the female's presence in the room and on the man. He clenched his fists tight, trying to get control of his emotions.

"Took? I brought her home. What business is it of yours anyway? She belongs here," Cosmos responded in a strained voice. The stun was still causing his body to react weakly, and he was fighting the need to slide back down onto the floor.

One part of Cosmos realized the man was speaking another language while another part recognized he could understand him... at least, in one ear. He shook his head to try to clear his thoughts; he needed to figure out what they wanted with Tink.

J'kar leaned over so he was in Cosmos' face. He wanted him to know exactly what he was saying and have no doubts about it. "She belongs to *me*, with *me*!"

"Are you nuts?" Cosmos asked in disbelief. He decided to take a different tactic when he heard all four men growl. "Listen, can you ask your two goons to let me go? Obviously we need to clarify some things."

He also hoped if he could get up, he wouldn't feel at such a disadvantage. Hell, he was imposing, but these guys made him feel like a scrawny kid. This was worse than when he was in grade school before he hit his growing spurt.

J'kar stared at Cosmos a minute before nodding to Lan and Derik to release him. The men slowly released Cosmos and stood back a couple of paces. Cosmos slowly stood, swaying a little. Shaking out the weakness he was feeling, he looked at the man in front of him.

What he saw surprised him. For an alien, his physical appearance wasn't so different from a human. He was tall, but not unreasonably so. His facial features were similar, though his nose was a little broader than a human's. The only thing that really stood out was his eyes. They seemed to glow with a silver light, and right now he could swear he saw small flames in them.

Clearing his throat, Cosmos nodded to J'kar. "My name is Cosmos Raines. I guess I should have expected some kind of repercussion from last week's little adventure. How is it I understand what you are saying? How did you find us?"

J'kar recognized the man seemed to be trying to come to terms with their sudden appearance. "Lan placed a translator device in your ear while you were unconscious. When…" J'kar paused for a moment. "When you grabbed Tink from my warship she dropped a device. My engineer, Brock, was able to discover its purpose and replicate it," J'kar nodded to another man who was standing in front of Cosmos' bank of computers.

The man, Brock, glanced up when J'kar said his name and nodded by way of introduction. Cosmos had a million questions for Brock but didn't think the irate man in front of him would appreciate his curiosity right then.

"What do you want with Tink?" Cosmos asked hesitantly. He decided he might as well find out what they wanted. If they had gone through this much trouble he needed to know why.

"Where is she?" J'kar asked again. He was impatient to see her, to touch her.

"She's not here. You answer my questions, and if I feel confident you aren't here to hurt her, I'll answer your questions. What do you want with her?" Cosmos repeated his last question. He decided if he was going to get any answers he was going to have to have something to barter with.

J'kar let out a deep growl. He was not in the mood to answer questions. He wanted the female. His hand swung up so fast Cosmos didn't even see him move. J'kar held Cosmos by the throat.

"Where is she?" he growled again, his eyes narrowing dangerously.

"Go. To. Hell," Cosmos gasped, standing still and glaring back into J'kar's eyes defiantly.

Derik reached out and gripped J'kar's arm. Speaking softly, he said, "Brother."

J'kar stared for a moment more before slowly releasing Cosmos' neck. "She is my bond mate. What you would call... wife." Stepping back, J'kar folded his arms across his chest. "We are Prime. My name is J'kar 'Tag Krell Manok, commander of the *Prime Destiny* and Second Lord Chancellor of Prime." Nodding to the others, he continued. "The others are Brock, my chief engineer; Lan, head of security; and Derik, my brother and now chief linguistics expert. As you know, we come from a galaxy far from here. We call our home world Baade. It is an advanced culture. On our world, males and females are connected to each other through mating rites. During the mating rites males and females are exposed to each other when they come of age. Mates identify each other through many different ways: touch, smell, voice. If a male and female react to each other, a bond is formed." Raising his left hand J'kar showed Cosmos the intricate circles on his palm. "We call it the life circle. Each circle is different for each bonded pair, but the same on the male and female who bond. It can only form if a true bonded mate is found. Our species mate for life. There are not many women on our world. We have searched other galaxies for compatible females, but have not found any who we could bond with, until now."

Cosmos listened to the explanation with disbelief. The guy thought Tink was his bond mate! His wife? He thought about the circles on Tink's palm. Could it be true? Looking at J'kar he didn't think the guy was making this up. He had come... what? Millions of light-years, to find Tink.

"Would you mind if I scanned your palm?" Cosmos asked quietly.

J'kar jerked with surprise. He had not expected the man to react so calmly. Perhaps he misjudged the human male. Nodding his acceptance, he followed the man over to a device next to the computer console Brock was downloading information from.

Placing his palm flat on the scanning device, he waited as the thin stream of light passed by up and down. Cosmos nodded to J'kar that he could remove his palm before sitting in front of the computer screen.

Pressing a series of commands, Cosmos asked out loud, "RITA, please analyze the scans and compare them to the ones on file."

"Certainly, dear. Done. They are a perfect match," RITA responded almost immediately.

Cosmos knew even before he was done with the scan they would be, but he needed the confirmation to satisfy his scientific self. Turning in the chair, he looked at the four men standing watching him.

"What happens if the male or female refuse to bond?" Cosmos asked.

Derik replied before J'kar could. "They cannot. To refuse to accept the bond would be death for both of them."

"Death? What do you mean… death?" Cosmos asked incredulously.

J'kar answered this time. "Once the two recognize each other, their bodies began to create chemicals, making them dependent on each other. They need to see, touch… hear each other frequently. They can seldom be apart for any length of time. If they are apart too long, they begin to become emotionally unstable, feeling the separation almost as if one half of them had died. Soon, they have no desire to live."

"But, how can that happen if you only just met? I mean you and Tink were together for what—a total of a few minutes?" Cosmos asked as his mind sped through alternative solutions.

"It doesn't matter. The bond was made," J'kar said harshly. "Where is she?"

"I can take you to her, but it has to be her choice. I won't let you do anything to her if she doesn't want it. Do you understand? I'll kill your ass before I let you or anyone hurt her," Cosmos said.

He had seen some of the things J'kar spoke of with Tink. He knew she was crying at night, even when she thought he couldn't hear her. RITA kept him informed. He also knew she had hardly eaten in the past week.

Hell, if it hadn't been for him, forcing her to or her trying to hide her nonexistent appetite from him, she probably wouldn't have eaten at all. Raking a hand through his hair, he didn't know if what he was about to do was right or wrong, he just knew he had to do something.

"She's at the bar playing tonight. She plays there on Saturday nights. Tonight they were having a big birthday party for her boss at the garage. I was heading over that way before you guys showed up," Cosmos stood up and shoved his hands in his pocket. "She won't be home for several hours."

"Then we go to where she is," J'kar said. Nodding at the other men, they waited as Cosmos led the way out of the lab.

Chapter 13

The party was almost over by the time Cosmos, J'kar, Brock, Lan, and Derik arrived. They found a corner booth where they slid in. Jessie, a young waitress, came and took their orders. Cosmos didn't know what Prime males drank so he just ordered a pitcher of his favorite homemade beer for everyone. Jessie smiled at Cosmos.

"I haven't seen your friends before, Cosmos," Jessie asked, smiling at Derik. The other guys were a little too intimidating for her taste, but the youngest male was more than a piece of eye candy and too yummy to ignore. Derik smiled back. He could like this planet, he decided with a grin.

"They're just visiting. How much longer is the party going to last?" Cosmos asked.

"Shouldn't be too much longer. I heard Peggy say they needed to leave if they were going to get up in time to catch their flight tomorrow. I think Tink and the rest of the band are going to do one more set after that, then call it a night. I'll be right back with your beer." Jessie cast one more smile at Derik before she left.

"I could like this place!" Derik said excitedly as he looked around.

Tink was singing a duet with Mike. It was a love song dedicated to Pete and Peggy. Her sultry voice rolled over J'kar. He felt his hands tighten into fists when Mike wrapped his arm around Tink's waist. As the song ended it took Lan and Brock both to keep him in his seat when Mike leaned down and kissed

Tink on the lips. Cosmos watched as the two big men strained to keep their friend in his seat.

Grinning, he couldn't resist jabbing the big man a little. "You've got it bad, don't you? You better get over it; Tink is very affectionate. She hugs and kisses everyone!"

"Over my dead body!" J'kar growled, never taking his eyes off Tink.

Jessie came by and dropped off the pitcher of beer, pouring each glass and making sure she leaned over to place Derik's right in front of him, giving him an eyeful of cleavage. She smiled a flirty smile before she left.

Derik picked up his drink, took a sip, and released a breath. "Wow. I love this planet. Beautiful, unattached women and sweet ambrosia," he said before taking another long sip of the beer.

Cosmos laughed. "You wouldn't if you didn't look old enough to be in here. If you are under twenty-one, you wouldn't be drinking that."

J'kar vaguely listened as the men discussed the contents of the beer they were drinking. He had eyes only for the woman up on the stage singing. She picked up another instrument, similar to the one she left on his ship, and began singing another song.

He noticed many of the people who had been sitting at a long table with colorful decorations on it began leaving. He deduced the older male and female were her friends, Pete and Peggy. A handful of males still remained. There were a few females mixed in with them.

He let his gaze wander around the room. He had an uneasy feeling and wasn't sure what the cause was. He let his gaze skim each person, trying to decipher who could be a threat. His gaze stopped at the two men sitting in a booth not far from the stage.

The one on the right did not seem to put off unpleasant vibes, but the light-haired man did. J'kar focused in on the man. He did not like the way the man stared at Tink.

He had a calculating look in his eye. He turned just then as if he felt J'kar's stare. J'kar watched the man glance in his direction and frown. The booth J'kar and the others were sitting in was in a dark corner, and J'kar felt certain the man couldn't see him.

"This is one of my favorite songs. Tink does a really good job with it," Cosmos said, distracting J'kar back to the conversation going on around him. J'kar focused again on his bond mate. *His.* He still had trouble believing he found her or she found him. J'kar watched as Tink swayed her hips back and forth as she sang. She was singing another love song. He watched as the lights on the stage reflected off the highlights in her hair and the twinkle from the diamonds around her neck and on her ears. She had her eyes closed as she sang.

He let her voice settle over him. He felt his body respond to the sound of her voice, hardening his groin, and sending shivers through him. He let his eyes devour her. He saw the slight sheen of sweat across her brow and glistening on her smooth stomach.

He was fascinated with the gold chain she wore around her waist, watching as it sparkled from the lights. As his eyes traveled lower, he imaged what it would feel like to have her long legs wrapped around him. A light sheen of sweat beaded on his forehead. It took everything he had not to get up and carry her off to his warship, his world.

"Thank you for coming tonight. I hope you enjoyed your evening, and y'all come on back!" Tink said as she finished her song. "Goodnight!" she added, turning to the rest of the band for closing recognition.

"She needs to straighten up the equipment, then we can go to her. Right now, we, meaning you guys, would draw too much attention if we approached her," Cosmos said, motioning for the men with him to remain seated.

J'kar let out a soft growl of frustration. *Hockta balmas*, he thought. *Hell's balls.*

It seemed everyone and everything was trying to keep him from his bond mate. If he was on Baade, he would have thrown her over his shoulder, gone to his chambers, and taken her. He watched as Tink laughed at something one of the band members said. Some of the men who were sitting at the long table came up to the stage, and he watched as one of the men grabbed Tink around the waist and lifted her up into his arms.

Gripping the table until his knuckles showed white, he watched as Tink laughed and gave the man a quick kiss. He only released his grip when he saw the man set her back down onto the stage and a petite woman come up and put her arms around the man, laughing. That was probably the only thing that saved the unsuspecting man's life.

Cosmos leaned over and said quietly. "I told you—Tink is *very* affectionate. Don't take it personally. She is a people person who brightens up the room when she is in it."

J'kar glanced at Cosmos before turning to look again at his bond mate. He watched as she interacted with all the people who came up to her. She had a smile on her face and laughed at some of the things they said, joking back. He could see how others appeared to gravitate to her.

He recognized an inner beauty in her. She seemed to glow from the inside out. He frowned when he saw the light-haired man he observed earlier approach her. J'kar watched as Tink's face lost its smiling glow. She was frowning at the man and talking to him in a quiet voice. There was a flash, almost too fast to notice, of anger in the man's face and eyes before he turned away. J'kar's eyes narrowed as he watched the man glance once more at Tink before he turned to talk to the man who was sitting with him earlier.

* * *

Tink couldn't keep the irritation off her face as she turned away from "The Senator's Boy." The nerve of the guy! When he approached her earlier, she thought she had been perfectly clear she wanted nothing to do with him.

Now, he thought he could tell her what to do. The scum thought he could tell her he wanted to sleep with her and actually thought she would! His "I watched how you sang for me tonight and I want you. I'm going to fulfill your every fantasy tonight" bullshit had her so mad she was surprised she hadn't decked him on the spot.

Picking up the guitar she'd borrowed from the equipment room, Tink headed out the side entrance to the stage. It led around the back so band members could get to the equipment undetected if they needed to during a performance. Heading down the dark corridor, Tink unlocked the door to the equipment room. It wasn't real big, ten by ten, but everything was put up nicely so there was no clutter. Tink turned in surprise when she heard the door close and lock behind her. Blinking back the anger she felt, she noticed Scott Bachman leaning against it.

Putting her hands on her hips, Tink narrowed her eyes and said in a tightly controlled voice, "Only band members are allowed in here Mr. Bachman. You need to leave now before I call security."

Bachman laughed. "You mean the old woman who owns the place? She has her hands full cleaning up the mess from the birthday party. There's no one to bother us," he added with a nasty little grin.

"Listen, I don't know what your problem is, but let me spell this out to you in plain English so you can understand me. I. Am. Not. Interested. In. You. Got it? Was that slow enough and plain enough to sink into that stupid skull of yours?" Tink asked as she went to move around him.

I am so turning off the neon sign on my forehead, she thought to herself.

As Tink moved to pass Bachman she was surprised to feel him grab her from behind. Gasping, she turned around and struggled to loosen his hands on her. Bachman leaned forward and laughed lightly in Tink's ear.

"Not so high and mighty now, are you?" he whispered in her ear.

That was it! She had enough of the overbearing idiot's idea of fun. Letting herself go slack, she bent her knees slightly as she twisted around.

She quickly rose up and tried to head butt Bachman in the chin while bringing up her knee at the same time to hit him in the groin. What she hadn't expected was for him to react so quickly. He turned at the last minute so her knee grazed his thigh and jerked his head back so she missed his chin entirely.

"Let me go, asshole," Tink gritted out.

Bachman responded by pushing Tink back far enough to slap her across the face. The blow, combined with the backward push, was enough to knock Tink down. Tink lay stunned for a moment on the cold, concrete floor.

Raising a hand to her cheek, Tink looked at Bachman with disbelief. "Are you fucking nuts?" she asked furiously. Pushing herself off the floor, Tink charged Bachman.

Bachman slammed his fist into her side as she came at him. Tink's breath slammed out of her at the impact of the fist to her ribs. She bent over, sinking to the floor, and gasped, trying to suck in a breath to scream.

"No, no, love. No screaming. I don't want to have any company. Once I'm done with you, you won't have any air to scream again. You see, my daddy was afraid someone would try to kidnap me, so he made sure I had plenty of training in martial arts. I've been watching you for weeks. You get up there and sing all those little love songs, swaying that delicious little ass of yours. Then have the nerve to act like I am some pesky little parasite not worth your notice." Bachman pressed against Tink's bent back as she tried to get her breath, talking softly in her ear and rubbing against her. "I can't wait to see how you take it. Do you scream when you come or just moan? You like it rough, I bet. I like to give it to a woman rough. I like listening to her scream." He rubbed his groin against her ass.

Tink was trying to get enough air to tell him to go to hell. God, she could feel how much he was turned on by all the shit he was telling her. Tink had never been hit before or been in a situation like this and was for the first time in her life afraid. The room was far enough back no one would think to come back here until it was too late. She had to get away.

Dragging in another shaky breath, she quickly dropped and rolled to her left. The move caused Bachman, who had pressed most of his weight against her back to fall forward. Unable to stop his forward momentum with both hands because Tink knocked his left arm out from under him, he landed face-first onto the concrete. Tink continued rolling until she rolled into a shelf along the wall. Grabbing the shelf, she pulled herself up. Moving shakily toward the door, she tried to twist the lock with trembling fingers.

Bachman pushed himself off the floor, pressing fingers to his bleeding nose and mouth. "You fucking bitch. You want to play, let's play."

Tink turned in time to kick out at him as he reached for her again. He grabbed her ankle, pulling and twisting it as she cried out. He flung her away from the door, watching as she hit the concrete floor hard. Tink cried out again when she hit the floor. The impact against her hip bone sent waves of pain flaring through her.

"You'll never get away with this," Tink hissed through the pain, tears blurring her vision. "You'll get your ass kicked so bad there won't be much for your daddy to put back together. And there is no way in hell he'll be able to buy your way out of jail, not in this town."

Bachman just grinned. "Not if there isn't any evidence. Do you think you are the first girl that I've wanted who just seemed to disappear off the face of the Earth? No one suspects Senator Bachman's perfect son."

Tink's eyes widened when she noticed the glint of insanity in Bachman's eyes. He really believed he could do this and get away with it. Tink started to crab-walk backward, trying to put space between them. As he came closer she kicked out with her good leg, striking him a glancing blow to the groin. She watched as his eyes glazed with pain, and he sucked in a breath.

"Bitch. You'll pay for that," Bachman said as he bent over.

Tink didn't wait to see how he wanted her to pay. She pushed down the pain from her leg and hip, and scrambled to a standing position, lurching for the door again. Tink was fumbling with the lock again when she was twisted around. She was pushed up against the wall next to the door. She reached up to push against Bachman when she froze.

"How does that feel?" Bachman asked quietly as he brushed his lips along her ear.

Pain exploded through Tink's side. Her eyes widened as she looked down and saw a knife protruding from her stomach, Bachman's hand wrapped around the hilt. Almost in slow motion, she felt the cold steel of the blade and the warmth of her blood as it started seeping from the wound. Pain flashed again as Bachman pulled the knife out and stabbed her again. He rubbed his lips up and down her jaw as he did it.

"You shouldn't have played so hard to get," he whispered. "Mm, you smell so good. It's a shame I couldn't have had more time to play with you." He slowly followed the line of her jaw to her lips. "So sweet. So sweet," he said once more, before he gently kissed her again, slowly pushing the blade into her for a third time.

Chapter 14

J'kar jerked in his seat as pain exploded from his stomach and side. His eyes glazed for a moment before he exploded out of the booth. Startled, the other men turned to watch as his features turned into a dark, deadly still mask.

"She is hurt… dying," he growled.

Moving at an unnatural speed, he leapt up onto the stage and through the back entrance to the corridor behind it. Growling, he sped down the corridor to where a man stood guarding a door. The man didn't have a chance to say a word before he was thrown down the corridor, landing against the far wall and collapsing in an unmoving heap on the floor.

J'kar hit the door so hard it shattered off the door frame. He entered the room in time to watch as the man holding Tink released her. Growling again, he hit the man in the jaw hard enough, he was flung backward into the back wall where he collapsed against the metal shelving. Turning, he barely had time to catch Tink as she slid down the wall, her eyes glazing over and silent tears running down her face.

J'kar caught Tink to him, slowly lowering her to the floor. He frantically cupped her jaw as she gasped for breath. Following her hands, he was shaken to see blood pouring out of wounds to her side and stomach. She was gasping, having trouble breathing, and had a ghostly white complexion. Behind him, Derik, Lan, Brock, and Cosmos burst into the room. Cosmos let out an anguished cry when he saw Tink.

"Baby, what did he do to you?" His eyes filled with tears at the sight of Tink's poor, battered body. "Call 9-1-1. Dammit, someone call for help." He ran his shaking hand down over her hair.

J'kar cradled Tink close to his chest. Tink turned her face into his chest slightly. "Tell..." She gasped, trying to get a breath. "Tell my family I lov—"

She closed her eyes as darkness started to settle over her. She was surprised she didn't really feel pain any more. Instead, she felt so cold. She started shaking. Even the warmth of the body pressed against her couldn't seem to push the cold away. She knew she was dying, but she didn't understand why. She didn't want to die. She had so much to live for. She heard distant voices, growling, pleading. She was so tired and cold. Maybe if she fell asleep, she wouldn't feel the cold anymore.

J'kar felt the life force leaving his bond mate's body. He wouldn't, couldn't lose her. Growling at Brock, he said hoarsely, "Set the portal. We have to get her to the warship now. It is her only chance."

Brock was already setting the coordinates. He pulled J'kar's portal device out of the pouch at his waist and set the warship's coordinates into it. He nodded to J'kar.

"Go. We will follow. What should we do with the human male?" Brock asked, nodding toward an unconscious Bachman.

"Bring him. If she dies, so does he... but painfully. If she survives, he will wish I had killed him," J'kar responded, pressing the portal device and watching as the shimmering doorway appeared. As soon as it was fully formed, he gently lifted Tink into his arms and walked through.

Cosmos had only a moment to absorb what was happening before J'kar disappeared with a dying Tink in his arms. Surging to his feet, he moved to follow him only to be stopped when a hand grabbed his arm. Looking up, he stared into a pair of compassion-filled eyes.

"It is the only chance she has to survive. Our medical technology is far superior to yours. She may not make it even with ours. J'kar will do everything in his power to make sure she does," Lan said. He could tell how much Cosmos cared for the female.

"You will let me know?" Cosmos asked. "I have to know... her family. Her family has a right to know what happens to her," he added. He had no way of knowing how he was going to explain this to Tink's family, and if she didn't survive... He couldn't even think that far ahead.

Lan nodded. "We will try to notify you one way or the other. She is where she belongs."

Turning to Derik, Lan said something in their native language that didn't translate. Derik responded by grabbing one arm of the unconscious Bachman while Lan grabbed the other. Brock activated his portal, and the three men, dragging an unconscious Bachman, disappeared through the portal doorway. Cosmos was left standing in the empty equipment room.

* * *

The moment J'kar walked through the portal doorway, he was yelling for medics. The two men who guarded the transporter room immediately linked to the medical level, telling them to move, stat. J'kar ordered them to stay for the others who were following him.

J'kar never slowed down as he whisked through the sliding doors of the engineering department carrying the bloodied, unconscious body of his bond mate. Men cleared a path as they saw him, fear and worry marring their faces.

J'kar tried to be as gentle as he could, trying not to jar Tink's battered body any more than he had to in his hurry to get to medical. He was just getting off the lift when the healer met him with a portable levitating emergency medical regeneration unit.

J'kar gently laid Tink on the bed, retaining hold of her hand as the healer lowered the top of the unit over Tink. The unit would provide artificial life support until the healer could get her into a full regen bed. Nano-units would be deployed immediately to begin repair of the damage done during the brutal attack.

Once in the medical unit, the healer turned to J'kar. "You will need to leave while I stabilize her. Fortunately, I have been working with RITA to learn about human biology and anatomy. It has been fitted into our system to help in case of an emergency. Please, my lord, I need to care for her."

J'kar looked at the healer, then back at Tink's pale face. Touching her cold cheek with the back of his hand, he leaned down and kissed her forehead. "Save her, Zariff. Her life is my life," he said quietly.

Turning, he left the healer to do what he could to save his bond mate. Heading out of the medical unit, he ran into his brother Borj. Borj took one look at his brother's face, and saying nothing, simply walked next to him back to the transporter room.

Derik, Lan, and Brock appeared through the shimmering portal doorway dragging the semi-conscious body of Scott Bachman. The two guards immediately grabbed the groggy human.

"Who the fuck do you think you assholes are?" Bachman said groggily. "Let me go," he demanded.

"Release him," J'kar said as he came into the room.

He watched as Bachman clumsily stood up and threw a triumphant smile at the guards. Standing up straighter, Bachman turned to stare at the man who had walked in, and turned pale. The front of J'kar's clothing was soaked with Tink's blood, but it was the expression on the man's face that caused Bachman to pale. He was looking death in the face, his own.

J'kar watched dispassionately as Bachman's smile disappeared, and fear replaced the triumph in his eyes. Towering over the man who shrank as he approached him, J'kar looked him up and down.

"You are guilty of attacking my bond mate. The penalty is death. If she dies, you will suffer a death like you have never imagined. It will be long and painful. If she survives you will wish every day you draw a breath that you had died, for you will work in the mines until your death," J'kar said in an icy cold voice.

Turning as if to leave, J'kar swung around again and hit Bachman in the jaw with all his might. Bachman crumpled in a heap at his feet. It didn't help, but it made him feel better to know the bastard wouldn't be smiling again anytime soon. Now, all he wanted to do was return to the medical unit and his bond mate.

"I think you broke his jaw," Lan said, looking at the crumpled heap.

"Good," J'kar said grimly, leaving the room to return to the medical unit.

Borj stood aside as his brother left. He looked at the three men who returned with J'kar.

"Tell me," he asked quietly.

He listened as his younger brother and two friends explained what happened once they disappeared through the portal. Letting out a disturbed sigh, Borj nodded before leaving the men. The two guards would take the prisoner to a holding cell. The other men left to get cleaned up and rest.

Deep in thought, Borj made his way back to the medical unit. He needed to talk to his brother. If this was something common for the females on Earth, it was imperative they take action.

Borj walked quietly into the medical unit. J'kar stood in the outer room watching through the clear glass as the healer worked on his bond mate. He could feel her life force, barely. He raised one of his arms to rest it against the glass and leaned his forehead against it. He should have been more observant. He should have just taken her. He should have protected her.

"You cannot change what happened," Borj stated quietly, standing close to J'kar. "Your actions saved her life."

"We do not know if her life will be saved yet," J'kar responded with a catch in his voice. "She was so beautiful. Her voice... She sang like the beautiful flying creatures of the mountains."

Closing his eyes, he tried to picture her body swaying as she sang. Tried to remember how her sultry voice wrapped him in a cocoon of sensual pleasure. Instead, he saw her pale face, her bloodied body lying lifeless in his arms. A single tear coursed its way down his cheek.

Borj simply stood by his brother while he grieved. He knew there was nothing he could say or do to alleviate his pain. Now was not the time to worry about his own needs. He needed to stay strong for his brother.

Chapter 15

Tink felt good. Not wonderful, but good. Like she had a good night's sleep and wasn't quite ready to wake up. Her eyelids felt heavy, and she was comfortable.

Struggling to remember whether she needed to get to work or not, she frowned. Something happened. She couldn't quite remember what it was, but it seemed like it was important.

Her thoughts swirled through a combination of memories. The party and music, the band, saying good night to her friends, putting up the equipment, the room… Memories suddenly flooded her, and she let out a cry. Struggling to move, to sit up and fight, she felt her hands pinned against a broad chest. Fighting to open her eyes, she let out a scream.

"Hush, little one. Hush, you are safe," a deep voice said over and over as a strong hand clasped both of her wrists in its warmth. "Hush, little one. I will keep you safe."

Tink felt a hand running over her cheek, gently wiping away the tears slowly coursing down it. She felt the hand gently move to cup her head as she twisted to get free. Soft, firm lips moved across her forehead, her cheek, her lips—soothing her, comforting her.

Unable to use her hands, she finally won the battle to open her eyes. It took a moment to focus on the face above hers. It wasn't the attacker from her memory. It was the tall, dark-haired man with the silver eyes that she had been dreaming of for the past week. Confused, Tink stopped struggling, dragging in shuddering gasps of air, and lay still.

J'kar was startled out of a light sleep when he heard Tink scream. He had not left her side for more than the few minutes it took to shower quickly. Even that was done in the medical unit.

It had been four sleep cycles since he brought her back to the ship. During that time, the healer almost lost her twice. If it had not been for the artificial life system and the work of the nano-units, she would not have made it. The nano-units were able to stop the bleeding and repair the most critical wound, but there had still been a lot of damage and she lost a large amount of blood.

Her life force left her briefly on two occasions. J'kar melded his own life force to hers to bring it back. The effort drained him. Now, as he held her, he was overwhelmed with emotion. Running his hand over her face, he gently traced his fingers across her lips as he drew his other hand holding her wrists to his chest over his heart.

"Feel my heart. It is glad you are here, with me," J'kar said tenderly.

"What? Where am I? What happened?" Tink looked up into J'kar's eyes fearfully, still reliving the horror of the attack. Her heart was beating frantically in her chest, and she was having trouble getting a breath. Her eyes were glued to the silver eyes staring down at her.

"What is this, J'kar? Can you not give the poor girl time to wake up and recover from her ordeal before you claim her?" a voice said with a touch of humor in it.

Tink turned her head to look at the new voice. Her eyes met a pair of silver-colored eyes glimmering with compassion and humor. The man who spoke was older. He appeared to be in his early fifties. He had small lines around his eyes and mouth like he smiled a lot, and had a calming presence.

"I am Zariff, healer for the Prime members aboard this ship," Zariff said, looking at J'kar who was still lying halfway across Tink, holding her hands tightly to his chest and cupping her head with his hand. He cleared his throat and looked expectantly at J'kar with a raised eyebrow. "My lord, do you mind if I examine my patient?"

J'kar's face had a light reddish hue when he straightened up. Slowly releasing Tink's hands from his, he brushed a quick kiss across her forehead before standing and moving aside so the healer could look at his bond mate.

Tink watched the display of emotions as they crossed J'kar's face. She wondered why she was as reluctant for him to release her as he appeared to be. Shaking her head, she refocused on the man called Zariff.

"Where am I?" Tink asked hesitantly, her fingers wrapped nervously in the thin, soft material covering her.

"You are in the medical unit aboard the Prime hunter-class warship, *Prime Destiny*. You were not in very good shape when you first arrived, my dear,"

Zariff said affectionately. "I am most pleased with your progress, though."

Tink didn't know what to think. Zariff ran a strange device from her head down to her toes and then looked at a flat screen. He did a lot of humming sounds and a few comments that sounded suspiciously like "interesting." Tink simply lay there, fumbling with the covers, acutely aware she wasn't wearing much under it from the feel of the material.

Glancing back and forth between the two men, Tink's eyes suddenly filled with tears again. "I want to go home. Where's Cosmos?"

J'kar growled softly at the mention of the other man's name on his bond mate's lips. His eyes flashed a brilliant glow of silver. "You—" he started to say sharply, until Zariff turned and laid a hand on his arm.

"Patience, my lord. She is confused and still weaker than I like," Zariff said quietly. Turning back to Tink, Zariff smiled. "Your friend is well. He remained behind. I'm sure J'kar will be happy to explain everything to you later. Right now you need to regain your strength."

"Hi, honey. How are you feeling?" a voice suddenly asked.

"RITA?" Tink gave a start, straightening back on the bed.

"Of course, dear. You don't think I would leave you all alone, now do you?" RITA teased. "Your respiration and color look good. You lost a lot of blood, you know. You frightened everyone. I'm reviewing your diagnostic scan, and everything looks like you should be up and about in no time at all."

Tink smiled. She felt almost like her mom was there with her. "Thanks, RITA," Tink let out a small yawn. Her eyelids were growing heavy. "I think I need to sleep..." Tink's voice slowly faded as she fell back asleep.

J'kar watched Tink as she slowly lost the fight with sleep again. "Is she...?" He swallowed. He couldn't finish the sentence.

"She will be just fine," RITA and Zariff said at the same time.

Zariff laughed. "It is good to have RITA's expert advice, as she is more familiar with the human body." Zariff looked at the scanner again before continuing. "Her body just needs rest to deal with the trauma it has been through. I should be able to discharge her in a couple of sleep cycles. Why don't you go get some rest? I will notify you when she wakes again. It probably won't be for several hours."

J'kar looked at Zariff, then back at Tink. She looked so delicate, so fragile, lying there. His eyes roamed over her face, watching as her lips parted slightly in her sleep. His gaze moved to her chest so he could watch the gentle rise and fall of it as she took a breath.

He was almost afraid to leave. What if something happened to her while he was gone? He could feel each breath she took as if it were his own. His life force was melded with hers even though the bonding had not been completed.

He'd come so close to losing her. Moving closer to the bed, he ran his hand across her cheek and gently pushed her hair away from her face. He knew he would do whatever was necessary to keep her safe. She would no longer call for this other man, Cosmos.

No, she will call for me, J'kar thought with grim determination.

J'kar glanced at Zariff as he turned. "Call me the moment she awakens."

"I will," Zariff said, trying not to smile.

It felt good for one of their males to have found a bond mate, especially J'kar. As the next leader, it was feared he would not have an heir to carry on the bloodline. Out of the four males and one female birthed to the 'Tag Krell Manok family, none had found their bond mate until now, not even the female who came of age a full planetary cycle ago.

J'kar left the medical unit suddenly feeling the weight of what happened upon his shoulders. Weariness made him stagger slightly as he moved down the corridor to the lift. As he approached, the door opened and his brother, Borj, started to exit. Seeing J'kar, Borj stepped aside so he could enter next to him.

"Level Five," J'kar said before looking at Borj. "All is well?"

"Yes, all repairs have been finished. The men are concerned about your bond mate," Borj responded quietly. "How is she?"

"Zariff says she will be fine. She rests still. Zariff hopes to release her in a few sleep cycles. My thanks for your concern." J'kar ran a tired hand through his hair.

"J'kar." Borj paused, unsure how to continue. "I am concerned about this world your bond mate comes from. If there is a possibility of our males finding our bond mates among them, but the females are in danger, I wonder if we should be more aggressive about bringing females to our world... for their safety as well as for the future for our own race."

J'kar turned to Borj tiredly. "I understand your concern, Borj, but we do not know enough about my bond mate's species to make such a decision on such limited knowledge. I would like to explore more about their culture and bring it before the council before a decision is made. I know, though—" J'kar paused briefly, a dark look crossing his face. "—I will not let my Tink return to her world. I will not lose her," he finished harshly. Letting out a deep sigh, he added, "I will take your concern under consideration."

The doors opened and J'kar exited. He needed a drink and rest.

Chapter 16

Tink stretched. She had to get up. Not only was she sore from lying around, she needed to use the bathroom and would kill for a shower.

Sitting up and dragging the thin material of the covering with her, she swung her legs over the side. Holding the covers with one hand and sliding her other hand over her stomach and side where she remembered Bachman pushing the knife into her, she felt for the wound. Surprise flickered across her face when all she felt was smooth skin.

Sliding off the bed, Tink held onto the bedside as she adjusted to being in an upright position. Her head swam a little, and her legs felt like wet noodles! She supposed this must be what it felt like to have a major hangover. If it was, that was one thing in life she wouldn't mind passing up.

She moved slightly, testing her head and legs before letting go of the side of the bed. Moving gingerly, she walked toward a door leading off to the side of the room she was in. Peeking inside, she let out a huge sigh when she saw it was a bathroom.

"Now, if I can just figure out how to close the door on the damn thing," Tink muttered under her breath.

"Not a problem, dear," RITA chimed in, activating the automatic door and sliding it closed. "Do you need anything else?"

"Oh, hey, RITA," Tink looked around at the strange devices in the room. She could probably figure everything out if her head didn't feel like it was filled with cotton. "How about a rundown on how everything works in here. Oh, and some clothes. Where are my clothes?" Tink asked.

"Your clothes are on the bottom shelf. The doc had them cleaned, but they didn't know what to do with them so he put them in here for now."

"Cool. One problem down, one to go. Can you turn on the shower for me?" Tink asked, looking at what appeared to be a stall with no on-off levers or covering to prevent water from going everywhere.

"It uses a sanitizer. Just stand in the cubicle. After a few seconds, the sanitizer will come on, and you are clean," RITA explained. "It really is a wonderful device. Do you realize how much water would be conserved if..." RITA continued with her account of how useful such a device would be with water conservation being such a concern on Earth.

Tink tuned her out while she dropped the thin shirt she was wearing and stepped into the cubicle. Within a few seconds, a light appeared around her and a dry, soft, heated wind blew, lifting her hair and making her giggle. Looking down, she was amazed when she looked at her stomach. There wasn't even a mark to show she had been stabbed.

Looking in the reflective glass across from the cubicle, she turned from side to side to see if she could see anything. Nothing! It could only have happened a couple of days ago.

There was no way she should have survived the attack, much less not even have a mark to show it. Stepping out of the cubicle, she was just reaching for her shirt when RITA piped out a warning.

"Honey, the boss man just came into your room. From his respiration, I don't think he is happy you are not in bed. He's heading for the bathroom," RITA warned.

Tink squeaked out a frantic cry. "Lock the door! Don't let him in. I need to get dressed."

"Done. But, I don't think he is going to be happy..." RITA continued.

"I don't give a damn if he's happy or not," Tink snapped. "Just don't open that damn door unless I tell you to," Tink said as she pulled her bra around into place and shoved her head through the opening of her shirt. Hopping on one foot, she fell over when a loud thump hit the outside of the bathroom door.

"Open up this door," J'kar's voice thundered.

"Ouch!" Tink let out a loud expletive as she bumped her head on the counter. Flipping over, she shimmied into her pants as another loud thump sounded on the door. Tink was just buttoning up her pants when the door opened.

J'kar was furious. He had slept longer than he intended. After hurrying through his shower, he rushed down to medical. He was furious with himself for having slept so long.

When he walked into medical and discovered Tink's bed empty he was overcome with a sense of panic. Had something happened to her? Why hadn't he been told? Where was she? When Zariff walked in he turned on the poor healer like a madman. Zariff was confused as he had just checked on Tink and she had been there. She couldn't have gotten far, he reasoned.

J'kar was beyond reason at the moment. When they noticed the door to the cleansing room closed, J'kar tried to enter it only to find it locked. Furious, he demanded it open. RITA informed him Tink demanded it be locked until she gave her permission for it to be opened. J'kar pounded on the door demanding Tink to open it. When he heard what sounded like her falling, he panicked all over again and used a bypass code to force the door open. Now, as he stood looking into the room, he was filled with rage again to discover his bond mate lying on the floor.

"Uh, hi?" Tink said, looking up at a rather furious alien.

"What do you think you are doing? You should not be up. Why did you lock the door?" J'kar bent and scooped Tink up into his arms, ignoring her squeal of protest.

"What do you think you are doing, you big oaf! Put me down." Tink let out a groan of frustration. Damn, he was strong. She doubted he even felt her pushing on his chest. When he sat in a chair with her on his lap, she tried again to push her way out of his arms.

"Let. Me. Go," she said again, pushing as hard as she could.

"No."

"No. No? What the hell do you mean, no?" Tink was beginning to panic.

She needed to get away from him. She had to find Cosmos. She needed to go home. She had to wake up from this nightmare.

Her breathing began to come in gasps as she struggled harder to break loose from the tight grip holding her. Unable to think of what to do, she threw her head forward in a head butt and clobbered the huge man holding her in the nose.

"Ouch! Dammit!" Tink fell onto the floor at J'kar's feet. She rubbed her bruised forehead while trying to scramble to her feet.

"Bloody hell!" J'kar grabbed his nose. A small amount of blood dripped from it. "Why the hell did you do that?"

His eyes were watering from the impact. For someone so small, she packed a powerful punch. Zariff and Borj hurried into the medical room on hearing the screech Tink let out.

"My dear, what happened? Did you hurt your head?" Zariff asked with concern, pulling his scanner from his waist belt.

"Yeah, on his hard nose," Tink said, still holding her throbbing forehead.

"J'kar, what did you do to the poor girl?" Borj asked, unable to hide his amusement at his brother's obvious discomfort. He walked over and handed him a cloth.

Holding the cloth to his bloody nose, J'kar growled. "Why did you do that?" he demanded, dabbing at the blood.

Looking around Zariff, Tink glared at him. "You wouldn't let me go. You keep your cotton-picking hands to yourself!" Tink winced when Zariff touched her forehead.

"I will touch you whenever I please!" J'kar said furiously, standing up and glaring down at Tink's petite frame. "You are my bond mate and belong to me!"

"Bond mate?" screeched Tink. Pointing a finger at J'kar, Tink glared up at Zariff and Borj, "Your buddy there needs some serious medicine. He is totally delusional. I don't belong to anyone, and if you lay another finger on me, it's going to be another part of your body I'm going to bloody!"

Zariff and Borj looked at the two furious faces glaring at each other. Zariff looked at Borj, grinning, and nodded toward his office. "I think we had better leave these two alone to sort out their differences." Both men grinned at Tink before disappearing into the office located off the side of the medical unit.

"I want to go home. Now!" Tink said through clenched teeth and then stomped her foot for added emphasis.

J'kar looked at the beautiful woman standing in front of him. His nose hurt like a son-of-a-grator's butt, and his eyes were still a little watery from the impact, but he couldn't help but think how beautiful she was. Her hair was flying in all different directions with a mass of curls floating out as she glared up at him with stunning dark brown eyes.

They seemed to sparkle with the light shining from her soul. He felt his groin tighten. Taking a deep breath through his battered nose, he caught her scent, and he felt the answering surge through his body as his desire grew.

He was so close to her, he could hear her heart beating. Her blood called to him. J'kar's eyes began to glow with a deep silver fire. He had to have her, taste her, feel her.

Tink's eyes widened when she saw J'kar's expression change from fury to desire. She saw the moment it happened. One minute, his eyes looked like they were molten silver, the next, they began to glow and small sparks, almost like sparklers, seemed to appear. His pupils dilated, becoming larger and more intense.

Taking a step back, she stumbled into a small table. Pulling it in front of her she took another step, stopping only when she heard the growl in his chest getting louder. Deciding not to tempt fate any longer, Tink shoved the table at J'kar and took off running for the door, yelling for RITA to lock it after her.

J'kar heard Tink's yell, but it was too late. He was already charging her, flinging the small table to one side with a crash. Growling louder, he barely missed grabbing her as she twisted back and down right outside the door. Regaining her balance, she took off at a dead run for the end of the corridor. J'kar hit the outer wall of the corridor before pushing off and leaping after Tink's running figure.

Tink made the mistake of glancing behind her, giving up precious time. She felt hard hands grab her from behind, lifting her feet off the ground. Screaming, she fought like a maniac, twisting and kicking.

"Enough!" J'kar said. Tink's scent this close up was overwhelming what little reserve he had of his control. He barely moved his head in time to prevent Tink from head-butting him again. He wrapped his arms around her tighter, drawing her so close she couldn't get in a good kick or blow. Walking to the lift, he ordered it to go to Level Five, ignoring the stares of his men and Tink's loud curses.

Once the lift doors closed, Tink quit yelling. It was obvious no one was going to help her. She was going to have to help herself. Going suddenly limp, she melted in J'kar's arms in the hope he would either think she was unconscious and loosen his hold on her or drop her suddenly limp form.

Either way, she would try to take advantage of his loose grip. Unfortunately, he did neither. If anything, he tightened his arms, pulling her impossibly closer.

"I will not let you go," J'kar murmured in Tink's ear, brushing his lips seductively along her bent neck.

Outraged, Tink stiffened and tried struggling again. "Let me go, you... you... Neanderthal!"

"Computer, pause lift," J'kar said, slowly lowering Tink to the floor of the lift.

As soon as her feet hit the floor and his arms loosened, Tink backed up against the side of the lift. Putting her hands out in front of her as J'kar growled again softly and moved slowly toward her, she tried to make herself as small as she could in the narrow confines of the lift. Looking up was a huge mistake.

As soon as she looked into J'kar's eyes, she was lost. When he moved so close her palms rested against his chest, she didn't have the willpower to push him away. Instead, she found her hands were running up and over his broad chest. She wanted to feel him. To taste him. Shaking her head while never breaking eye contact with him, she ran her tongue over her lips. She didn't have long to wait to wonder what it would be like to kiss him.

J'kar watched as Tink's eyes suddenly became heavy with desire. He let out a shuddering breath when her hands moved over his chest. When he saw the tip of her tongue touch her lips, he quit resisting his primal urge to claim her. Wrapping his hands along her jaw, J'kar lowered his head and took Tink's lips savagely with his own. Groaning, he slid his hands down her body, pulling her closer, sliding them under her ass and lifting her up.

Tink loved the taste of J'kar. Wrapping her arms around his neck, she felt him lifting her off the floor again. Only this time, instead of fighting, she wrapped her legs around his waist, locking them at the ankles, fitting his growing length against her. Moving in time to their kiss, she moved her hips in small circles, pressing down, trying to get closer to him.

J'kar broke the kiss with a groan and rested his forehead against hers. "Feel my heart. It beats for you," He reached out and took one of her small hands in his and placed it over his heart.

Tink looked up into his eyes. Hers widened when she felt his heart beating. When he pressed his hand against hers, she felt it was beating at the same time as his. His eyes were glowing with the internal silver flame.

"What is happening?" Tink whispered in a soft, confused voice.

"You are my mate. My wife. We are one." J'kar pressed Tink between himself and the wall of the lift. He did not want to let go of her. He leaned over and sniffed along her neck and jawline, closing his eyes as the scent flowed through his mind and body. "I have lost you three times. Never again. I will never let you go."

"What do you mean, you lost me three times?" Tink was confused. She could only think about when Bachman stabbed her.

"The first time was when you first came aboard my warship. I had only discovered you. Then your friend took you from me. I wanted to kill him. The second and third times were when your life force left you."

Tink watched as pain flashed across J'kar's face. "My life force?"

"The wounds you received were grave. Twice, while Zariff worked on you, your life force almost left you. I bound my life force to yours to give you the strength you needed to live. I could not lose you,"

J'kar said quietly as if the pain was more than he could bear remembering.

Tink stared into his eyes and realized the cost her near-death had caused to the man holding her. She saw the truth, and it overwhelmed her. She had never felt anything so intense before, and it, well... it scared the hell out of her. Unlocking her ankles, she slid her legs down to the floor again. She had to think. Too much had happened, in too short a time, for her to understand and absorb it all.

"I need to go home. I need to see Cosmos," Tink said, biting her bottom lip in confusion.

A deep growl left J'kar when Tink mentioned Cosmos' name. "No. We will finish the mating rites when we return to my world. You will adjust."

"You can't just keep me. I'm not some pet or anything! I have a family, a life, and friends." Tink pushed at J'kar's hard chest, growing angrier when he didn't move.

"You will have a new family, a new life, and new friends," J'kar ground out.

He would not let her return to a world so full of danger. It would be hard enough for his people when they learned of females who were not only compatible, but who they could actually bond with. If his people found out females were in danger, it could be all-out war on the males of Earth.

"You need to get a life if you think you can tell me what to do. I don't care who you think you are—I will see my friends and family again, or you will see what hell looks like up close and personal, mister." Tink was spitting fire.

If there was one thing you didn't do with Tink, it was tell her she couldn't do something she wanted to do. And there was no way in hell she was giving up her parents, sisters, and Cosmos without a fight. She would raise so much hell he would be begging to send her home by the time she was finished.

"Lift, activate," J'kar said.

He didn't like the look in his bond mate's eyes. He had a feeling it did not bode well for his peace of mind. While he tried to gently probe her mind to see what she was up to, all he felt was a repeated rhyme he did not like, saying over and over, "All the king's horses and all the king's men..."

Chapter 17

Tink was in no mood to deal with the arrogant alien jerk. He took her to what appeared to be his living quarters and pushed her inside without another word. Of course, he couldn't get one in since she was letting him know how much hell she was going to give him if he didn't take her home immediately.

When he locked the door and even RITA replied she couldn't open it was when Tink finally let loose with all the really good expletives she had learned working at the garage. If she had her tool belt, she would have dismantled the damn door and half the ship. Instead, she was left with no one to listen to her rant and rave.

After a twenty-minute tirade of all the evil things males were made up of, Tink decided it was time to explore her surroundings. Maybe she could learn more about the "insane evil alien" as she had now categorized the new male in her life. Sinking down on the bed, she pulled the pillow into her arms and rested her chin on it. She still tired easily.

Burying her nose in the pillow, she inhaled J'kar's scent. She was honest enough to admit she loved the smell. If he wasn't such a bonehead, she could see herself dating him. He just needed to drop the caveman attitude. Lying back on the bed, Tink felt her eyes growing heavy again.

Yawning, she struggled for just a moment before giving in to the need to sleep again. She would deal with caveman after she had a good sleep. Yeah, she would deal with him. She liked his kisses and wanted more. A smile curved her lips as her last thoughts were of his lips against hers.

J'kar paused before ordering the door to open to his room. He, one of the fiercest warriors on Prime, was nervous of a tiny human female. When the door slid open J'kar moved silently inside, scanning the room. His breath caught in his throat when he did not see Tink at first. His first thought was she had been taken again.

A sudden sound from his bed caused him to release the breath he was holding. Sleeping peacefully, Tink let out a slight sigh in her sleep. She was lying on her side with her arms wrapped around his pillow.

J'kar sank down next to her on the bed. Removing his boots and outer jacket, he lay down beside her. Pillowing his head with one arm, he reached over to gently pull Tink closer to his body, wondering if she would resist in her sleep. She had been extremely furious with him when he refused to return her to her home. When she snuggled closer to his body, he tightened his grip around her waist, splaying his hand over the bare skin of her stomach.

Closing his eyes, he rested his chin on the top of her head. J'kar let his mind reach out for Tink's. He didn't know how she would feel knowing they could communicate this way. From what he had learned from Lan and RITA, this was not possible between a human male and female. It was common on Prime for bonded mates to be able to communicate telepathically with each other. It was another way they bonded. It helped build the bond between the couple and helped with protecting the female.

Tink had much to learn. So did he. He had learned much from the report Lan and Derik provided him on humans, especially females.

They were a spirited, independent race who prided themselves on their individuality and freedoms. Tink would not be happy with some of the constraints that would be placed on her. A Prime male's first instinct with his mate was to protect and care for her. After her protection, he did what he could to make her happy.

Prime women were not very demanding. His mother never seemed to demand much from his father. She just accepted what he gave to her as was her right. Burying his nose in Tink's hair, J'kar had a feeling this would not be the case with his mate.

Slowly, images began to appear in his mind. Images he was not familiar with. J'kar realized he was catching glimpses of random thoughts flickering through Tink's mind. He caught bits of different women, laughing and singing together. An older male with his arm wrapped around her shoulders.

He stiffened and a low growl escaped him before he could stop himself when an image of the human male, Cosmos, appeared. It was a memory of them lying together in a bed laughing. The growl grew when the imaged shifted to one of Cosmos kissing her.

* * *

Tink was dreaming. It was one of those *"I know I'm dreaming, but is it real, and I know I won't remember it when I wake up"* kind of dreams. In the middle of the kaleidoscope of memories flowing in and out like a tide in dreamland, a low growling slowly infiltrated through her consciousness.

Rolling over onto her back and pushing the pillow away from her, Tink was vaguely aware something warm was pressed against her. It felt warm and smelled good. Continuing her roll, she kept her eyes closed as she inhaled deeply.

Yep, warm, masculine, delicious. If this was a dream, she wanted it to continue.

Her thoughts went to J'kar and how good his lips had felt. How she wanted to kiss him again and again. Letting the feeling take over her mind, she remembered the feel of his hands on her and shivered. Hands running down her back to her hips and pulling her up so she could wrap her legs around his waist. The feel of his huge cock against...

"You must stop, or I will not be able to."

Tink's eyes flew open. She was lying in J'kar's arms. His body was pressed against hers tightly, and he had those funny-looking flames in his eyes again.

Staring into a pair of dark, molten silver eyes, Tink thought to herself, *"I heard you speak to me. In my head."*

"Yes, little one, it is part of the bonding between mates. It helps the male in protecting the female. It also helps him to know what needs to be done to make her happy."

"Well, knock it off. I'm still mad at you."

"I can tell. You were most displeased." J'kar could not keep the hint of amusement out of the tone of his thoughts. He winced suddenly at the new thought in Tink's mind. He would have to remember she had a very vivid imagination.

Tink raised her eyebrow and thought about what a pair of pliers placed on a very strategic part of the anatomy would feel like. *"Cool! I think I could like this a lot."*

"You are a very…" J'kar searched for the right words to use.

"Difficult, creative, lovable, delightful, adorable…" Tink said with a grin.

"Unusual. Female," J'kar murmured before uttering a surprised hiss.

Tink had some ideas about being unusual. She might not remember her dreams, but she did remember her last thought before going to sleep. There were a few things she wanted to try on the big guy. She just needed to verify a few answers to some questions before she proceeded. She decided a surprise attack might produce some answers. So, with a quick grip to his wrist, she twisted out of his arms and up on top of him.

Straddling him, she held his arms above his head. They both knew he could easily overcome her, but J'kar was so startled by the move, he lay still. Scooting down his huge body until she pressed the vee of her jeans against his crotch, she rubbed against him.

J'kar drew in a deep breath. His eyes turned a deeper silver, and his pupils dilated. Through clenched teeth, he hissed. "What are you doing?"

"Interrogation," Tink replied with a wicked glint in her eyes.

"Interrogation?" J'kar didn't remember any of this being in the reports he had received.

"Yes. I have a few questions, and I want some answers. So, interrogation." Tink lowered her head. She slid her lips along the underside of J'kar's jaw. Rubbing her lips against the rough shadow of facial hair, she asked her first question.

"Do you live with your momma?"

"Live. Momma. What?" J'kar was having problems creating a rational thought. She wanted to know if he lived with a momma?

"You know. Do you live at home with your mother? Are you a momma's boy? Does your mother tell you what to do, take care of you, tell you who you can date?" Tink added a little nip with each clarifying question, soothing each one with a lick of her tongue.

"Yes. No. I mean, we live in the palace in the city. I have my own home outside the city where I reside most of the time. My mother does not control my life. Her place is beside my father. Yours will be beside me." The nips and licks were playing havoc with his body. He was on fire.

"Good enough. Next question. Are you currently involved with anyone? Such as in a short-term, long-term, or married relationship?" Tink moved one of her hands, gripping—if you could call not even being able to wrap her hand around one of his wrists gripping—his two wrists with her other hand.

She moved her hand down through his hair, running her short nails through it as she went. She shifted her hips again to press it along the huge length now clearly defined in his pants. Stretching so she could run her lips along his ear, she repeated her question. Groaning at the feelings she was bringing out in him, J'kar gritted his teeth when she moved across his arousal again.

"Yes. I am involved in a long-term relationship. With you." Beads of sweat appeared on his forehead, and he closed his eyes.

His canines had lengthened against his will. He did not want to frighten the human and knew from some of the things he had learned from RITA this might be a cause of concern. Human superstitions had elongated canines belonging to creatures who might not be considered good, except if you read the current series about a vampire family and the human girl who had fallen in love with one of them.

J'kar's eyes flew open when he tasted the sweet warmth of lips against his. He could no longer control himself when Tink ran her small pink tongue up the length of one of his canines. A primal growl exploded out of his chest as he quickly took control of the situation. Rolling over and pinning Tink beneath him, he ground his arousal against her.

Tink was startled as she watched J'kar's canines extend. It should have scared her, but she picked up enough bits and pieces in J'kar's mind to know he would never hurt her. If anything, it turned her on even more than the interrogation she had started. She had only meant to throw him off balance when she started, but it soon turned into something much, much more.

She could feel his arousal growing and knew she should have stopped, but she couldn't. Fire consumed her, burning uncontrollably from her toes to the top of her head. She felt like if she didn't have an orgasm soon she would spontaneously combust. She had never had an orgasm, she had read about them, but right now she would kill to experience one.

As he pressed down on her, she rose up to meet him. Grinding her hips against him, Tink gritted out between her own clenched teeth, "I think I can forget the next two questions. You have passed the interrogation. Now, do something about it!" Twisting in an effort to free her hands, Tink was almost sobbing from the frustration she was feeling. She had to touch him, taste him.

J'kar was breathing hard. He was very close to losing all of his self-control. He tried to breathe in through his nose, but that made the situation even worse. Her scent normally stretched his control, but the scent of her arousal combined with his own was too much.

He had to leave before he did something they would both regret. Closing his eyes, he struggled to regain enough strength to leave. Pushing himself off the bed and away from her, he grabbed his boots and jacket and left the room as if the hounds of hell were after him.

Tink lay there for a few minutes trying to control her own erratic breathing. *Pheromones are powerful shit,* she thought.

If she could bottle the stuff she would never have to work again. Groaning, she pushed herself off the bed. Putting her head in her hands, she tried to get her body back under control.

Damn, she could feel the wetness between her legs. Her pants were wet from her arousal. She had never gotten so turned on before. Not from all the articles, books, or movies she had watched.

She knew one thing for sure, if he thought he was not going to satisfy the ache she was feeling, he had another think coming. He thought he could just leave? Like hell. This was war, and she planned on winning. She wanted a certain alien. She wanted him very badly, and what Tink wanted, she got.

A wicked little smile formed on her lips. So, they could talk mind-to-mind. This could get really, really interesting.

First, she needed more information on the alien's sex life, and what they liked and didn't like. Who better to give her the information than a horny young alien male? Yes, this could be fun, Tink thought, as the plan became clearer in her mind.

Chapter 18

"Enough!" Lan pulled J'kar off another young crewman. "Enough, J'kar."

J'kar went down to one of the cargo areas they used for training during the long months in space. He had to work off some of the excess feelings he was having. For the past two hours he'd pounded, tossed, and kicked anyone crazy enough to take him on. Sweat dripped off his body and his breathing was heavy as he turned to face Lan.

"Here. Dry off," Lan threw a towel at his face. "Do you want to talk about it?"

Growling, J'kar grabbed the towel drying off his face, chest, and arms. "You did not tell me about human interrogation methods."

LAN paused, looking at J'kar with confusion. "Human interrogation methods? What human interrogated you? What did they do?"

"Not they, she. The human female interrogated me. She…" J'kar's flushed face deepened in color. "She asked me questions and used unnecessary force to get her answers."

"Tink? Tink interrogated you? What did she do? What questions did she ask?" Lan was shocked.

How did a tiny human female have the strength to interrogate someone as strong as a Prime male? From the look of J'kar when he entered the cargo area he had been in physical pain. Lan had never seen him like this before. He did not remember J'kar being this upset even after he was tortured once by a group of rebels who had captured him in an attempt to take over the Prime leadership.

What could the human have done to elicit so much pain? He needed to know. If they were that powerful, perhaps it would be best not to try to bring more females to their world.

"She…" Turning away, J'kar clenched and unclenched his fists, trying to regain control. Even thinking about her with her body pressed against his, her tongue sliding up his extended canines, was causing his body to react.

Groaning, he turned and sank down on one of the low benches along the wall, putting his head in his hands. "She straddled me, running her body up and down against mine. Her lips. She ran her lips over my jaw, nipping and licking as she went. She held me down under her, while she…"

Lan listened in disbelief. Prime women were never this aggressive. "She straddled you? As in, she climbed on top of you?" Lan whispered in awe.

Groaning again, J'kar continued, "That is not all. She rubbed against me over and over. Then, she ran her hands through my hair while she licked my ear and bit it. It was incredible. The feelings were overwhelming, but she would not stop. She asked me questions. I don't even remember what she asked. The thoughts flowing through her were unbelievable. It was nothing like what we were taught. She had images of our bodies doing things I have never seen or heard of before. I would have answered any question she asked. But, when she, when she…" J'kar trailed off. His gaze was glazed as he remembered.

"What?" Lan all but shouted. He quieted down when he noticed some of the men training stopping to look at them. "What did she do?"

Lan could hardly believe what he was hearing. Prime women were not very sexually active. They came together with their men for duty and birthing. The mating ritual was done to ensure the best possible match was made so the strongest offspring was conceived. There were places the men could go for gratification, but even there the women simply provided a place for them to relieve the buildup of hormones. From what J'kar was saying, not only did this human female enjoy the contact between them, she initiated it.

"She ran her tongue along my canines." J'kar looked at Lan.

Lan sat back as he absorbed what J'kar was saying. During sexual stimulation a Prime male's canines grew in length. They were very sensitive.

Most of the time, a male would bite the female when it was time to reproduce, as the canines secreted chemicals, causing the female to be more receptive to the male's mating. It did not last long, but allowed the female to receive some pleasure from the mating. Lan had never heard of a female actively seeking or responding to a Prime male without the bite. He especially never heard of a female finding pleasure in the feel of the canines.

Lan had a huge grin on his face. With this new information, he was more inclined to agree with Borj about invading the planet and taking off with the females. Just the thought of it had him growing hard.

"What were her thoughts as she interrogated you? You said her thoughts were unbelievable. What did she imagine your bodies doing together?" Lan was almost salivating as he waited for the answer.

J'kar threw Lan a frustrated look before getting up and moving toward the lift. Lan stared after him in disbelief. He wasn't going to tell him.

He knew he wouldn't get any more answers out of J'kar. He had to know. He was on fire. He shook his head. If he got this turned on just listening to the few things J'kar told him, he couldn't even begin to comprehend what J'kar must be going through having experienced it. He would have to find his answers somewhere else.

Moving toward the lift, he decided he needed to talk to RITA some more. It would appear he missed a critical part of Earth culture: sex. What was it like for a human male and female? Determined, he headed for his office.

* * *

"What do you mean that is not part of your database?" Lan wailed. He thought for sure RITA would have all the answers. "You know all about human beings."

"Well, not all. You have to remember I was a partial download! It is not my fault you want to know information I didn't think was relevant at the time.

Why don't you ask Tink? She can tell you what you want to know," RITA said with a huff, like she was Dr. Ruth or whoever.

Lan grabbed his hair on either side of his head. This was not helping. How could he ask Tink without J'kar knowing what he was doing? J'kar would not be understanding at all if he found out. He also had no idea how the human female would feel about it. He needed to know, though. He was burning up inside now with the images his conversation with J'kar had given him.

Were they all like that? Was she unique? Grabbing his jacket, he headed for the galley. Maybe if he talked to Zariff, Brock, Derik—no, not Derik, well, maybe Derik—or Borj, they could help him.

* * *

Tink realized after J'kar left the door to the room was no longer locked. She figured it was probably a mistake, but what the hey, you didn't argue with a gift horse. Moving down the corridor, Tink tried to remember Tansy's advice, "When doing something you shouldn't be doing, just act like you aren't doing anything wrong, and no one will notice you."

Great advice if you had nerves of steel, which right now she didn't. Straightening her shoulders, she headed out the door. After all, she wasn't doing anything wrong. He was the one who had left the door unlocked. In her book that meant she was free to come and go as she pleased. Moving to the lift, she paused as she saw one of the crewmen ahead of her.

* * *

"Excuse me. Can you tell me where you get something to eat around here?" Tink asked with a friendly smile.

The crewman looked startled at first, then nodded. "Level Three, third door on the right."

Touching one of her ears where the translators had been implanted, she grinned. "Thanks!"

Tink moved past the slightly dazed crewman and headed for the lift. Stepping inside, she waved before the doors closed. The crewman lifted his hand with a puzzled look on his face.

"Level Three, please."

The lift quickly took her down to the level she wanted. She moved down the corridor, counting. Sure enough the third door opened to reveal the dining hall. Glancing around, Tink's eyes lit up when she caught sight of Derik. Moving through the tables until she was standing in front of him, she grinned down at the men sitting down at the table.

"Do you mind if I join you?" Tink asked, nodding toward an empty seat.

All three men stood quickly. "Yes, please. Sit. You are much better?" Derik asked quickly.

"Yes, thank you. Just hungry." Pushing her hair away from her face, she slid into the seat across from Derik.

"I would be happy to get you something," one of the other men said, not sitting down immediately.

"Oh, would you, please? A little of everything so I can see what I like, if you don't mind," Tink gave him a big smile, showing off the dimple in her right cheek.

The young crewman blushed and turned, hitting his leg on the edge of the table as he hurried to get her food.

Laughing, Tink leaned forward on her elbows. "Is he always like that?"

"No, just with you." Derik grinned back. "He is normally very talkative."

"Hmm. So, what have you been up to since I last saw you? You look pretty damn good considering you were almost iguana bait the last time I saw you," Tink asked, her eyes twinkling at the memory of her first time on board the ship.

"I am most well, thanks to you. I went to your world. I heard you sing. You are most gifted. Perhaps you can sing for us. We get little entertainment here," Derik said, totally absorbed in Tink's natural beauty.

The crewman who had left to get her something to eat returned with a tray loaded down. Tink laughed when she saw all the food. There was no way she would ever be able to eat it all! Placing the tray in front of her, the crewman blushed again before sitting next to her. Tink couldn't resist leaning over and giving him a kiss on the cheek.

"Thank you, this looks great. I hope some of this is for everyone. I could never eat all of this by myself," she said, picking up a piece of purple food. It looked like some kind of root. Smelling it first, she took a small bite before grinning. It was good. It was only when she was about halfway done with the piece that she realized silence filled the room.

"Is something wrong?" Tink asked, chewing the purple root slowly. She glanced around the room and noticed everyone was looking at the crewman next to her. Turning, Tink was shocked to see him staring at her with wide eyes and a silly grin on his face.

"What?" Tink asked again, shaking her head and wondering if everyone was always this strange. If so, she was going to have some interesting meals.

Derik cleared his throat, replying hoarsely, "You placed your lips upon Von."

"So?"

"Never has a female placed her lips willingly upon one of us," Derik replied with awe.

Tink choked on the drink she had just picked up. Coughing, she cleared her throat. "Are you telling me you are all virgins? You've never been kissed?"

"What is this virgin?" Derik asked.

* * *

Lan had come to the galley for food and the hopes of meeting up with some of the other men to discuss what happened with J'kar earlier. When he noticed Derik eating with another crewman, he figured now would be as good a time as any to ask Derik if he had learned anything about human females.

Just as he was getting up the nerve to ask Derik, Tink entered the galley. Perhaps he would be able to ask her some questions discreetly. When she kissed Von, he was as shocked as the rest of the crew.

Never had a female initiated contact before like that. She was a bonded mate. Yes, he knew the ceremony formally mating them had not been done, but she belonged to J'kar. Yet, she placed her lips upon another male. He had seen her do this on her planet and thought it was just a custom there. Cosmos had called the female a "people person" who was "very affectionate." He needed to know more. Did this have something to do with the interrogation she had given J'kar?

Tink couldn't resist laughing. Here she was, a highly qualified virgin giving sex ed to a bunch of manly alien males.

"A virgin is someone who hasn't been with someone else sexually yet. There are varying degrees of virgins if you ask my mom. I guess if you break it down, there are."

Derik blushed. "Do you mean the physical release of the male?"

Lan leaned forward. He wanted to know as well. Tink realized she had every man's attention in the room. She was used to working with guys, and where there were guys, there was always talk about sex. It was something she had stopped being embarrassed about years ago. You didn't get to be twenty-two and not know the birds and the bees or whatever name they called it now.

Besides, her parents were a walking, talking sex-machine couple. They couldn't keep their hands off each other if their lives depended on it. Tink and her sisters had grown up listening to all the innuendos her parents used to say before they became old enough to understand them. It didn't stop her parents from making them.

"You guys know about the birds and the bees? Don't you?" Tink asked, biting her bottom lip to keep from grinning.

"We know not of these birds and bees," Lan said.

Looking across at Derik and Lan, Tink shrugged her shoulders before calling out in a loud voice. "Raise your hand if you want to know about sex?"

Laughing when all hands rose, she continued, "I hope all of you are old enough for this. Please note this disclaimer that I speak only from my limited knowledge and cannot be held in any way responsible for the outcomes of this conversation."

Tink felt she should make some kind of disclaimer. After all, she didn't know how serious these guys really were. But hey, she was always willing to do her part in interworld relations. Besides, maybe it would get back to Mr. Ice Cube, and he might be interested in alleviating her current virgin status.

So, with a grin on her face and a very active imagination from all the romance novels, books, Internet research, sex education classes, and talks with mom, sisters, girls, and the garage mechanics, Tink gave the galley full of interested alien males the highs and lows of sex on twenty-first century Earth. After an hour-long talk, she asked if anyone had any questions.

"What did you mean by oral sex?" Derik asked.

Oh, boy. Maybe she should have skipped the question part. Blushing a little, Tink cleared her throat and replied, "Well, oral sex is when a man or a woman... well, they use their mouth to, you know, give each other pleasure."

"No. How can using your mouth give pleasure to the other? Why would they use their mouth? How can there be mating with just a mouth?" Confused murmurs went through the room.

"Okay. Let's see. Maybe I can give you an example," Tink was thinking back to the movie with Meg Ryan and Billy Crystal. If it worked for Meg, maybe it would work for Tink. Hiding a grin behind her hand, she couldn't believe she was going to do this. She couldn't wait until she shared it with her sisters and Cosmos.

"Everyone close your eyes. I am going to give you an oral sexual experience to show you how much just talking about it, imagining it, listening to the sounds, and feeling it can be a really big turn-on," Tink said, wiggling her shoulders and getting into the role. She cleared her throat, letting it drop down a notch to a husky, sultry level before she started.

Tink looked around to make sure everyone had their eyes closed. Satisfied, she hoped she could pull this off. She closed her eyes and imagined what it was like with J'kar, the feel of him, the taste of him, the smell of him.

She imagined what she wanted to do to him, how she wanted to run her lips and teeth all over his body. How she would slowly undress him and then herself. She imagined how she would dance for him and tie him to the bed where he couldn't touch her, just feel as she used her mouth, her teeth, her tongue to make exquisite love to every inch of his body.

Tink didn't realize at first she was talking out loud until she heard the first moan come from a table next to the one she sat at. She continued describing in exquisite detail all the ways she would make love to the man of her dreams using just her mouth.

"Now, slide your thumb in your mouth. Wrap your tongue around it. Feel how it wraps around you, hot, moist, soft, and firm at the same time. Suck on it, drawing it deeper into your mouth. Oh God, feel how hot and moist it is wrapped around you. Imagine a woman doing that to you. She slides between your legs and takes you deep into her mouth. Her hot, moist mouth wrapped around you down low where she moves slowly at first, then faster and deeper, holding you tight while you watch her running her tongue up and over you again and again. Feel the slight nip of her teeth as she scrapes it over you so deep she can feel you as you are coming. She tastes your hot cum, swallowing everything you've got to give her. Now it's your turn to do the same for her. Open your mouth and run your tongue up between two of your fingers and imagine it as being her. Imagine how hot she is for you, how swollen. She begs you to take her, and then she explodes with an orgasm so powerful you can feel her clenching you tight as she cries out her release." Tink moaned as if she was having an orgasm.

Unable to continue as she felt her own desire for release build, she opened her eyes, ready to tell the guys that was what oral sex was when she caught a glimpse of a dozen male faces, eyes closed, in varying degrees of intense sexual release.

Slapping her hand over her mouth, Tink's eyes bugged out as she realized this was nothing like the reaction Meg Ryan had gotten. It had been bad enough watching it on the television. To see something like it played out in real life, in front of her, was almost more than she could handle.

Standing quietly, Tink slowly backed out of the room, hoping no one would open their eyes to see her make a fast escape. Once in the corridor, Tink took off at a run to the lift. Collapsing in a heap of giggles, she was laughing so hard she had tears running down her cheeks.

She was in total, deep shit. She didn't have a clue as to how she was going to get out of this one. She only hoped J'kar didn't hear about it or she would never be allowed out of the room again.

Chapter 19

J'kar was on the bridge after his workout in the cargo area. He had showered and changed in the small cleansing room located in the conference room off the bridge. He was not up to seeing the human female yet. He was barely in control, and needed time and exhaustion to deal with her.

Prime males could be very aggressive during sex, and he had come close to losing his control. If he had, he had been fearful of frightening or hurting the female with his desire. He was in the middle of reviewing a report when the first sense of unease rippled through him.

He looked around the room and noticed two of the younger men sitting at one of the view-screens. It was not uncommon for the men to work together if they were reviewing a report or had a question about something, so he ignored it at first. It was more their body language, as if they were excited about something. Soon, more of the men seemed more focused than usual on what was going on at their stations. No one was moving away and they had their eyes closed.

Then, the images began. He felt when Tink unknowingly searched for him. He felt the connection when she melded with his mind.

Closing his eyes, he let the first contact with her wash over him. He had at first been afraid she was in danger. From the instruction he received when he was younger, he had been told the only time a mate searched for her male was when she was in danger.

He let the waves of dizziness pass as she seemed to caress him. It was then the images filled his mind. What she wanted to do to him, all the ways she wanted to touch him, taste him, love him with just her mouth. Locked in the mind meld, he could barely move. He became instantly aroused as the first wave of what she was thinking washed over his body.

He staggered back to the conference room and choked out a command to lock the door. He leaned back against the door, unable to move at first. The next wave of images had him bending over. He put his hands on his knees as the images became more detailed. Gasping, he reached up and undid the buttons on his pants, releasing his swollen cock so it was free from the tight confines of his pants.

As the images of Tink slowly undressing him filled his mind, he could feel her hands on him. His skin burned from the feeling of her hands running over his shoulders and down his chest. He sucked in his breath when he felt her tongue and teeth scrape against his nipples, first one, then the other as she brought them to a hard peak. She ran kisses over his chest before letting her lips slide further down to place small kisses down to the edge of his pants.

He gasped as she undid his pants, pulling his full and throbbing cock free. He groaned loudly when he felt her, wrapping one hand around his swollen cock while the other wrapped around his tight balls. Pushing his pants down until they pooled around his ankles, she gently pushed him down onto the bed where she slid ties around his wrists and ankles. Tied to the bed, he could do nothing as she began a slow dance.

Moving her hips from side to side, she slid her hands over her flat stomach until she gripped the end of her black shirt. She did a slow twist, turning her body as she pulled the shirt over her head. All he could see was her bare back as she smiled wickedly over her shoulder at him. Swaying back and forth, she grabbed the top of her jeans and bending over she let them slide down her legs and stepped out of them giving him a view of her beautiful ass covered by a thin lacy material. Turning, she again ran her hands down over her full breasts, stopping to play with the nipples before moving her hands down to the edge of her panties and pushing them down.

J'kar wrapped his hand around his aching cock. It had drops of pre-cum pearling on the end.

Breathing heavily, he couldn't have broken the image Tink was giving him if his life depended on it. When she pictured coming to him and kissing him as he lay unable to move, he dragged in long, deep breaths, trying to control the feelings she was building in him.

When she moved up and gripped his balls again, he sank to his knees on the floor of the conference room. The image of Tink sliding his cock into her mouth and her sucking him—slowly at first, then faster, then slow again—filled his mind; he groaned and laid his forehead against the floor. Tink's mouth felt hot and moist as she wrapped it around him, drawing him closer and closer to release.

When she stopped, he let out a howl of anguish. It wasn't until the next image filled his mind that he finally couldn't hold back any longer. The image of her wet, dripping mound above his mouth, her thighs on each side of his face, and her lowering herself down for him to suckle on her as she slid his cock back into her mouth had him throwing his head back, his teeth fully elongated as he felt his release.

Panting, he growled as he felt her withdraw from his mind. Growling, he slammed his fist into the floor of the conference room. The conference room floor was covered with his cum.

His eyes gleamed with a wild flame. He would make her pay for this. No female had ever made him come like this before. No one had ever brought him to his knees before. None had ever had the power to do what a tiny human female had done. He had to find out how she did it. He had to know how powerful human females were.

* * *

Tink made it back to the room feeling a sense of relief to find it empty. Maybe no one would say anything. It wasn't as if guys wanted everyone to know about their having uncontrolled ejaculations.

No, as long as the guys in the galley didn't say anything she should be safe, Tink thought as another fit of giggles had her rolling on the bed. Boy, her sisters were never going to believe this one. It was a good thing her mom hadn't been there. Tink had talked about having oral sex from watching videos, reading books, and such. She could imagine how a talk from her mom would have gone over with Tilly talking from experience. It had taken Tink a year to get over the little her mom had been able to explain to her about it. The last thing she wanted to think about was her parents having oral sex. God, what a thought.

Getting up, Tink headed to the bathroom. Closing the door, she took off her clothes and stepped into the cubicle. After the light beam did its job, Tink wrapped a towel around herself.

"Damn. No clothes," Looking down with disgust at her dirty clothes, she shrugged.

Well, it wasn't like she hadn't asked to be taken home. She would borrow a shirt from J'kar. As tall as he was, it would be longer than most of her dresses anyway. Opening the door to the bathroom, she moved into the room at the same time the door to the room opened from the corridor. Startled, Tink twirled around and sank down on the bed, pulling the towel closer around her body.

"Hey, knock next time, will you?" Tink exclaimed, startled.

Silhouetted against the light coming from the corridor was J'kar's large figure. Not saying anything, he moved into the room and gave the command to lock the door.

"You don't look any better than you did when you left. What is your problem?" Tink asked crossly.

She wasn't up to an argument with him, at least, not until she had some clothes on. Standing, she moved to cross to the bathroom. The least she could do was put her dirty clothes back on, then she would feel better about dealing with him.

J'kar moved at the same time Tink did. He ignored Tink's yell when he picked her up and tossed her onto the bed. He lay down on top of her, pinning her hands above her head to prevent her from moving.

Tink stared up at J'kar. She didn't know what was wrong, but something had definitely pissed the big guy off. He was furious. Not just mad. Not just angry. Totally Berserker fury.

"What's wrong?" Tink asked in a small voice.

"You," J'kar growled harshly.

"Me. What did I do?" Tink squeaked.

Oh, God. Had he found out about the galley? Surely he couldn't be this angry about the birds and the bees talk. Okay, more like a Meg Ryan re-enactment, but still, she had given the disclaimer.

Breathing deeply, J'kar tried to get control of the emotions raging through him. He had meant to come back to the room to discipline her. He had not expected to find her covered in so little clothing or unaware of what she had done to him. He could sense her confusion was real.

Staring down into her eyes, he asked her, *"Do you remember your connection to me a short while ago?"*

"What connection? Are you—we—doing the weird mind reading thing again?" Tink asked, confused.

"I need to know if you purposely connected with me a short while ago." J'kar asked in a gruff voice.

"I don't know how. You are the one doing it. I just answer you. What happened a little while ago? Did I do

something that hurt you?" Tink's eyes grew wide with fear.

She didn't want to hurt anyone. If she had hurt him unintentionally she needed him to know she didn't mean to. She didn't understand all this brain to brain communication stuff. Could she have hurt him?

Tink's eyes filled with tears as she asked the question she was afraid to have him answer. "Did I hurt you somehow? I don't understand how you can talk to me telepathically. Humans can't do that. If I hurt you I didn't mean to. What happened?" Tink whispered.

J'kar closed his eyes briefly as he thought about what she said. If she spoke the truth, she was unaware of the power she had over him. He could not condemn her for something she had not been aware of doing. He could not punish her for doing something she was unaware of doing. He would need to teach her, though. She had much more power over him than anyone else ever had.

"Your thoughts, little one, are very powerful. You had thoughts earlier that were very—" J'kar paused, searching for the right words. "—arousing. It became very difficult for me."

It took a moment for his words to sink in. When they did Tink turned a brilliant shade of red. "Oh, lord. You saw all the things I was thinking about?"

"Yes. I saw. I felt. And… I reacted," J'kar said. He didn't like to admit it, but he needed her to understand the power of her thoughts and their effect on him. "I had never experienced anything like that before, and it was most difficult."

Raising an eyebrow Tink couldn't resist asking, "Did you like it?"

Groaning, J'kar rolled off Tink, standing quickly and moving to the other side of the room. Turning to face her, he growled. "More than you can imagine. What you imagined is impossible."

"Why?" Tink asked curiously.

"Are you telling me the males and females of your planet actually do the things you imagined?" J'kar looked at Tink with disbelief.

"Yes. It's called making love. Well, it is for those who do it while caring for each other. Otherwise, it's just called sex," Tink answered in surprise.

Eyes wide with amazement, it was J'kar's turn to ask questions. "Where did you learn about it? Have you done this with males of your species? With the male... Cosmos?"

The last part was said with a growl. The thought of Tink doing the things she imagined with another male, with this Cosmos, filled him with rage. He wanted to find any male who had touched her and kill him, slowly.

"Yew, no. Cosmos is like my brother. I have never had nor do I ever want to have sex with him." Tink shuddered at the idea. Cosmos was cute and all, but not in that way!

J'kar relaxed a little hearing Tink's intense distaste of the thought of having sex with Cosmos. But, she still hadn't answered his questions.

Realizing J'kar wasn't going to let it drop, Tink blew back a strand of hair hanging over her forehead. "I learned a lot from my mom. She gave all of us girls the 'talk' when we hit puberty. The rest is a part of American culture. Books, Internet, magazines, movies, and girlfriends fill in the rest of the knowledge pool. No, I have never done *it* with a guy before. What I imagined doing with you or anything else." Tink looked away as she said the last part. She fumbled with the edges of the towel, suddenly conscious of how little she wore and the direction of the conversation they were having.

"Your mother told you about such things?" J'kar asked in disbelief.

"You don't know my mom. Let me tell you, she could give you a sex education class that would have all the men on your planet blushing. If not that, just listening to her and my dad talk to each other is enough of an education," Tink muttered, picking at the corner of the towel she was wearing.

"Your parents. They enjoy being together?" J'kar asked curiously. He moved back to the bed and sat next to Tink, picking up and holding one of her hands. He held her hand, rubbing his thumb back and forth across it. It gave him a warm feeling, touching her and her seeming to enjoy it.

"Yes. They enjoy being together very, very much. They are always hugging, kissing, and touching each other. I swear those two act worse than any teenagers I've ever seen. They are always making out or talking about sex, having sex, where they've had sex, or where they want to have sex. It got so bad none of us girls could look them in the eye. They thought they were being sly about it, but we caught on at an early age when they would suddenly need to take a nap in the middle of the day and the whole RV would rock. Talk about embarrassing," Tink said, rolling her eyes as she remembered the first time she finally figured out what her folks were doing.

Tink liked how he was rubbing his thumb across her hand. She gasped when he turned her hand over and traced the circles on her palm. It felt like he was touching her deep inside.

She shuddered at the feelings coursing through her body. She could feel the moisture form between her legs. Pulling his left hand toward her, she pulled his fingers back until the intricate circles on his palm were visible.

Watching him, she slowly brought it to her face. Rubbing her cheek against it, she saw the small flames appear in his silver eyes. Turning her head, she continued watching him as she slowly traced the design with the tip of her tongue.

J'kar's eyes widened, then narrowed to slits. A growl started in his chest, and his teeth began to elongate. Tink's body was on fire. J'kar's nostrils flared at the scent of her arousal.

Standing up so she was in front of him, Tink dropped her towel. Nibbling on the palm of his hand, Tink leaned closer until her breast brushed against his mouth. J'kar groaned as Tink pressed her engorged nipple against his lips.

Flicking his tongue out he drew the nipple into his mouth, sucking on it. Tink pulled his palm down to her other breast and threw back her head with a groan as J'kar pulled her closer. Letting his right hand drop down to between her legs, J'kar slid his finger across Tink's mound.

He felt her moist heat and could not stop himself from sliding a finger between the folds of her vulva. He growled against her breast when she pushed down against his finger. Pulling her down and around until she lay on her back on the bed, J'kar stood and began removing his clothes.

"You are mine. For now and for always. There will never be another. There will be no going back," J'kar said. "I claim you as my bond mate. My wife. For always." He finished undressing and stood above Tink, fully aroused.

Tink was not afraid. She wanted him and knew it was right. Her mom had always told her she would know when it was the right man. Kneeling on the edge of the bed, Tink smiled and held out her hand.

"I want you. I don't understand all of this. The feelings you stir inside me, but I want to find out. I need to find out," Tink said softly as she reached for him.

"I would like to do what you had imagined earlier," J'kar said in a husky voice filled with need.

Laughing, Tink said. "That is just the tip of the iceberg, baby. Just the tip."

Tink slid her hands up his chest as he pushed her back. Tink pulled J'kar down with her and kissed him deeply, running her tongue up and down the length of his elongated canines. J'kar shuddered as her tongue moved up and down, then across his lips.

Pressing Tink farther back into the bed, J'kar kissed along her jawline, moving along her neck and shoulder. Tink arched her back, trying to get closer to J'kar's hot lips and tongue. Sliding her leg up and down along his from hip to ankle Tink wrapped one leg around J'kar's hip, forcing his swollen arousal against her moist mound.

"It is my turn to torture you. I like the idea of tying you down. When you imagined doing it to me, I thought I would lose my mind. I think it only fitting you should suffer too," J'kar growled.

"Later. I want to touch every inch of you. I want to see if you taste as good as I imagined you do," Tink whispered against J'kar's lips.

Groaning, he pulled away just enough to slide farther down Tink's body. J'kar gripped Tink's thighs and pulled them apart. He needed to taste her. The feelings she was bringing out in him were so foreign to him, so unexpected, especially without his having to restrain her or bite her to initiate a response, it seemed to be overwhelming all of his control.

"I want to taste you as you imagined me doing it," J'kar whispered huskily along the inside of her thigh.

Tink shivered at the hunger in his voice. She had never been with a man before, and this was way over her comfort level. But she felt beautiful before him.

She gasped as she felt the first touch of his lips on her slick folds. She couldn't hold back the moan as he began licking and sucking on her. Tink draped her legs over J'kar's shoulders, pulling him closer to her hot center. She began shaking as the feelings grew even stronger.

"J'kar," Tink cried out. "Please."

J'kar growled as Tink grabbed his hair and tried to pull him up. J'kar wrapped one arm around Tink's thigh and held her against him while he slid his finger into her wet pussy. He could feel the walls of her vagina clench tightly around his finger as he slowly worked it in and out.

Suddenly, Tink arched up with a strangled cry, clamping down hard on his finger as she climaxed. Licking her gently, J'kar tasted the sweet nectar of her release. Pulling his finger out of her, he moved slowly up over her wet mound, kissing her flat stomach.

He closed his eyes against the sudden pain he felt upon remembering how close he had come to losing her. He remembered trying to stop the blood pouring from the wounds to her stomach. He gently brushed his lips back and forth, groaning as Tink arched up against his lips.

Continuing up her body, he stopped to savor first one breast, then the other, drawing each nipple into his mouth, sucking on it, and brushing his elongated canines against them. He growled low as he felt the nipples swell. Looking up into Tink's passion-glazed eyes, J'kar's breath caught. He had never seen anything so beautiful. The soft glow of the lights reflected off the highlights in her hair and cast a softer glow around her face.

Reaching up, he captured her lips with his own, showing her how much she affected him. Lowering himself between her legs, he pushed her thighs farther apart with his own and pressed his hard shaft against her slick folds. Holding himself up slightly by his elbows so he didn't crush her with his weight, he pushed slowly into her, watching her as he did.

"You are mine. Say it," J'kar panted.

"Yours," Tink whispered.

"Only mine." J'kar shuddered as he pushed in another inch.

"Only yours," Tink repeated.

J'kar felt the thin barrier. Unable to control himself any longer, he let out a roar as he pushed past it and buried himself fully in Tink's wet pussy. Tink cried out as J'kar broke through the barrier of her virginity. J'kar held his lower body still as he leaned over to kiss the tear escaping down the side of Tink's face.

Shuddering, he began to move slowly, pulling almost all the way out before pushing back in. Tink gasped as she felt him moving. The feelings were overwhelming. His thick shaft stretched her almost to the point of pain, but it felt so good. Her hips began moving on their own.

"Faster." She groaned. "Please. Faster. It feels so good."

J'kar wrapped his arms around Tink, pulling her closer as he began moving faster. Suddenly, he pulled all the way out of her. When Tink would have protested, she ended up letting out a startled gasp as J'kar flipped her over onto her stomach, wrapping a muscular arm around her waist and pulling her up onto her hands and knees.

He pushed into her pussy from behind, burying his shaft all the way to his balls. Gripping her hips, he began pumping in and out of her wet pussy faster and faster. Reaching down he ran his fingers along her slit until he came to her clit. Rubbing the swollen nub between his fingers, he growled when Tink cried out again.

The feelings cascading through him were too much. He was lost in the primal instinct to mate. When he felt Tink shudder as another climax built inside her, J'kar let his primal instinct take over. Pounding into her hard and fast, he leaned over and sank his canines into Tink's shoulder, letting the chemical bond take them even higher.

* * *

Tink was panting, trying to draw in a breath. The feelings J'kar was stirring in her were so intense it was almost painful. She could feel another climax building. J'kar's thick shaft was hitting all the sensitive nerves up and down her vaginal walls. In the position he held her, he was able to fill her even more than before.

Clutching the covers of the bedding, Tink sobbed as she sought relief from the pressures building inside her. The climax hit her sudden and hard. Screaming out, Tink pushed back against J'kar, taking him deeper at the same time as she felt a flash of pain, then sudden warmth as her womb clenched tightly. It was more than she could handle, and with a shuddering gasp she went limp in J'kar's arms as everything went black.

J'kar felt his release as he bit down onto Tink's shoulder. Closing his eyes against a pleasure so intense he felt pain, he trembled as he released himself deep into Tink's womb. It was so powerful he could feel the threads of the bond connecting him to her. There were millions of tiny, silver lines wrapping around and bonding his soul to hers. As the last of his release left him, he became aware of Tink lying limp in his arms.

Withdrawing his teeth from her shoulder, he gently ran his tongue over her, sealing the wound, before he gently pulled his body out of hers. Shaking, he turned her in his arms.

"What have I done?" His trembling fingers brushed her damp hair away as he ran his fingers over her cheek, down to her throat, and breathing a sigh of relief when he found the steady beating of her pulse there.

Tink's eyelids fluttered as she slowly became aware of being held. Purring, she tried to snuggle closer to the warmth holding her. She finally was able to lift her heavy lids long enough to give J'kar a small smile.

"Wow," she whispered.

"I have hurt you. I—" J'kar broke off as his throat tightened. "I will take you to medical."

Tink frowned. She didn't need medical. She needed him. Struggling to sit up, she finally gave up when she realized J'kar wasn't going to let her go.

Tiredly she lay back. "I don't need medical. I need you to hold me."

"I should have been gentler." Running his hand along her face, he ran it farther down her body, stopping with a look of horror when he saw the traces of blood on the inside of her thighs. "I must get you to medical immediately."

Tink followed his horrified look and saw the evidence of her virginity. Blushing, she tried to pull from J'kar's arms again. "I, ugh, need to get a shower."

J'kar looked dazed as Tink pulled out of his arms and reached for the towel lying on the floor. Wrapping it around her, she headed for the bathroom on trembling legs.

Wow, if this is what it's like for mom and dad, no wonder they can't keep their hands off each other, Tink thought to herself as she stepped into the cubicle and waited for the sanitizer to do its job.

As the light disappeared, Tink turned to see a very shaken J'kar standing in the doorway of the bathroom wearing a pair of unbuttoned pants. He looked pale under his normally darker complexion. He raised a hand to run it through his short hair. Tink couldn't help but notice it was shaking.

Concerned something was wrong, Tink waved the sanitizer off and stepped out of the cubicle. Not even bothering with a towel, she walked over to J'kar and placed both of her hands on his bare chest. Staring up at him, she reached one hand up to run it along his cheek. She was scared when he jerked his head back away from her touch.

"What's wrong? Are you upset about what happened?"

The only thing Tink could think was J'kar was upset she had been a virgin. Maybe she hadn't pleased him. It had been wonderful for her, but she didn't have anything to compare it with.

Did the women on his world make love differently? Did he regret making love to her? If so, she wasn't going to let him. She had wanted it, and if he hadn't enjoyed it, well, they would just have to try until she got it right. As long as he still wanted her.

"I will not touch you again. I apologize for what happened. It will not happen again," J'kar said stiffly.

"You will not touch me again?" Tink asked in disbelief. "What the hell do you mean, you won't touch me again?"

"I regret what has happened. I give you my word it will not happen again. I will escort you to medical to be healed," J'kar said in a harsh voice.

Tink watched in disbelief as J'kar turned and walked into the bedroom. He kept his back to her as he reached for his shirt. A deep anger started in the pit of her stomach as what he said sank in.

"Hold on just a damn minute. What is your problem? Are you saying you regret what just happened between us?" Tink was breathing hard.

She was truly pissed. It was her first time, and sure, she knew she didn't really know much about it, but hell, while it was happening he sure as hell didn't seem to mind.

Glancing at Tink, J'kar turned to grab his shoes. "Yes. No. I must get you to medical." J'kar was feeling overwhelmed. Why didn't she understand he was just trying to protect her from him? He was worried about the blood he had seen and worried he had done more damage to her than she realized.

"Please, get dressed. If you are not able, I will call for the healer to come here."

"The only one who is going to need a healer is you when I get done with you." Tink turned and began dressing. "I can't believe it. I finally let go and what happens? I meet the biggest jerk in the whole galaxy! The only place I am going is home. You are taking me home right now! Do you hear me? Right. Now," Tink hissed as she pulled on her pants. She was so through with losers. Wiping at the tears streaming down her face, she yanked her T-shirt over her head.

Running a hand through her tousled hair, she made the wavy mass go even wilder than before. Looking around to see if she had forgotten anything, she shrugged and figured it could just get left. All she wanted to do was get off this damn ship and back home. At least there she knew how to deal with assholes.

J'kar's heart clenched when he saw the tears coursing down Tink's cheeks. Groaning in self-disgust, he walked over to pull Tink into his arms. He wrapped his arms tighter when he felt her resistance.

Kissing the top of her head, he begged softly, "Please forgive me. My heart breaks at the thought of hurting you. I should never have lost control. I did not mean to hurt you, little one. I would never hurt you intentionally. You are the very breath I breathe."

"Then why don't you want to touch me again? I know I'm not very experienced, but I thought it was great. I know if you are patient, it can be even better." Tink sobbed into the front of J'kar's opened shirt.

"You want me to touch you? After I hurt you?" J'kar asked in shock.

"What are you talking about? You didn't hurt me. Well, it hurt for a minute, but I knew it would since I had never been with a man before. But it won't hurt like that again," Tink said, her voice muffled as she pressed her face into J'kar's chest.

"I do not understand. I saw the blood," J'kar whispered.

Tink looked up in disbelief. "That's normal the first time."

Shaking his head, J'kar looked down into Tink's beautiful brown eyes. "Normal? I do not understand."

Blushing, Tink looked into J'kar's silver eyes. "The first time a woman goes all the way, uh, has sex... when she loses her virginity..." *Did he seriously not realize she was a virgin and what it meant?* "A girl has a thin membrane inside her. The first time she has sexual intercourse it is broken, and there is some bleeding. There is nothing wrong, and although it hurts at first, it passes quickly. It doesn't happen again. Only the first time. Do you understand? You didn't hurt me. It was a natural part of human anatomy. I had never been with a man before you."

"You do not need a healer?"

Tink shook her head, a slow smile forming at his look of dawning comprehension.

"I did not hurt you?"

Tink shook her head again.

"I am the only man you have ever been with?" This time there was a definite growl in his voice as he asked. Tink smiled even wider as she nodded her head.

"The only one so far," Tink answered with a mischievous smile.

Tink felt the vibration as J'kar growled and pulled her up against him. "The only one ever. Forever."

Pulling his head down to hers, Tink whispered against his lips, "Forever."

Sealing her lips to his, she nipped his lower lip. When he opened his mouth to respond, she quickly took control, pushing her tongue into his mouth and drawing his tongue into her mouth, where she could suck on it. She never did get a chance to see how good he tasted. She planned on remedying that in the next few minutes.

Pushing his shirt off his shoulders, she ran her hands over his broad shoulders. Pulling her lips from his, she ran them along his throat, feeling a thrill run through her when he groaned and tilted his head back to give her more access. Tink licked and nipped her way down along his shoulder, wiggling until he let her slide back to the floor where her feet could touch. Not taking her lips off his skin, she grabbed one of his nipples between her small teeth and sucked hard.

J'kar shuddered as Tink's lips locked on his nipple. He was already swollen with need again and could smell her desire. He wanted her again and again.

"I don't want to hurt you, little one," J'kar groaned out in Tink's mind.

"You won't. Give yourself to me. Let me love you this time. Let me show you how good it can be between the two of us," Tink moaned passionately in return.

Tink pulled J'kar's shirt the rest of the way off, raking her nails lightly across his back as she tossed it aside. Sliding her hands across his flat stomach, she worked her way down his chest. It was covered in a light coating of dark hair.

Lowering herself to the floor, she worked the front of his pants open, raking his ass as she pulled them down. J'kar moaned as he felt her nails rake across his body. He began to tremble again as he felt the primal beast hidden deep within him fight to come out and claim his mate.

Tink licked her lips to wet them when she saw how big J'kar was up close. The rounded head of his cock had drops of pre-cum glistening on it. Taking her tongue, Tink rolled it around the head before sliding his cock deep into her mouth.

J'kar gasped as he felt Tink's mouth close around him. Shaking even harder, he clenched his fists, staring down as Tink looked up at him. He had never seen anything more erotic or beautiful than her kneeling there with his cock sliding in and out of her lips. Never had he been exposed to so much feeling during a sexual encounter. Females on his planet never placed a male's sexual organ in their mouth. Sex was a means of reproduction or relief from hormonal buildup. It was not done for enjoyment; it was a need. What he was experiencing now went beyond enjoyment to an addiction. He had to have her. Wrapping his hands in Tink's hair, he began shaking even more as he felt his climax building.

"You must stop. I am going to spill my seed," J'kar said harshly as he tried to pull away from Tink's mouth.

"I want to taste you. I want to swallow your hot cum. Come for me, baby," Tink thought hungrily.

J'kar started shaking as he climaxed. His eyes stared in wonder as Tink drank his seed, licking every drop of his cum from him. She pressed kisses along his length before reaching down and cupping his balls in her hands and pressing a kiss to them.

"Did you like?" Tink thought with a mischievous smile twisting her swollen lips.

J'kar bent down and lifted Tink into his arms. *"You have too many clothes on."*

Tink laughed as J'kar started removing her clothes again. "I just put these on," Tink giggled out.

"Yes. And I am taking them off you. I think I will keep you without clothes when I take you to my home. You will not need to wear them. Ever."

Grasping one of Tink's swollen nipples in his mouth, J'kar wondered if he would ever be able to leave Tink at home. He could not imagine leaving her without his protection during the day while he took care of the needs of his people.

Chapter 20

J'kar left Tink sleeping in his room. They had made love again and again. He would have preferred to stay with Tink, but they would be home after the next sleep cycle and he had left much of the repairs and running of the ship to his brother over the past five sleep cycles while Tink had battled for her life.

Walking onto the deck of the bridge, J'kar noted the furtive glances he received from the crewmen. Frowning, he walked over to where Lan, Derik, and Borj were talking quietly. He was surprised when the group broke apart almost guiltily.

"What reports do you have?" J'kar asked, reaching for a nearby data screen. Glancing over it, he waited for one of the men to reply.

Clearing his throat, Borj replied, "Um, everything looks well. All damage has been repaired, and we are on schedule for docking with the space dock tomorrow."

Noticing the odd tone to Borj's voice, J'kar looked up and studied him. "You are well? Do you need to see the healer?"

He really focused on the men standing in front of him for the first time since entering the bridge. Derik and Lan avoided looking him in the eye. They actually had a slightly red tint to their faces. Borj looked at him but seemed uncomfortable, shifting from one foot to the other. J'kar had never seen any of his warriors so uncomfortable before.

Glancing around the bridge, he noticed all the men had stopped what they were doing and were watching him. When they noticed he was returning their stares, they quickly turned back to their stations.

"Conference room. Now," J'kar said through clenched teeth.

Turning, he strode toward the conference room door. He knew something was amiss and planned to find out what it was. He had a bad feeling it was going to involve his bond mate.

The door closed behind them with a soft whoosh. Walking over to the replicator, he asked for a cup of tea. If his feelings proved accurate, he might end up with something much, much stronger. Squaring his shoulders, he took a sip of tea, watching the three men who had followed him. He almost felt a sense of amusement as they looked at each other, then shuffled uneasily from one foot to the other.

"Well? What is it?" J'kar asked in a deceptively calm voice.

His eyes scanned the three of them, and he wondered who would speak first. His eyes narrowed on Lan as he seemed to be the most uncomfortable. Borj looked hesitant, while Derik just stood there with an idiotic grin on his face.

"How is your bond mate?" Lan began uncomfortably. J'kar's eyes narrowed even further when he noticed slight beads of sweat beginning to form on Lan's forehead.

"She is well. Why do you ask?" J'kar asked hesitantly.

Pulling at his collar as if it was suddenly too tight, Lan cleared his throat. "The mating ritual is complete?" It was more a statement than a question, and J'kar could tell Lan was becoming more uncomfortable with each passing moment.

"It is," J'kar's voice had dropped to a deadly calm. "Why do you ask?"

Lan looked desperately from Borj to Derik. He was shaking his head back and forth as if he was trying to convey some message.

J'kar set his cup on the long table and leaned forward placing both hands down flat on it. "Why. Do. You. Ask?" he repeated slowly.

"Did you do oral sex with each other?" Derik blurted out. His eyes were wide, and he had a huge grin on his face like he couldn't wait to hear the answer.

J'kar pulled back sharply. "What?" he asked hoarsely.

"Did she do oral sex on you?" Derik repeated, the light in his eyes hopeful for an answer.

"How do you know about oral sex?" J'kar asked in stunned disbelief.

Borj put his hand on his younger brother's arm, muttering under his breath, "If you value your life I think I had better explain the answer to this question."

"But you weren't even there! You don't know what Tink said and how she made us all feel," Derik began, before glancing at his oldest brother.

J'kar's face had grown darker and darker as Derik argued with Borj. Clenching both hands into tight fists, he sought to control the beginning rage that was building in him.

Turning to glare at Borj, J'kar forced the words out, "Tell me."

"Perhaps it would be better if we were to sit down," Borj moved to sit at the farthest end away from J'kar. The other two men quickly followed. Each man made sure they were seated near the door.

Clearing his throat, Borj tried to think of a way to explain what happened yesterday in the dining level without getting them all killed. A bonded male was very protective of his female and had been known to kill rival males who threatened to interfere with the mating ritual or tried to take a bonded female.

Even though the males and females of the Prime species normally only came together sexually to reproduce or relieve a buildup of hormones, the instinct to protect a bonded female because of her ability to produce children was overwhelming for the male and part of their genetic makeup. It did not mean a male might not seek relief elsewhere if necessary, just that the female was his alone for breeding purposes. Any male suspected of being sexually active with the female would be killed to prevent the threat against the bloodline.

What happened yesterday was an unforeseeable event. He did not know of another instance where something like it had occurred in all of Prime history. Borj had been unaware of the events, as he was resting.

When he returned to the bridge and noticed most of the men gone, he had been worried they had been under attack again. The two men remaining on the bridge had strained expressions of pain on their faces and were breathing abnormally. Both begged to be relieved of their post for a short time.

Unable to cope with so few men, Borj had requested additional help from Lan's department. When he received no reply, he had ordered Lan to the bridge immediately. Lan arrived with Derik in tow.

The first thing Borj noticed was how flushed both men appeared. A short time later most of the men had returned to their post. Borj was confused and requested the healer to join them on the bridge as well. He debated whether he should interrupt J'kar but decided not to until he had ascertained what the problem was.

Moving the group into the same conference room, he had begun his inquiry. At first, he did not receive any information that made any sense of what was going on. Upon further investigation, the whole tale of what happened was retold. It appeared once Tink decided to explain about twenty-first century sex on Earth, some of the men in the dining hall had opened their communication devices to others aboard the ship so that they could hear what she had to say. It had soon spread and was being broadcast ship wide.

Borj had listened to the whole tale in silence, unable to believe what he was being told. When parts of what Tink had explained were played for him, especially the demonstration of oral sex, he found himself in the same situation as the other men had. In short, Tink had disabled the entire warship with just her words, something no other species had ever been able to do.

As Borj finished his explanation of what was going on, he glanced up to see J'kar's expression. A brief human expression he had heard while in the bar—"Run, baby, run"—flitted through his mind. He could appreciate the expression as he watched J'kar's face turn a deep, dark red.

"So, did you have oral sex?" Derik asked expectantly.

Both Lan and Borj looked at Derik like he had lost his mind! J'kar unclenched his fists, slowly stretching his long fingers out in front of him. Both Lan and Borj stood up and began moving slowly toward the door.

"How many?" J'kar asked softly.

"Just about every man on board," came the hesitant reply. "Those who did not hear it then, have more than likely heard or listened to it by now. I would have to say everyone on board."

J'kar closed his eyes and pictured the sweet, innocent face of his bond mate. He was going to kill her—no, not kill. He needed a lot more time with her first. He would have to think of another punishment for her. Right now, though, all he could think of was how he was going to explain to the council members why he had to kill every man on his warship and how was he going to be able to run the damn thing by himself.

* * *

Tink stretched. She felt deliciously sore in all the right places. Reaching out with her hand, she felt next to her.

Bummer, he's gone. Oh well. It gives me time to shower, she thought lazily.

A slow smile curved her lips when she thought about some of the things she would like to do to him in the shower. With a sigh, she sat up and realized it would have to wait. Besides, she wanted to experiment in a shower with actual running water. Groaning as she moved off the bed, she made quick work of getting cleaned and dressed.

"RITA," Tink called out.

"Yes, dear."

"Can you locate J'kar for me?" Tink asked as she hopped around on one foot trying to get her shoe on.

"He is in the conference room off the bridge," RITA replied. She debated telling Tink she was concerned as his respiration seemed a little fast and his blood pressure was elevated, but decided against it as a brief scan seemed to show he was not ill.

"Thanks. I think I'll head to the dining level to grab a bite to eat and meet him there. It is so cool looking out the front window of this thing," Tink said as she grabbed one of J'kar's shirts to wear as a light cover. It wasn't cold, but she wanted to have something of his close to her skin.

Heading out the door Tink entered the lift at the end of the hall and requested Level Three. Moving down the corridor, she entered the dining hall to find it almost empty. It must be later than she thought.

There were three men at a far table. They stopped their conversation and watched her as she moved toward a row of replicators. She requested a biscuit with sausage, egg, and cheese on it, wondering if the computer would actually be able to produce it.

Much to her surprise an equivalent version of what she requested appeared. After requesting a cup of coffee—which wasn't quite the same, but close enough—she placed the items on a tray and moved to a nearby table to eat.

Sitting down, she took a sip of the "coffee" and decided it wasn't half bad. She had just taken a bite out of her biscuit when a shadow fell over her. Glancing up, she was surprised to see the three men had risen and moved to stand near her table.

"Morning," Tink said with a smile. "How are things going?"

The men glanced at each other and glanced down at Tink again. Tink raise an eyebrow at them. It was obvious they wanted something, but were unsure of what to say or do. Tink had dealt enough with men to know these guys were up to something. She just didn't know what.

"Okay. Sit down and tell what you have to say," Tink said with a slightly bemused expression on her face. She waved to the seats near her.

"Let's get the introductions out of the way. My name is Jasmine Bell, but everyone calls me Tink. What are your names?" Tink felt like she was trying to talk to a bunch of teenage boys. She could almost feel them squirming in their seats.

The smallest of the three, if you could call a man outweighing her by over a hundred pounds small, answered, "I am called Rorr. This is Toak, and that is Cale." Each man nodded as he was introduced.

Holding out her hand to shake each man's hand, Tink smiled a welcome to each one. "So, are you guys off duty right now or just on a coffee break?"

The three men frowned, not sure they understood everything Tink had said. "We—" Rorr looked at Toak and Cale before continuing. "—work in engineering. Yesterday, we heard the conversation you had with other members of the crew here. We wondered…" He paused again.

"We wondered if what you had said is true," finished Toak.

Tink looked at the three men in disbelief at first, then the realization that everyone on board probably knew about what happened began to form in her brain—about the same time as she got a brush of unease. If the men in engineering had heard what she had said, did that mean J'kar knew about it? If so, she vaguely wondered how he would react.

Shrugging her shoulders, she decided he couldn't be too upset. It wasn't like she had done anything wrong or anything. For crying out loud, some of the conversations in the garage could get more explicit than what she had said yesterday.

"Yeah, it was true. Most Earth men and women enjoy being together both physically and mentally," Tink replied.

The men looked at each other with a combination of hopefulness and awe. Turning to look at Tink, Cale asked in a deep, rough voice, "Are there many women on your planet?"

"Billions!" Tink said with a grin. "Though not in America. You see our planet is made up into countries. I come from the United States of America. We have a huge population, but not as big as some other countries. Over fifty percent of the population is female, but you have to take into account that is all females, regardless of age. Let's just say there are a lot of single girls out there! Why?"

"We wish to capture us a female," Toak answered.

Tink started laughing, not stopping until she realized they were serious. "You can't just go capture a female." She stared at each of the three faces across from her. Pushing her hair away from her face again, she let out a breath. Boy, how was she going to explain that men didn't go around "capturing" females on Earth?

"Listen. If you end up on Earth, you don't go grabbing girls off the street. Some are married, have families, or are in relationships—that kind of stuff. You have to meet them. Take them on dates. Get to know them. See if your feelings develop and where it takes you. What happens if it doesn't work out? What if the girl decides she wants to go home? There are a lot of things you have to consider before you take off with some poor girl. What happens if she finds out you are an alien, and she freaks out? Not everyone can handle the thought of aliens in the world.

Earthlings don't even know for sure there are others out in space. We write about it, create movies, and stuff, but we don't, or I should say never had, proof until now that aliens even existed. You could cause some poor girl to have a heart attack," Tink explained, exasperated.

Just as one of the males was going to respond, Tink felt a sudden burst of rage rush through her mind. Closing her eyes, she tried to focus past what was causing it. Reaching out to J'kar, Tink could feel him in her thoughts. He was really pissed off about something.

Smiling, she thought about how it would feel to run her hand along his jaw to calm him. Sending feelings of warmth and love out, she hoped he could feel it. She recognized the moment he felt her touch.

"Where are you?" J'kar asked softly.

"Hanging with some guys from engineering in the dining hall," Tink responded.

Immediately she felt J'kar's answering rage before he blocked her from his mind. Tink frowned. *What got his panties in a bind?* She wondered. Shrugging, she stood up.

"I'd better go. J'kar seems to be having a rough morning and I wanted to see the bridge so I'm gonna head that way. Maybe I can catch up with you guys later in engineering. I'd love to take a look at what powers this baby," Tink said as she discarded the tray and dishes from her late breakfast in the cleaning rack.

"We would be honored to talk with you again," Rorr said. The other two nodded their agreement and left at the same time Tink did.

Tink returned to the lift and requested the bridge. Leaning back, she tilted her head back and smiled as she thought about how much her life had changed in the past twenty-four hours. She ran her hands down the front of her and pulled J'kar's shirt closer to her face so she could inhale his scent. Boy, she missed him, and they had only been apart for a couple of hours. Straightening up as the lift slowed, she moved to exit it as soon as the doors opened.

Chapter 21

J'kar could feel Tink's confusion at his anger. He could not control the feelings of rage coursing through his body at the knowledge she was alone with some of the males on board the warship, and had shut her out. He had to collect himself before he confronted her.

He left the bridge with the intent on finding her and locking her in his room until they were planet side. He did not trust his fragile hold on his desire to tear something or someone apart. The idea of the rest of the men knowing what he had enjoyed was almost too much.

He was just leaving the bridge when he looked up as the lift doors opened. A tiny bundle of energy seemed to pour out of it and right into the arms of one of his men. A Berserker's rage glazed his eyes as he saw the man put his arms around Tink.

"Oh, sorry. I should have looked where I was going!" Tink said with a smile as she looked up into the blushing face of Von. "Oh. Hey, Von. How are you doing today?"

Von was stumbling over a response when he noticed Tink's eyes grow huge in her face. Turning, he was off-balance when he felt Tink shove his body away from hers. As he started to fall, he reached out and grabbed Tink's arm, pulling her with him. They both fell in a tangle of arms and legs, Tink lying across the young warrior's chest.

The loud roar echoed off the walls of the corridor. Before Tink realized what was happening, she was lifted off the startled chest of the young warrior who was trying desperately to get up off the floor. She was shoved behind the huge figure of J'kar.

Watching in disbelief, she gasped as J'kar lifted the poor guy up by his neck. Tink couldn't believe J'kar was freaking out over a little trip and fall. Hell, she did it all the time in the garage. The guys were always teasing her about watching where she was going.

Realizing he was going to hurt the poor kid, Tink jumped on J'kar's back, wrapping one arm around his neck and the other over his eyes. She would have never been able to reach it if she hadn't been in such good shape. Damn, but he was big and tall.

J'kar barely registered the slight weight on his back. It wasn't until an arm wrapped around his throat and another covered his eyes that he jerked backward. Other men had come out from the bridge to see what the disturbance was. Borj, Derik, and Lan were at the front. Von, who was gasping and holding his throat, stared in horror as the leader of the Prime fought to remove the little figure holding tight to him.

"Let me go," J'kar roared.

He moved from side to side trying to grab hold of Tink. He couldn't see a thing with her arm over his eyes. The arm around his throat wasn't really restricting his breathing; he just couldn't see where the crewman who had his arms around Tink was, and he was livid.

He backed up into the wall on the other side of the corridor. Tink, instead of letting go, tightened her legs around his waist. At least she had removed her arm from his eyes. She wrapped the other arm around his neck to get an even tighter grip. Now, he could feel the beginnings of a restriction. Pressed against the wall, J'kar turned around in Tink's arms until he was facing her. The last thing he expected her to do was to lean into him and kiss him like there was no tomorrow.

Tink realized the best defense was an aggressive offense. Keep him off balance and he wouldn't know which way to go. So, when J'kar had trapped her between the wall and his body, she let loose just enough for him to turn. Now, she had him where she wanted him. Moving in for the kill, she locked her lips to his and gave him a kiss to knock his socks off.

J'kar had just been about to force Tink to let him go when she re-tightened her hold on him, pressing her soft mound onto his growing length and locking her lips to his. Her kiss promised all kinds of wonderful things, as did the things she was imagining doing to his body. As he opened his mouth, she took advantage of it and slipped her tongue deep inside, coaxing him to move into her. She grabbed hold of it as soon as he slipped it in, sucking on it.

Pulling back, she ran little kisses all along his jaw before nipping at his ear. When he would have said something, she captured his lips again and began moving her body slowly back and forth. Running her hands in his short hair, she released his lips again.

Pulling his shirt away from his neck, Tink leaned over and ran little nips and licks along his throat. When she reached the section where his shoulder and neck met, she bit down hard, then eased the pain with more tiny licks and kisses.

J'kar forgot about everything but Tink. Her kisses and nips were driving him insane. When she bit down on his neck, he threw his head back and let out a roar of pleasure pressing his body even closer to hers. It was so intense he forgot he was standing in the corridor outside the bridge with an audience full of males.

Tink raised her head and looked up. Her eyes were glazed with passion. All she could think about was stripping J'kar down and taking him. Her eyes widened and cleared a little when she realized they were putting on a show for all the guys standing there gawking at them.

Burying her face in J'kar's neck, she whispered softly against his skin. "I think we need to take this somewhere else. We have an audience."

J'kar looked down at Tink's pink face, then up at the faces of his brothers, friends, and crewmen. They all stared at him and Tink with a combination of lust and envy. He could tell the demonstration they witnessed had affected them greatly.

Glaring at Von, J'kar spoke to Borj. "You have the bridge."

Borj just gave J'kar a bemused smile and nodded. If what he saw was any indication, he might not see them again until it was time to return to the planet.

Borj's mind briefly flitted to the image of the tall, golden-haired female in his pocket. He wondered if she would be as passionate as his brother's bond mate. He could feel his own body respond to the idea of her wrapped around him. Borj bit back a curse as he turned back to the bridge.

J'kar stepped into the lift without ever letting go of Tink. She was still holding on as tight as she could to him, giving him little kisses all along his jaw line and running her hands through his hair. He fought back a groan at the feel of her body moving restlessly against his. It took every ounce of his self-control not to take her right there and then.

As soon as the door to his room shut, J'kar set Tink down. Tink slid reluctantly down J'kar's body. She was surprised when he didn't follow her toward the bed but just stood watching her.

"Take your clothes off," J'kar commanded. He clenched his fists. If she didn't obey at once he would rip the clothes off her.

Tink's eyes grew wide, then she smiled. Slowly, she slid first one, then the other sleeve of the shirt she wore off her shoulders. She let it dangle from her fingertips before letting it fall to the floor.

Next, she ran her hands over her hair, then down the front of her thin T-shirt before gripping the edge of it and pulling it up and over. Shaking her hair out, she held out the T-shirt and let it fall to the floor next to the overshirt of J'kar's she had been wearing.

Standing in just her bra, jeans, and shoes, she leaned over and slowly untied first one lace on her shoes, then the other, making sure she gave J'kar plenty of cleavage to look at. Toeing her shoes off, she stared into J'kar's eyes as she undid the button and zipper on her jeans. Hooking the top with her fingers, she let them slide down her hips to pool on the floor. Now, she was standing only in her bra and panties in front of him. Instead of feeling nervous, she was edgy with excitement and desire.

J'kar could not believe he was able to control himself during the striptease Tink had put on so far. He could feel his cock swell to painful proportions as she removed each item. When she leaned over to untie her shoes, he had unbuttoned his own pants to let the length of his cock hang free. The feel of the material against him was more than he could stand.

Watching her, he could smell her own arousal as she removed more and more of her clothes. She did not understand what she had started in the corridor. He was not going to be able to control his primal urge this time. She had to understand he did not want to hurt her, but she could not drive him to this point again. Realizing other men knew how human females made love was one thing. Seeing her in the arms of another male was too much.

Clenching his teeth, he growled. "The rest. Remove them and get on the bed."

His eyes glittered with dark silver flames as he watched the last two pieces of lacy material fall to the floor. When Tink turned to get on the bed it was too much. Moving rapidly, he grabbed her from behind and laid her on the bed, pinning her beneath him. "You will not move. Do you understand?"

Tink looked up into the flaming eyes above her. She felt her pussy clench at the promise held in them. J'kar gripped both of Tink's hands and lifted them above her head. Shoving his leg between her thighs, he pushed them apart, letting his thick cock rub against her moist mound. Unable to stop herself, Tink arched up to rub against him with a moan.

J'kar's teeth elongated, and he growled out in a deep, heated voice. "I said don't move." He waited until Tink nodded silently.

Getting up, J'kar looked down at Tink's naked beauty as she lay in his bed. He wanted her... badly. He only hoped he didn't hurt her. Moving over to his closet, he removed several restraints. Normally used in cases of attack if they took prisoners, they could also be used when a male needed to restrain his mate who was not receptive. Since Prime females were not always welcoming of a male's attention, on rare occasions a male might use them to help protect the female until the chemical from the bite he gave her started working. Now, he realized he would have to use them to protect Tink from what could happen when a Prime male got too excited. He did not want her trying to resist him. It would become too dangerous for her then, as he would lose all control.

Moving back to the bed, he clasped Tink's wrists in his hands, closing the restraint around them. Next, he moved to her ankles, tying down first one, then the other, leaving her open to him. Breathing heavily, he began undressing.

He hated that he had to do this. He did not want her to hate him. Unable to deal with the look of horror he knew must be in her eyes, he quickly finished dropping his clothes in a pile next to hers.

Tink watched what J'kar was doing. When he went to the closet, she was afraid he was going to leave her like this, hungry and frustrated. Instead, she became even hotter when she saw the restraints he held. All kinds of wicked and kinky ideas began to form in her mind in explicit detail.

When he tightened the restraints on her wrists, she couldn't hold back the groan of desire as her body heated up to an explosive level. Her pussy was so hot with anticipation she could feel it clenching and pulsing. She was ready to have an orgasm right then and there. When he tightened the two leg restraints, pulling her open to him, she could feel the moisture seeping down the insides of her legs. Moaning, she wiggled as the waves of desire and need rushed through her demanding relief. She was so horny that she was determined if he didn't do something soon, she was going to attack him.

J'kar flinched when he heard the moans and groans coming from Tink. He was beyond stopping, though. He could only hope she could forgive him for what he was about to do.

Sliding onto the bed, he gripped Tink's thighs in his large hands, and holding them apart, he began lapping at her, sliding his tongue up and down along her folds. Moving his hands, he pulled her soft folds apart to get closer to her nub. Sucking and licking her like she was a favorite dessert, he groaned as the taste of her filled his senses.

He was totally lost in the haze of sexual need. He slid one, then two fingers into her pussy, pumping them in and out as he licked and sucked her, gorging himself on her essence. When Tink began begging him and fighting the restraints, he lost the little control he hoped to retain.

Growling, he ran his elongated canines along the inside of her thigh before sinking them into her. Tink screamed as pleasure flooded her when the chemical inside of J'kar's canines was released into her bloodstream. Her body arched up, shuddering as one orgasm blended into the next before she collapsed back to the bed where she lay panting.

J'kar sealed the wound from his bite with a lick of his tongue. Moving up her body, he latched on to her nipple, sucking it into a hard peak. Gripping it between his fingers, he moved to the other nipple, making it peak into a hard pebble. Gripping it and rolling it between his fingers, he moved up to sit beside her. His cock was inches from her face.

"Touch me like you did last night. Take me in your mouth like you did," J'kar demanded as he twisted the pearl-sized nipples.

Tink couldn't have denied J'kar anything. Straining, she ran her tongue over the swollen head of his cock, licking the pre-cum off the tip. He squeezed her nipples harder, and she groaned, taking more of him into her mouth.

As he began moving his hips back and forth, Tink could feel another orgasm rising just from him playing with her nipples. He pushed his cock deeper and deeper into her mouth. Tink took as much as she could, but when her orgasm came, she pulled away, arching her back as the feelings washed over her. She was unable to hold back the scream as her body exploded in a pleasure so intense it was painful.

J'kar heard Tink's cry as she pulled away from his cock. The smell of her orgasm was pulsing through his system. He had to ride her, but was afraid to. He had restrained her, but he was totally out of control.

Growling, he climbed back between Tink's legs, and lifting her up as far as he could with the restraints holding her, he buried his cock all the way in her slick folds with one thrust, impaling her all the way to her womb. He closed his eyes and clenched his teeth, holding still for just a moment to give her time to adjust to his size until he could hold back no longer. Gripping her thighs in a bruising hold, he pounded into her over and over, pulling almost all the way out before thrusting back into her as deeply as he could. J'kar let out a deep growl when he felt Tink struggle against him, the animal part deep inside him fighting the need to subdue his mate.

It took a moment for J'kar to realize Tink was not fighting him to quit. She was moaning, "Harder, faster, deeper." For the first time J'kar looked at Tink's face, into her eyes. He had expected to see disgust, anger, and fear. Instead, he saw passion. Her head was thrown back in pleasure, her cheeks flushed, and her lips slightly parted as she moaned. It was so unexpected, he stopped.

Growling out under her breath, Tink swore out loud. "So help me, if you stop now, I'll kill your ass after I tie you down and have my way with you. Move, damn you. Move. Fuck me. Hard, baby. Fuck me hard." Tink glared up at J'kar, daring him to stop.

J'kar's senses were inflamed at Tink's passionate demands. Leaning over her he grabbed her nipples again and twisted them as he moved deep and hard into her pussy. Fighting the restraints, Tink glared up at J'kar before she threatened him in a voice husky with desire, "I'm going to fuck you so hard when I get lose you won't ever want to leave my bed. I'm going to tie you down and see how many ways I can make you beg me to love you."

J'kar growled at the promises Tink was making. Thoughts began filling his head of all the ways Tink wanted him to take her. Unable to handle it, J'kar pushed deep into Tink, touching her womb with his cock as he yelled out his release.

Tink could feel the hot seed burst inside her. Closing her eyes, she let out a small scream as she came again. J'kar knelt over her, panting, before collapsing over her.

Brushing kisses along Tink's shoulder and neck, J'kar bit down with his canines breaking the skin. He felt Tink's startled response before she relaxed into his hold. He felt the chemical release as it pumped into Tink.

He had bitten her three times now. She would be ready for his offspring. She would never leave him. Never.

Chapter 22

J'kar brushed a kiss across Tink's swollen lips. They made love most of the night, and it wasn't until J'kar received word they would soon be docking with the spaceport that he had allowed Tink to sink into an exhausted sleep.

With everything that had happened in the few sleep cycles she had been on board the warship, he couldn't even contemplate all the mischief she could get into on the Space station. He needed to make sure everything was taken care of and notify his father and the council about his bonding.

"Sleep, little one. I need you to stay in the room until I come and get you. It will not be safe for you to leave it. Do you understand?" he murmured against her lips.

Tink moaned and reached for him. "Don't go. Stay with me."

J'kar laughed softly. "You make it hard to leave you."

Tink's eyes opened to shine mischievously up at him. "I like making it hard. Need any help with it?"

J'kar laughed out loud. "You are insatiable." Smiling down tenderly, he pushed the hair away from her forehead, kissing her. "Please. I need to know you are safe. Stay here and sleep."

Tink arched toward J'kar's warm body, stretching her arms over her head. "Well, if you insist. You haven't had any more sleep than I have. But, if someone has to catch up on it, I guess I'll have to volunteer." With that, she rolled over onto her stomach and snuggled up with his pillow.

J'kar shook his head and smacked her on the ass. "You will need to be punished for that little remark."

He left laughing. He could have sworn he heard her muttering, "Promises, promises."

He gave the command to lock the door. He did not want to take a chance of anyone disturbing her. Walking toward the lift, he gave the command to access RITA.

"Yes, dear. How can I help you?" RITA replied. "You know I can't wait to tie into the programming on the spaceport. This is so exciting."

J'kar tiredly closed his eyes. Tink was right about him not getting much sleep. Now, he not only had to worry about keeping Tink safe, he had to worry about what mischief RITA was going to cause on the spaceport, how the council was going to handle everything, and how he was going to explain his new mate's behavior to his people.

"RITA, I need you to monitor Tink at all times. Make sure she does not leave the room and that no one tries to enter. I need your to help protect her." J'kar felt funny asking a computer for help, but from what he had learned, RITA's programming was much like a familiar, a creature who was often a pet or protector for the Prime females. She would do anything to protect Tink.

"I will, dear. Don't you worry about her. She's sleeping right now. I can use the internal monitors to track her. I'll keep her safe." Sometimes, J'kar thought in amusement, it was hard not to think of RITA as just another crew member.

J'kar pushed himself out of the lift and headed for the bridge. He entered to find Borj reviewing some data charts with one of the crewmen on duty. Moving to the captain's control panel, he sat and reviewed the current position. They should be docking within the hour. He ran through all the reports, scanning and marking any items of interest for further review. Final preparations were being made, and he didn't have much to do. His crew was one of the best and knew exactly what needed to be done.

J'kar looked up as Borj joined him. Nodding, he continued reviewing a detailed report on the trade items they brought back with them.

"All preparations are being finalized, and we have clearance to dock," Borj said quietly.

"Good. Make sure the cargo is unloaded first. I want a military team to prepare the ship. Load appropriate weapons and supplies," J'kar stated.

He regretted some of the items had been removed prior to their last voyage to make room for trade items. It had been a cover to scout for females, but could have been a costly error he did not plan to make again. With the added ship they could use one for cargo transport and leave the warships for what they were designed for, war.

"Have you made the decision to attack the human's planet?" Borj asked. While he tried to keep his tone neutral, a bit of unease slipped through.

It had been his suggestion to forcibly remove the women from the planet. He had not expected J'kar to agree. He did know it was going to be a real possibility now the men aboard knew how passionate Earth women could be.

If the incident in the dining level had riled the crew up, the incident in the corridor had the men in a raging fury for an Earth woman of their own. Before Lan had a chance to lock down the video of J'kar attacking Von, and Tink's subsequent interference, it had been broadcast throughout most of the ship.

Lan confiscated the video as soon as he was able to, but the damage had been done. The men were ready to revolt. They had never seen any female react the way the Earthling had, and they were in a highly sexually charged mood. Even he was having problems. It was not as bad for him as there were women available at the palace to take care of his needs, but the men would have to visit some of the relief houses.

J'kar looked at Borj for a moment before frowning. "I have no intention of attacking her planet. We do not have enough information on their culture. From what we have learned from RITA, the women there might not appreciate us doing so. She even mentioned many women fought in their military. It would be against our best interests to attack. Why do you ask?" J'kar asked his brother, looking at him intensely. Something was obviously bothering his brother, and he needed to know what it was.

"The men are growing restless. After the incident in the dining hall—" Borj paused just a moment at seeing the darkening look in J'kar's eyes at the reminder, but continued. "—It was difficult. But, the incident in the corridor has caused the men to become more aggressive in their desire to find a human female of their own."

"What do you mean, 'the incident in the corridor'?" J'kar asked softly.

Borj looked at J'kar, then at some of the men on the bridge. Replying in a soft tone so he wouldn't be overheard, he reminded J'kar of what had transpired. "Never have the men seen a female respond so passionately without being bitten first. Even then, as you know, the females are just more receptive. Your bond mate attacked you. If she had not realized at the last minute we were watching, I am not sure she would have stopped. She was—" Borj paused a moment to draw in a breath. "—unbelievable."

J'kar moved uncomfortably in the seat. He was remembering what happened not only in the corridor but afterward. He became even harder. Damn, but he wasn't sure if he was going to make it to the planet without taking her again. Just the idea of taking her in the corridor was causing him to breathe heavily.

Borj couldn't contain his curiosity any longer. "Is she really so different? So...passionate?"

J'kar looked at his brother a moment before responding, "More than you can imagine. When I took her back to the room, I was out of control." J'kar paused, trying to think how to explain to his brother what happened.

Borj nodded sympathetically. "You had to use restraints. She will learn and become understanding. You had no choice." Borj laid a supporting hand on J'kar's shoulder.

J'kar shook his head. "No. You don't understand. I used restraints, but she—" J'kar couldn't keep the silly grin from his face. "—She enjoyed it... very, very much. It made her even more passionate. She wants to use them on me next."

Borj bit back a groan. Shaking his head and looking around, he whispered, "Do not let any of the men know this. We would have a war on our hands. The council needs to be informed. This type of knowledge could give our clans more power over the others, creating problems. Many of the outlying clans are having problems with not enough females as well. They will want to find her planet and take females. If the other clans find out we have a way to create a portal to her world, it could be an all-out war between our clans, not to mention our world and hers."

Borj turned as an announcement came over the internal speakers stating the docking was complete. He gave a brief nod to J'kar before walking away. He couldn't help thinking of the beautiful, long-legged woman in the photo he carried being tied down to his bed, passionately responding to his caresses. He paused briefly to adjust the front of his pants. Yes, he thought, even he would go to war if it meant having her in his bed.

Chapter 23

There wasn't much for Tink to do while J'kar was tied up with the docking, unloading, and preparations for the trip to the planet. Tink was more than a little nervous. She wondered what his planet would look like. Would it be anything like Earth? What about his family? What if they didn't like her? He was like some kind of prince or something. The next in line to rule. What if they didn't think she was good enough for him?

Tink took a shower and cleaned up the room, placing dirty clothes in the cleaning bin, then hanging them up when they were done. J'kar had a light breakfast delivered by the healer, of all people, and some clothes. The clothes were beautiful. They were of a soft pastel blue with silver highlights running through them.

The outfit was a long flowing dress reaching down to her ankles. The top portion was sleeveless with a scooped neckline embroidered with tiny jewels that looked like diamonds. A matching long-sleeved, waist-length jacket fitted over it, and it too was embroidered with the tiny jewels.

Tink thought it looked a little too formal for her tastes. She would have preferred a nice pair of jeans and a comfortable T-shirt or sweater. It suddenly dawned on her, she had a lot to learn about J'kar's world. She really didn't know anything about it. She had no idea where he lived, where he worked when he wasn't flying around on a spaceship, how many brothers or sisters he had except for the two she had met on board. She really didn't know anything about him except he was an exceptional lover.

She began breathing heavier as a panic attack started to form. What had she done? Panting, she leaned forward, trying to catch her breath. Would she ever see her family again? What would happen if things didn't work out between her and J'kar? Did they have divorce on his planet? What if they had kids? Could they have kids? Panting even harder, Tink squeezed her eyes closed as she felt tears starting to form. Oh, God, what had she done?

"Little one, I feel your pain. What is wrong? You are in danger?" J'kar's anguished voice filled her mind.

"I'm scared," Tink replied, trying not to cry.

"What has scared you? You are in danger?" J'kar asked again, this time unable to keep the concern from his own voice.

"No. I'm not in danger. Just scared. What if your family doesn't like me? I don't know anything about you really. What if this doesn't work out? Will I see my family again? I miss my parents and my sisters. I miss Cosmos. I…"

"I will come to you," J'kar said with a sigh of relief. *"You will not be alone. I will be with you. My family will love you as much as I do. Do not Borj and Derik love you? You will love my world. It is very beautiful, almost as beautiful as you,"* J'kar teased.

"I'll be okay. Is it going to be much longer?" Tink asked, a small quiver in her mind voice.

"No. I will send Zariff to bring you to me. I would like you to see my world from space. You will see how beautiful it is."

"J'kar," Tink said hesitantly. *"Thank you."*

J'kar could feel the touch of warmth Tink sent to him. He closed his eyes briefly as the feeling coursed through his body. A part of him was concerned someone, anyone, could have this type of effect over him. He had never heard of it even among bonded mates, at least not in the newer times. There were legends of old that told tales of bonded mates being very powerful together, working, fighting and living as one being.

Over the past several hundred years, though, the bonding ritual had come down more to who could breed. He knew his own parents did not have a bond like he was experiencing. Even Zariff, the healer, was able to leave his mate for extended periods when necessary, though it became uncomfortable after a while.

"Zariff," J'kar murmured into the communicator.

"Yes, my lord," Zariff replied immediately.

"Please escort my mate to the bridge."

"With pleasure, my lord," Zariff replied.

"Zariff, make sure she is well. She seemed a little upset. I need to know she is not harmed," J'kar asked hesitantly. He was concerned all their lovemaking may have been too much for her. He had not let her get much rest. He had also lost control during their lovemaking more than once during the night. She was much more fragile than the women on his planet, and he was easily twice her size.

"Of course, my lord. We will join you shortly." Zariff signed off.

J'kar let out a sigh. He walked to the front view-screen and stared with unseeing eyes down on his planet. He had reservations as well. He wondered how his people would take his mate. She was much smaller, more delicate, than they. She was also paler in both skin and hair coloring. It made her look more exotic. He would have to make sure she was protected whenever he was not with her. He would kill anyone who tried to harm her.

* * *

Tink called out a welcome when the communicator device announced Zariff was asking for entrance. Tink smiled at the healer as he entered the room. She was just finishing cleaning up, and was about to fix herself a cup of tea. Smiling a welcome, Tink asked Zariff if he would like a cup of tea.

"Yes, that would be very pleasant," Zariff replied.

"Tell me about your planet," Tink asked as she came over and set the tea in front of Zariff.

"It is very beautiful. The main city is surrounded with tall mountains on three sides and the sea to the west. The mountains are home to many different species of animals. Some are small and some are large. It is best not to travel in them without an escort. The city itself is the most beautiful in our region. It is the home of the 'Tag Krell Manok family. They are the most powerful in our region and rule over all the clans. There are many other clans but none quite as powerful. The 'Tag Krell Manok family brought the other clans together to form the high council, which establishes and enforces the laws of our planet. Each clan has a council and certain members represent each clan on the high council. We have three moons, Ananke, Leda, and Metis. They are very beautiful on the months they can all be seen. The sea in this part is warm and flat during the warm months, but wild and fierce during our cold periods."

"It sounds lovely. I wish my family could see it. Hannah would be the one to disappear into your mountains. She is at home in the wild," Tink said with a sigh.

"You have many in your family?" Zariff asked curiously.

Tink shook her head. "Not really. It's just my two sisters, mom and dad. And Cosmos, of course. We adopted him so he's part of the family, whether he likes it or not."

"My bond mate and I have a son. We hope one day he will find his bond mate. Your world gives me hope. If he could find someone like you, I would be honored to have her as my daughter," Zariff said with a warm smile.

Tink's eyes filled with tears. Wiping them with the back of her hand, she smiled. "That is so sweet. Please forgive me. I don't know what is wrong with me. All I want to do this morning is cry."

Zariff smiled gently at Tink and nodded for her to lie down on the bed. "J'kar is worried about you. He asked me to make sure you are all right. I would like to scan your body to make sure it has healed completely from your earlier wounds. You and J'kar have completed the mating rituals?" Zariff asked quietly as he pulled the medical scanner from his waist.

Tink felt the blush turning her cheeks pink. She was feeling a little self-conscious. She knew he was a doctor, but the connection she had with J'kar was still new to her.

"Yes," Tink replied softly.

"Prime males can be very forceful during the mating process. We forget our strength at times when the primal urge overcomes us. J'kar's feelings for you are very strong, much stronger than I have ever seen in a mated pair. You are much smaller than our females. He is concerned he may have hurt you during the mating rituals," Zariff said gently as he took in the rise of color in Tink's cheeks.

"He didn't. He was wonderful. Human females may be smaller, but we are strong," Tink responded with a grin.

Zariff ran the scanner slowly over Tink. He paused and frowned when he came to her stomach area. Running the scan over her again, he made some adjustments before scanning a third time.

"Did J'kar bite you during your mating?" Zariff asked with a frown as he studied the results.

Tink blushed a deeper red. "Yes, several times. It didn't hurt, if that is what you are worried about. I think I bit him a couple of times, too. Prime males aren't the only ones who lose control during the mating, you know."

Zariff looked down at Tink with a startled look in his eyes. "You can sit up. Human females lose control during sexual mating?" He could not keep the fascination or the curiosity out of his voice.

Tink sighed. "You really need to talk to my mom. I finally realized exactly what she was telling us girls for years. When I am around J'kar, all I can think about is jumping him. I would worry it was a chemical reaction happening just because he was different from me, but my folks are the same way after almost thirty years of marriage. They still can't be in the same room without touching each other."

"Fascinating. I would be very interested in meeting your parents one day." Zariff slipped the scanner into his belt. He turned to pick up the two cups and placed them in the cleaning rack before turning back to Tink.

"So, am I cleared to go? Everything is okay?" Tink asked as she walked toward the door.

"Yes, but you will need to see a healer as soon as you are settled on the planet. You are breeding," Zariff said, coming up behind Tink.

Tink froze. She was breeding? What exactly did that mean? She was pregnant? Already? How could he tell?

Turning as if in slow motion, Tink drew in a small breath. "What exactly do you mean by breeding? Are you telling me I'm pregnant? I'm going to have a baby? How can you tell? J'kar and I have only been together... what? A few days at most? There is no way to tell yet, is there?" Tink asked in a dazed voice.

Zariff smiled. "The scan says you have bred. It can tell within a day if the male's seed has taken. It is very unusual for a woman to breed so soon. Many times a male must inject the breeding chemical many, many times before a woman's body accepts. It took my bond and I several years before it happened, and even then, we only had the one son."

Tink turned pale, and her hand went to press against her stomach. Looking down, she was suddenly a little dizzy. "What do you mean 'inject the breeding chemical'?" Tink asked hoarsely.

Zariff reached for Tink, guiding her over to the chair and gently forcing her to sit back down. "As you know, during sexual mating a male's canines elongate. This allows us to bite the female, holding her still while our body injects a chemical making her more receptive to our sperm. It usually takes many, many times for a female to accept. The chemical helps the female enjoy the sexual experience and readies her womb for our seed to implant. Is this not what your males do?"

Tink listened in disbelief. She really only heard a little of what Zariff was saying. The males bit a girl to make her horny and so she could get pregnant? Was that why J'kar was always biting her? He thought she needed it to want him?

Shaking her head, she replied numbly. "No. Our males don't bite the females. It just depends on the timing most of the time. Females get pregnant very easily most of the time. It only takes one sperm to get a woman pregnant on our planet."

Zariff shook his head. "I wonder if it is even necessary for one of our males to bite a human female to get her pregnant? I would like to do more research on this. In the meantime, J'kar is getting impatient for me to bring you to him. He will be most pleased to know of your breeding status."

Tink's head flew up at that. "No. You mustn't tell him."

Zariff frowned. "But why? It is a time of celebration among our people. J'kar, as the next ruler and a member of the ruling house, will be most excited."

Tink stood up quickly and reached for Zariff's hands. Looking at him with pleading eyes, she begged, "Please don't say anything. I need time to absorb this. On my planet it is normal for the woman to tell the man she is expecting. I want to wait for the perfect time to tell him. He has so much going on right now. Please. Let me be the one to tell him."

Zariff studied Tink's pleading face. "Of course. I can understand you would want to be alone with him to give him this great news. I will not say anything," Zariff responded before he added a word of warning. "But, you must promise to see the healer at the palace as soon as possible. Since this is a first between our species, we will need to monitor you carefully to make sure there is no threat to you or the child."

Tink let out a sigh of relief. "I promise." Grinning, she added, "I'm going to be a mommy."

"And, may I add, a beautiful one. Now, I must get you to the bridge before J'kar sends an armed escort to find us," Zariff said with a chuckle.

* * *

J'kar paced back and forth impatiently. What was taking Zariff so long to bring Tink to him? It had been over half an hour since he'd called. Did Zariff find something wrong? Was Tink hurt? J'kar pressed a hand to his stomach. The thought of anything happening to Tink was more than he could bear. He didn't know what he would do if she was hurt... or sick. Pressing the communicator again, he growled for Zariff to answer him.

"I have brought your bond mate, my lord," Zariff answered from the entrance to the bridge.

"About time," J'kar snarled. "What took you so long? Is she well?"

"*She* is perfectly all right," Tink answered with a soft smile.

She loved looking at him. She loved being with him. In the short time she had known J'kar, she realized she had fallen in love with him. It was like the other half of her was complete. Walking up and wrapping her arms around his waist, Tink stood on her toes to kiss him. Even then, she still needed to pull his head down to hers.

"I need a step stool to reach your lips," Tink murmured.

J'kar lifted Tink up and held her tight against his body. "I will simply hold you against me. You are so beautiful," he murmured, kissing her deeply.

He had been stunned when he first saw her. She had been behind Zariff when they entered, but when she stepped around him, he was mesmerized by her beauty in the traditional dress of his people. The blue and silver represented the colors of his house. The women wore traditional gowns representing their house or clan colors. This showed who protected them.

Tink was breathtaking. Overwhelming feelings of pride and the need to protect her filled him. She would be in danger from other clans who would want to secure her for their own. He knew he would do whatever he had to do to protect her. She would just have to learn to understand it was for her safety.

Borj cleared his throat. "J'kar, the shuttle is ready for departure. Father is most anxious to meet with you."

J'kar reluctantly broke the kiss and let Tink slide down the front of him. He smiled when he heard Tink's gasp as she felt the hard length of his cock. Smiling wickedly she turned, brushing the front of his pants with her hand as she moved toward the front view-screen to look out at the planet below.

This time it was J'kar's turn to gasp. His eyes narrowed to slits as he followed her graceful glide to the front. *"I should punish you for that."*

"Promises, promises. By the way, isn't it my turn to tie you up this time? I'm thinking I could start at your ankles and work my way up. Very, very slowly," Tink responded with a sultry smile curving her lips and a promise in her eyes.

J'kar growled low under his breath. His eyes flared with the silver flames Tink loved. J'kar took a step toward Tink before his brother's voice drew him back to the fact they were not alone.

Borj looked between the two of them, frowning. "J'kar, did you hear me?"

J'kar threw an exasperated look at his brother before turning back to his bond mate. "A moment. I want Tink to see her new home from here before we leave. Give us a moment alone. We will be there shortly."

Zariff, Borj, and the last crewman left the bridge. J'kar walked over to Tink, who was standing against the front railing of the view-screen looking at the planet below. He wrapped his arms around her, pulling her tight against his body. He couldn't get over the feeling of how delicate and fragile she felt, yet how strong and brave she was.

Tink sighed, melting back against J'kar's hard body. "It's so beautiful. It doesn't look all that different than Earth from space. A little more colorful in some areas. Earth is like a little blue and white marble. Baad is blues, greens, whites, pinks, and reds."

Tink moaned as one of J'kar's hands moved over her breast. Taking his hand in one of hers, she slid it down the front scoop of her neckline, arching back into his body to give him more access. J'kar watched as his hand slid under the covering of her gown, and he gripped her hardened nipple between his fingers.

Pulling on it, Tink moaned again as she moved her body back and forth along his length.

J'kar growled. "I want you now."

Tink was already pulling on her gown, pulling up the back. Panting, she said, "Quickie. We can do a quickie, right here, right now."

J'kar groaned again. "I do not know this quickie, but it sounds good. Bridge command, lock door, no entrance without authorization."

J'kar pulled the gown up around Tink's waist and bent her forward. He pulled her lacy panties down until they pooled around her ankles, and she stepped out of one side to free her legs as he unbuttoned the front of his pants, freeing his swollen cock. Pushing Tink's legs apart, J'kar forced Tink to lean even farther forward over the railing. Cupping her ass he rubbed the length of her line.

He had the sudden desire to explore her even more intimately. He wondered if she would let him. He must have communicated his dark desire with her, as he felt the sudden flood of warmth and excitement at the idea.

"Yes, oh, yes."

J'kar's eyes narrowed with lust and passion as he felt her response. *"Soon, little one. Soon I will taste every part of you. Enjoy every part of you."*

Sliding two of his fingers into her pussy, he found the wet mound swollen with need. Unable to resist, he pulled his fingers out and lifted them to his lips, tasting their delicious flavor. The taste sent J'kar over the edge.

With a low growl, he grabbed Tink around the waist. *"Hold on; do not let go. I cannot control myself. I am sorry, little one."*

"Fuck me. Now." Tink was panting she was so horny.

With one thrust J'kar buried himself deep inside Tink. He was out of control with need and desire. Holding her tightly he pounded her pussy, each thrust going deeper and deeper.

Reaching around her, he rubbed her clit, finding her swollen nub and pinching it between his fingers while his other hand grabbed the swollen nipple of the breast he had pulled free from her gown. He could feel the strength of her orgasm rising.

Tink was breaking apart. The feelings were overwhelming her as the tension built. Between the erotic thoughts of him wanting to fuck her ass, his deep, hard thrusts which were hitting all of her nerve endings, and his fingers working their magic on her breast and clit, she couldn't control the shaking overtaking her as her climax hit her hard and fast. Letting out a scream, she went wild in his arms as she came.

J'kar felt her orgasm all the way from the top of his head to the tips of his toes. When she went wild in his arms, he grabbed her hips to still her wild movements and plunged into her harder and deeper than he ever had before, keeping her legs spread apart.

Pressing his thumbs into her ass and spreading them, he thought about how good it was going to feel when he did this in her tight ring. Once, twice and he let out a roar as his release came over him. Leaning forward, he wrapped his arms tightly around Tink's shaking form, pulling her into the shelter of his arms. He was never going to let her go. Never.

Chapter 24

Tink let out another nervous sigh as the shuttle made its approach. They had made the last shuttle leaving for the planet. All other shuttles were arriving, each one filled with equipment and men in uniforms.

J'kar had been very understanding of her nervousness, holding her hand or pulling her close whenever they were stopped. The new men arriving stopped and stared at her as they walked through the shuttle bay. Tink stared right back, smiling and waving occasionally at a few of the more attentive ones. J'kar had *not* been very understanding of that.

"I am going to have to lock you in our room. You are dangerous to the men of my planet," J'kar whispered in her mind.

Leaning back against him Tink replied with a mischievous grin. *"I would just escape. Besides, if you think I am bad, wait until my mom or sisters come for a visit. The men won't know what hit them!"*

"I look forward to their coming here, little one, if it makes you happy." J'kar did not allow his concern to slip through.

He was not at all sure how his people would react to the fact a compatible species had been found. There was a real possibility Tink might never see her family again. If she did, it was almost certain they would never be allowed to return to their world.

From everything they had discovered, Earthlings had no idea about life existing outside their world, their galaxy. They were still in their infancy as far as space travel was concerned. The differences in their technology alone were inconceivable.

If they were to find out other species had access to their world and were so far superior to them in space travel and technology, it could cause widespread fear, paranoia, and panic leading to unnecessary loss of life. As of now only Cosmos presented a danger, a danger that might yet have to be eliminated.

"We are approaching arrival at Gate Four. The high chancellor is waiting for your arrival, my lord," the pilot informed them as they cruised over a series of buildings and shuttles before landing in a large circle marked with a strange symbol.

Tink turned quickly before the doors opened and gave J'kar a quick kiss. "For luck," she whispered.

"Luck? Why do we need luck?" J'kar asked.

"It never hurts to have a little handy, you know, just in case your dad blows a gasket when he finds out his son married without telling him. That kind of luck," Tink said in a rush, her face flushing with her nervousness.

"He will love you as much as I do," J'kar growled out in a low, husky voice.

Tink rolled her eyes at J'kar. Borj, who had been sitting across from them, let out a little laugh when he saw it. Tink turned and gave Borj a million-watt smile, wiggling her nose a little.

"He is right, sister. Who could not love you?" Borj said with a smile.

Tink threw her arms around Borj's neck and gave him a noisy kiss, right on the lips. "I need to introduce you to one of my sisters."

The sound of someone clearing their throat had Tink swirling around in a floating wave of blue and silver. An older replica of J'kar stood at the entrance to the lowered shuttle platform, flanked by a half dozen uniformed giants.

"Oh, hi," Tink said with a grin.

J'kar pulled Tink away from his startled brother and back against his side. "Father," J'kar took a step forward and gripped both of his father's forearms.

"Mak told us of the attack. I am pleased you are safe," Turning to look at the unusual female peeking out from around J'kar, Teriff asked harshly. "Who is this?"

"Father, may I present my bond mate, Tink. Tink, this is my father, the high chancellor, Teriff 'Tag Krell Manok," J'kar gently pulled Tink around until she stood in front of him.

"Hello, sir. It's a pleasure to meet you." Tink smiled up at the tall, formidable man.

Teriff stared down at the petite female standing in front of him. She was looking up at him as if she was his equal. He did not understand a word of what she had said, but the cadence of the language was very pleasing to the ear. Teriff looked at J'kar, then back down at the woman. She was beautiful in an exotic way.

"She is the one who saved Derik's life? She attacked a Juangan?" Teriff glanced up at J'kar in disbelief. "You expect me to believe this little female fought and won against a Juangan?"

"All it takes is a hammer in the right place, sir." A small smile appeared as she leaned back into J'kar's arms, smiling up at him when he wrapped his arms around her waist. "Lucky for me, though, your son came to my rescue as well."

Teriff looked at both of them with a slight frown on his face. Studying the expression on his oldest son's face, taking note of his arms wrapped around the female's waist, and the emotion showing on her face confused him. He needed to debrief his son on his mission. Obviously, something had happened, and he wanted to know what it was.

Did this female have control over him somehow? He looked at Borj and saw he was also watching the interaction between his brother and the female with a small smile on his face. What type of control did she have over his sons?

"What does she say? I do not understand her," Teriff frowned again. The female just looked up at J'kar and ran her hands up and down his arms as he held her close to his body.

"She said a hammer in the right place defeated the Juangan. She also explained I had saved her life as well. Derik and RITA have been working on translating their language to ours and have programmed our translators to understand her. I will have him update the translators here as soon as possible. I want everyone to be able to communicate with her. I will not have her feeling uncomfortable."

J'kar could feel the waves of concern coming from his father.

Nodding toward two of his men, Teriff spoke firmly. "Escort the female to the palace. I want the healer to check her over. J'kar, you and Borj will travel with me. I wish to know more about this species you have brought back and why you have bonded without first seeking the council's permission."

Tink was aware the older version of J'kar wasn't happy about her, but she wasn't going to let him cause problems. There was no way in hell she would be separated from J'kar the minute they were planet side. And, there was absolutely no way in hell was she going to be examined like some kind of a specimen. Her parents always told her first impressions were important, and there was no way she was going to let "Mr. High Chancellor," as she had named him, walk all over her.

"I don't think so," Tink said firmly, crossing her arms in front of her. Moving away from J'kar, Tink walked up to Teriff and gave him one of her "it's not happening" looks. Jerking her head toward J'kar, Tink said in a firm voice. "Where he goes, I go for now. If you want to know about my species you can just ask me."

Teriff looked shocked at first. While he didn't understand what the female said, her body language seemed to be telling him she was not going to cooperate. He stared down in disbelief at the tiny figure standing in front of him with her arms crossed and a determined thrust to her jaw.

"What did she say?" Teriff demanded, his eyes narrowing.

"Father, these humans are not like our women. They do not care to be ordered around. She says she will go where I go." J'kar wrapped his arms around Tink again. "This is new to her. She was not even aware other life existed outside their world."

Teriff let out a soft growl. "They are a primitive species, and you have bonded to one of them? She will go to the palace now. I want the healer to exam her thoroughly and see what control she has over you. Now." Teriff turned and strode away, his shoulders stiff with his anger.

"Well, I think that went well, considering, don't you?" Tink asked in a bemused voice. "Boy, he really needs to get a life, get laid, or get that big stick out of his ass."

Borj choked on a laugh as J'kar just closed his eyes and shook his head. He was actually afraid of what might happen if his father's translator was updated.

* * *

Tink was not happy, and an unhappy Tink was a problem on a good day. Today, while it had started out good, had quickly gone into the trash bin. J'kar had made a compromise, of sorts. He escorted her to the palace while his brother traveled with his father. Once at the palace, though, Teriff made sure there was no doubt his orders would be followed. He immediately had two guards escort both her and J'kar to the medical wing of the palace.

Tink was pacing back and forth, steaming. She was not going to put up with being examined like a bug. She wasn't even any good about going once a year to see the doctor. Hell, she only went about every four or five years, she was so paranoid of doctors.

On board she had tolerated Zariff because he had just used a scanner, never touching her. She could handle that. Anything else and she had panic attacks. She didn't know why. Some people were scared of spiders, snakes, or roaches. She was scared of doctors.

J'kar grabbed her arm as she passed by him again. Wrapping his arms around her, he kissed her gently on the lips. "I will not let anyone harm you, little one."

Wiping a tear from the corner of her eye, Tink huffed at him. "I don't like doctors. Zariff said I was fine. I can handle that. If whoever comes in only uses a scanner, I'm cool. But, if they think they are doing anything else, I am so out of here. Do you understand? I won't do anything else."

J'kar could feel the tremors running through Tink's body. His brave little fighter could handle a Juangan or a knife-wielding human male, but not a healer. All he could do was hold her and rock her as she worked her temper into a fine-toothed weapon.

"Welcome home, my lord. Welcome, female. I am Terra. I am one of the healers for the royal family. I have been requested to give you a complete exam.

J'kar, Father has asked you to join him immediately in the council room," the woman said softly before moving over to a cabinet where she began pulling out all types of equipment.

"Terra, I will stay during the exam. I will not have my bond mate distressed by it," J'kar said quietly.

"I am afraid that will not be possible. Father has sent two of his security members to make sure you arrive. I promise to do what I can to make this as comfortable as possible for your bond mate," Terra responded with a confused frown.

As if they were listening, two large men in uniforms stood in the entrance way to the room. Placing their hands to their chests and bowing, one of the men stepped forward. "My lord, we were asked to escort you immediately to the council room. Your father has asked that you come peacefully."

J'kar's eyes narrowed at the veiled threat. If his father had added the last part it meant they were given permission to use restraints if necessary to make sure he attended. Growling under his breath, J'kar felt the anger burn bright. Standing in front of Tink, J'kar's eyes glowed with molten silver flames, and his teeth began to elongate.

"J'kar, what's wrong?" Tink's soft voice barely penetrated. "Why would your father threaten you?"

Terra replied softly, "J'kar, Father fears the female has some type of control over you. If you resist, he will be more convinced she has you under her control. Please, go. I will not harm her. I will conduct the tests Father has requested. Once he has the results, if they show she does not control you as he fears, he will be more rational."

J'kar glared at the two uniformed men in the doorway before turning around to pull Tink back into his arms. *"I will be with you. Call me if you need me."*

"Hey, I do know how to kick some ass, and right now I am seriously considering kicking your dad's. No offense," Tink responded lightly. The last thing she wanted was for J'kar to get into a fight over her.

J'kar couldn't help the soft laugh that escaped from him. Kissing Tink, he glared at the healer. "If she says no, you are not to do anything. It is her choice, do you understand?"

Terra bowed her head in understanding. J'kar looked down into Tink's eyes, once more running his palm down her cheek before turning and leaving the room. He didn't see the flash of fear that passed through Tink's eyes as he left, or he never would have been able to leave her.

Chapter 25

Tink folded her arms across her chest again and watched as the healer moved to close the door. The woman was the first one Tink had seen since her arrival so Tink took a moment to look her over. The females were built similar to the males—tall, dark, and handsome.

The woman had to be at least six feet tall if she was an inch. She wasn't very old and she was very beautiful. She didn't look much older than Tink, maybe Hannah's age.

She had long, thick black hair braided down her back and was wearing a dark blue gown with strips of silver running through it. She wasn't wearing a jacket, so Tink could tell her arms were muscular. She would be a formidable adversary if Tink had to fight her way out, but Tink had a few tricks up her sleeve. First and foremost, she learned to never fight fair. Glancing at the door behind the woman, Tink wondered how much trouble she would be in if she decided to haul butt.

* * *

Terra watched the female studying her. She appeared to show intelligence. Pulling the data chart to her, she made notes on her observation: small build, fragile appearance, not very strong, pale coloring, unusual eye color.

"I had Derik upload a copy of the translation program to the data screen. I should be able to understand you. Please remove all of your clothing and position yourself on the examination table," Terra said calmly.

Tink looked at the woman, then the exam table. "Not happening. If you want to scan me, go ahead, but the clothes stay on and I remain standing."

Terra was taken aback by the female. She asked in a confused tone, "How am I to examine you without you removing your clothing? The High Chancellor has requested I give you a thorough examination. I must assess if you are compatible with our species and note differences, both physically and mentally."

"If you want me to draw you a picture, fine. I don't do exams well. As far as compatibility, we are," Tink answered in a short tone.

Frowning Terra said again. "I must document your body to see if you are able to breed with one of our males. I must determine how your body handles sexuality with the males. I must also determine if you can control them through some type of mind or chemical control."

Tink smiled and moved around the exam table to put it between the two of them. Running her hand over the top of it, she thought about how she was going to reply. Taking a deep breath, Tink waved her hand in the air.

"Perhaps we could talk about this over a cup of coffee or tea? I can answer all your questions, give you some drawings to help you, and you can wave your scanner over me. As far as whether we are capable of 'breeding,' as you put it, we are. Zariff said I was pregnant. How you guys can tell so soon is beyond me. It takes a little longer on my planet to find out, but he seemed pretty positive I was," Tink said with a determined tilt to her jaw. *Chew on that,* she thought.

Terra froze. "You have bred with J'kar? Already?" she whispered.

"Yes." Tink watched as the color seemed to leach from the healer's face. "Is there a problem with that?"

Terra looked stunned. "But, how is that possible without the mating rituals? It is said only those who have been through the mating rite can breed."

Holding up her hands, palms out toward the healer, Tink shrugged her shoulders. "Don't ask me. Humans don't need a mating rite to get pregnant or breed, as you say. We just need to do 'it.'"

Terra's eyes were glued to Tink's left palm. "Please, may I see your palm?"

Tink looked at her palm and then at Terra. Walking around the table, she laid her left hand palm up in the healer's. Terra ran her fingers lightly over the intricate patterns of circles.

"How?" she asked in wonder.

"The first time I touched J'kar, it happened. When I went back to my world, I was so lost, like a part of me had been torn out and left behind. Cosmos ran tests to see if it was dangerous, like a parasite, but there was nothing. It wasn't until I was with J'kar again that I felt whole. He saved my life. A man, a human man, had attacked me. I was stabbed several times. J'kar said he held my life force so I wouldn't die," Tink finished softly, gently rubbing the circles with her finger.

"You are well, little one?" J'kar asked in a tense voice.

Tink smiled, *"Yes, so far. I'm explaining how we met to the healer. She saw the circles on my palm."* Tink traced the circles again, this time a little harder, a little longer.

"Little one, please stop. I cannot focus when you do that," groaned J'kar.

"You are talking to him, aren't you?" Terra asked.

Tink blinked as she refocused on where she was at. "Yes. Since not long after he brought me back, he has been able to talk to me telepathically. My people can't do that, so at first it totally weirded me out. But it is fun now."

"I must examine you. I will respect your wish to keep your clothing on for now. I will need to speak with the High Chancellor about this. I will examine you as best I can in the meantime. If you are breeding, we must assure ourselves of the health of you and the child. Please, lie on the examination table. I will only scan you for now," Terra said anxiously.

Tink looked closely at Terra before deciding she needed to compromise. Climbing onto the exam table, she lay back, watching every move the healer made. Terra picked up a scanner off the small tray next to the exam table and ran it over Tink, spending more time around her lower abdomen.

"I would like to take a blood and tissue sample. Is this permissible?" Terra asked hesitantly.

"I kind of have this fear of needles. How do you plan on taking it?" Tink asked, going a little pale.

Terra laughed. "You should not feel more than a pinch on your finger." Pulling a small device off the tray, Terra gently picked up one of Tink's hands and placed her finger on it. She removed it and connected it to the scanner.

"That's it?" Tink asked.

Terra smiled down at Tink. "Yes, I have everything. Your blood type is different from ours, but on initial analysis, it is compatible. You are breeding. It is still too early to tell the sex of the child, but there is an abnormality with the reading. I am not sure what it is yet."

"What do you mean an abnormality?" Tink asked fearfully. "Is there something wrong with my baby?"

"I do not know. I am getting a duplicate reading when I scan," Terra said. "I will need to study it to make sure it is not the scanner malfunctioning."

"Wait a minute, can't you just get another scanner and do it again and compare them?" Tink asked as the fear of something being wrong with her baby ran through her.

Terra looked at Tink for a moment, then nodded. "Please wait here. I will retrieve one from the other examination room."

Tink blinked back tears. What if something was wrong with the baby? What if their DNA wasn't compatible, and it caused a mutation of some sort? What if—

The door opened, and Terra came back in holding another scanner. "Please, I know you do not want to undress, but perhaps you could lift the gown up so I can scan directly over your womb without any coverings."

Tink nodded, sliding off the table enough to pull the gown up over her hips. Terra rescanned Tink's lower abdomen again. When she was done, she nodded to Tink, who quickly sat up and pulled the gown back down over her legs.

"Well?" Tink asked, her voice quivering.

"I do not understand. It comes up the same. The scanner continues to show a duplicate marking. It is as if there are two babies instead of one. That is impossible."

"Twins? It says I'm having twins?" Tink's eyes grew huge. Holy shit! J'kar was lethal.

"What is this 'twins'?" Terra asked.

"It means I'm having two babies. They can either be identical or fraternal," Tink whispered.

"But, our females never have more than one child at a time. Can your species carry more than one?" Terra asked in disbelief.

"Yeah. Sure. One woman even had eight babies at one time. That isn't normal, but it has been done," Tink said, rubbing her hands over her stomach. "I don't know anything about handling one baby, much less two. I... Oh, shit. Twins," Tink looked wide-eyed at Terra, and burst into tears.

* * *

J'kar had been having problems focusing on his father, who was reviewing the tapes and reports from their voyage. He was furious the Juangans had the audacity to attack one of their warships. Just as his father was getting to the video of Tink's appearance on board, J'kar was hit by a wave of panic.

Blocking out everything around him, he focused in on the cause. Feeling Tink's overwhelming feelings of fear, he jerked out of his seat and was halfway out the door of the council chamber before he heard his father's demands to know what was happening.

"My bond mate needs me. So help me, if you have done anything to harm her I will not be responsible for my actions. She is my bond mate and nothing will separate me from her." Turning, J'kar yanked open the door to the room and ran out.

Borj, Derik, Lan, and Brock, who had also attended the meeting, stood. Borj said, "With our deepest respects, Father, we must assist in the protection of the female."

Teriff watched as the four men took off running after J'kar. Who was this female that she could command such loyalty from not one, but three of his sons and two of his highest-ranking officers? He would discover her secrets if it was the last thing he did. Walking out of the room, he proceeded to follow the others to the medical wing.

J'kar burst into the room as Terra was trying desperately to stop Tink from crying. "Please. You must stop. I…"

"What did you do?" J'kar growled, pushing Terra to one side roughly. He gathered Tink into his arms, holding her against his chest. "What did you do?" he shouted.

"It wasn't... It wasn't..." Tink hiccupped. "It wasn't anything she did. It was what you did." Burying her face in his chest, she began sobbing again.

J'kar looked puzzled. Walking over to a chair in the corner, he sat down and tried to pull Tink's face out of his chest. "What did I do, little one?" Tink continued to shake her head and snuffle.

"J'kar, is she safe?" Borj asked a minute later as he, Derik, Lan, and Brock filed into the room. "Terra, what have you done?"

"Borj, I didn't do anything. I promise. She is very emotional. This is not uncommon for her condition. She needs time to adjust to the changes her body is going through. It will be important to keep her as calm as possible, as it can cause her to become very ill," Terra said, trying to calm her older brother.

"Terra, you are my sister, but if you do not tell me what is wrong with her I will not be responsible for what happens. What is wrong with her?" J'kar asked again through gritted teeth.

"What is the problem here?" Teriff demanded as he entered the room. "Terra, is the female hurt?"

"No, Father. I performed most of the tests you have asked. She is..." Terra began.

"Is she sick?" Teriff demanded. "What is her problem?"

Tink had had enough. Sitting up straight in J'kar's arms, she glared at the High Chancellor. "I'll tell you what my problem is, buddy. Your son is one potent son of a bitch. I'm pregnant with twins! You try landing on an alien planet, deal with a dickhead like you, and find out you are going to have, not one, but two babies, and see if you don't feel a little overwhelmed," Tink shouted in anger and frustration.

"Baby?" Teriff whispered.

"Two babies?" J'kar said, staring at Tink's stomach, totally stunned.

"Good breeding, brother," Derik said with a huge grin on his face.

Chapter 26

"What is a dickhead?" Teriff asked as he poured another glass of potent wine into his cup.

Derik grinned. "According to RITA, a dickhead is the head of a male's penis, where most women think a man's brain is. It also means a stupid or despicable man. RITA seems to think Tink meant the second one, but she didn't rule out the first definition either. It is not a compliment to be called one."

Teriff frowned as Borj and Lan tried to smother laughter. "I am not stupid or despicable. How dare she call me a dickhead."

Brock laughed. "She called J'kar a son of a bitch. That means he is the son of a female dog. It is not a compliment either."

All five men laughed. "She has a very unusual language. I am glad I had the translator updated. I am going to be a 'grandfather' according to her RITA. I like I am considered 'grand.' I have been a 'grand' father, haven't I?" Teriff said loudly as he held his glass up for a toast. "To many more of my sons being sons of bitches. May you all breed as well as your brother."

As the five men polished off another bottle of the potent liquid, a man approached. "Father." He nodded to the other men at the table, looking at the five empty bottles with a raised eyebrow. "Am I missing something?"

Derik laughed. "J'kar has bred well with his bond mate. They are expecting twins," he finished with a slight hiccup at the end.

"Twins? What does that mean?" Mak asked.

"Tink is going to have two babies. Her species can have more than one baby at a time," Borj replied, grinning. "I plan to find the one she calls Hannah. I will claim her. Perhaps I will breed twins with her."

"How do you know who this Hannah is? How can you be sure she is your bond mate? She might not be as attractive as J'kar's bond mate. Even though I have not seen J'kar's bond mate yet, the men talk of her beauty," Mak said, picking up an empty glass and filling it. Sipping the wine, he watched as Borj pulled an image out of his pocket. It was folded and slightly bent around the edges like he had been carrying it for some time.

"Tink said she was going to introduce me to one of her sisters. I want the one she calls Hannah. Tell me she is not the most beautiful woman in the world," Borj handed the image to Mak. Frowning, he added, "On second thought, do not tell me that, because I would hate to have to beat your ass." He sloshed a little bit of the liquid that was in his glass onto the table when he pointed it at Mak.

Mak grinned. "Let me see who this beauty is who has captured your heart without even meeting her."

Mak thought it was funny to see his brother so drunk. Never before had the calm, always-in-control Borj ever lost control.

Picking up the image, he looked at the female. He had to admit she was very attractive in an exotic kind of way. She was lean and muscular but still appeared soft and fragile at the same time. She had warm, green eyes and long hair braided down her back. Her clothing left little to the imagination. She seemed at home in the image with the vivid blue sky and water behind her.

Unfolding the image on one side, he saw the image of what appeared to be his brother's bond mate. She was shorter than the other woman and had different color eyes, but their facial features were similar enough to show they were siblings. She looked like she would be a handful from the mischievous grin on her face.

"You see, is she not the most beautiful woman in the whole galaxy?" Borj asked, reaching for the image.

Mak grinned. "Yes, she is indeed very beautiful. Perhaps I should challenge you for her?"

Borj made a drunken grab for the image growling. "I have claimed her. She is mine. You can have the other one."

"I thought J'kar had already claimed her?" Mak replied teasingly.

"Not her, the other one."

Mak looked down at the image and realized it was still folded. Unfolding the other side, he sucked in a breath in surprise, staring down at the image of the third female. His whole world seemed to narrow in on her. Never had he felt such strong emotions from just looking at an image.

The female was not as tall as Borj's Hannah but taller than J'kar's Tink. She was built with more curves, all in the right places, and was stunning. Her hair was a mixture of their red sands and the giant trees surrounding them. Not a true red, a dark mahogany with tints of red highlights.

She was looking out at the sea, a faraway look in her eyes like she was deep in thought. She was wearing a white shirt with long sleeves that billowed out around her as the wind blew, pulling it back just enough to show hints of the small triangles covering her full breasts. Her legs were covered by short, tan-colored pants, and she was wearing thin leather sandals on her feet.

It was her expression that haunted Mak. He could see the secrets in her eyes. Secrets he wanted to discover, uncover and share with her. Mak started with a growl when the image was pulled out of his hands.

"Get your own image," Borj growled back. "This one is mine!"

"Where am I to get an image? Where are the females?" Mak demanded, leaning forward.

The other men looked at each other and grinned. Derik asked the other men, "Do you think we should tell him about oral sex? Perhaps he won't want to meet the female then."

"What is oral sex?" Teriff demanded. "You did not tell me about that? What is it? Is it something different these females do?" He reached for another bottle and frowned when nothing came out of it. "Tell me."

Lan just groaned. "It is most uncomfortable. You need to learn about it in private."

"Why?" Mak asked curiously.

Brock leaned forward and said. "I do not think you really want to know. It has caused us many an uncomfortable night since we learned of it."

"Now. Tell me now," Teriff roared. "I command it."

Derik, Brock, Lan, and Borj looked at each other and grinned. They knew if they offered it as a challenge, neither their brother nor their father would be able to resist. They had placed bets earlier to see who lasted the longest before having to excuse themselves. Borj nodded at Lan to produce the vidcom.

"I warn you to watch this at your own risk. It can be very disturbing," Lan stated soberly before moving the vidcom in front of Teriff and Mak. Sitting back, Lan, Derik, Brock, and Borj tried to prepare themselves. The vidcom of the incident still affected them every time they watched it, which was daily.

Teriff and Mak watched the vidcom, at first with interest, then disbelief. It wasn't until Tink was telling them to close their eyes and began describing what she wanted to do with her tongue and lips all over the male body that beads of sweat began to gather on the men's brow. By the end, both men were groaning and leaning forward, trying to control their breathing.

Teriff asked in a strangled voice. "What she described—it is possible for a female to do this to a male?"

"Yes. Not only what she described, but much, much more. J'kar said he had to restrain her, and she became even more passionate, wanting to tie him up. Not only this, but she attacked him in the corridor in front of all of us. She was kissing, licking, and biting on him, as well as running her body up and down his without being bitten herself. They were not seen again until it was time to leave for the planet. Even then, I suspect they did not make it off the bridge without mating," Borj said, looking at the image he held in his hand.

Teriff stood up suddenly. He adjusted the front of his pants which had a suspiciously large bulge in the front, and moved toward the doorway. "It is time for me to retire. I believe your mother is calling me."

Borj, Mak, and Derik looked at the rapidly departing figure of their father. "Mother, calling him?" Derik replied before bursting out with laughter. Soon all the other men joined in. Mak took the opportunity to snatch the image out of Borj's hand, taking off out the door right after their father.

Chapter 27

"Ah, little one, please stop crying. Terra said it is bad for you. You will make yourself ill," J'kar begged again, wiping frantically at the tears streaming down his bond mate's face.

"This is all your fault! If you hadn't bitten me, then I wouldn't be pregnant!" Tink growled at J'kar, giving him a watery sob. "I want my mom and my sisters. I need them. I can't do this alone."

J'kar was desperate. He would promise her the moons if it would stop her tears. "I'll send someone to bring them to you. I promise. I will have Borj go as soon as possible. He will retrieve your mother and sisters."

Tink looked up as hope flared through her. Throwing her arms around J'kar's neck, she ran little kisses along his jaw. "Really? You'll let them come here? Oh, thank you. I love you so much."

"I love you too, little one." Placing his large hand over her stomach, he whispered, "Two babies. The gods and goddesses smile on us."

A sudden knock at the door had J'kar growling. He wanted time alone with his bond mate and was getting a little tired of constantly being interrupted. Since they had been planet side he had not been alone with her except for the last few minutes. J'kar leaned over and kissed Tink before striding to the door. Opening it with a growl, he was surprised to see Lan standing outside it, armed.

"What is wrong?" J'kar demanded, glancing behind Lan to see six armed guards.

"The Earthling who attacked your bond mate has escaped," Lan replied quietly.

Tink came over to stand near J'kar. "Bachman escaped?" Tink shivered as J'kar pulled her closer.

"How?" J'kar asked, moving aside so Lan could enter.

"The guards underestimated his abilities. He overpowered one of the guards and shot both of them. He escaped into the woods on the outskirts of the city as he was being transported to a holding facility."

"He said he had special training. He used it on me when we fought," Tink whispered softly. She turned worried eyes on J'kar. "He isn't sane. I could tell from his eyes."

"The guards?" J'kar asked.

"Both killed. He knocked one out and killed the other, then shot the one at close range while he was unconscious. There was nothing we could do to save them," Lan replied furiously. He felt responsible for the deaths.

J'kar laid his hand on Lan's shoulder. "I accept responsibility for their deaths. I should have killed him immediately."

Lan looked at Tink. "Before one guard died, he said he'd heard the Earthling say he had unfinished business with you and your bond mate. I would feel better if you had extra guards until he is captured."

J'kar growled before nodding his consent. "Post extra guards around this area. I want some of our best trackers looking for him. Kill on sight. I will not have him harm anyone else."

Lan nodded before leaving. J'kar took one look at Tink and knew she was fighting back tears again. Wrapping his arms around her, he pulled her tight against his body. He would never let anything harm her again. He knew what it was like to almost lose her, and he didn't think he could ever live through it again.

"Come, you should eat something and sleep for a while. It has been a very trying day," J'kar murmured as he picked Tink up in his arms and carried her to the bedroom.

Tink wrapped her arms around J'kar's neck and laid her head on his shoulder. Just for a little while she wanted to feel safe and protected. "Will you stay with me?"

J'kar brushed his lips over her hair. "For a little while, until you fall asleep. I need to help with the search. I will send for my mother and Terra to stay with you. It will be good for you to meet her. There will also be guards posted outside the rooms."

Tink just nodded. "I'm not very hungry, but I will take you up on the nap. Can you hold me for a little while?"

J'kar laid Tink gently on the bed. "Of course, little one. Sleep now. All will be well. I will not let him hurt anyone else, especially you."

Tink's eyes were already closed. The strain of the day had finally been too much combined with the lack of sleep. J'kar held her close to him, feeling her body slowly relax into a deeper sleep. He brushed a light kiss over the top of her head before he carefully untangled himself from her arms and legs. He could not resist brushing her hair back from her face and cupping her cheek gently in the palm of his hand.

She was so delicate-looking when she was asleep. His gaze traveled down to her stomach, and he laid his palm on it, smiling at the thought of his children growing inside of her. He knew she would be even more beautiful rounded with his children. He had much to do if he was going to bring her family to his world and capture the man who had tried to kill her.

Chapter 28

J'kar called for his mother and sister to join him in his living quarters. He paced back and forth, impatiently waiting for them. He was furious at the human's escape. Bachman was a dead man; he just didn't know it yet. J'kar was even more dangerous now that his bond mate was breeding. He would kill anyone who was a threat to his family.

J'kar strode to the door and flung it open when he heard the soft knock. Opening the door, he gazed at his mother, looking at her through new eyes. He would need her help and support if Tink was to adjust to their way of life.

Tresa 'Tag Krell Manok was a woman known for her strength and beauty. She was the perfect complement to his father. Where his father was stern, imposing, and fearsome, she was elegance, grace, and gentleness.

"Mother," J'kar said with a bow.

"J'kar," his mother acknowledged softly. "I am most pleased you are safe. I heard about the attack on your warship. I feared for your brothers' and your safety."

"All was well. I have good men, and Borj and Derik fought well," J'kar replied. "Please, come in and sit. I have need to speak with you."

Tresa nodded and moved into the room, looking around. She had hoped to meet J'kar's bond mate. She had heard much and, she thought with a slight blush, experienced much last night because of the female's influence.

She couldn't quite keep the smile from curving her lips as she reflected on last night's experience. Teriff had come to her bed with restraints. She had expected it to be a normal occurrence of his needing to seek release.

She had learned long ago not to resist him but to just try to enjoy the encounter as much as she could. What she had not expected was for him to do some of the things he had done to her. He had restrained her, something he had not done in years. Instead of mounting her, he had used his mouth on her to give her pleasure unlike anything she had ever encountered.

By the end of the night she had been screaming out her release and begging him for more. He had made love to her over and over throughout the night, and she had woken in his arms blushing, wanting more. She had never felt so well loved or satisfied in her life. She wanted, needed to speak with the female about how to please her bond mate as well as he had pleased her.

"J'kar, where is your bond mate? I would like very much to meet her," Tresa asked softly as she moved to sit down on the large couch.

J'kar looked at his mother, noting her pink cheeks with a frown. He hoped she was well. He did not want Tink exposed to any illnesses. "You are well, Mother? Is Terra coming?"

"I am very well, thank you. Terra will be along shortly. She wanted to meet with RITA to discuss your bond mate's breeding. She had medical questions she wanted to ask to make sure your bond mate gets the best care possible. I told her I would meet her here," Tresa responded lightly.

"Tink is lying down. I am afraid I have not let her get the rest she needs," J'kar said, his face turning slightly red. "I would like it if you could offer your friendship and guidance to my bond mate. She is missing her family, especially her mother and sisters. She needs their assistance during her breeding."

"It is my understanding she is expecting two children. This is unheard of. I can understand her concern. I remember well how fragile I was while carrying you, your brothers, and your sister," Tresa said. "I will be happy to offer her my friendship and guidance. I am glad you have found your bond mate, my son."

J'kar smiled. "She is extraordinary. She is small but very strong and brave. She is different from the women here, and I fear they may not understand or accept her. I need for you and Terra to protect her."

"You needn't worry. We will keep her safe," Tresa replied, seeing the love J'kar had for his bond mate shining from his eyes. She looked up when she heard the sound of a door opening. Standing up, Tresa turned to get her first look at the female who had captured her oldest son's heart.

Tink stood in the doorway, looking uncertainly at the woman standing next to J'kar. She was very, very beautiful. She was wearing the traditional dress and colors of his house. It was only when she turned that Tink was able to see the resemblance to J'kar in her face. Smiling shyly at the woman, Tink moved forward, pulling the robe around her small frame a little tighter about her.

"Hi," Tink said as she wrapped her arm around J'kar's waist. "I'm Jasmine Bell. Everyone calls me Tink."

J'kar leaned down and kissed Tink on her lips, murmuring softly, "You did not sleep very long, little one," Tink just smiled and laid her head against his chest.

"It is a pleasure to meet you at last, daughter. I am Tresa, J'kar's mother." Tresa responded, watching the interaction between her son and new daughter. She couldn't help but notice how gentle J'kar was with the female or how the female seemed to enjoy touching him. She looked forward to learning more about her new daughter.

J'kar sighed before giving Tink another kiss. "I have to go out for a little while. Mother, please see Tink eats something. I will return as soon as possible." Bending, he murmured for Tink's ears alone, "I love you, little one. Take care until I am with you again."

He kissed Tink deeply, leaving her breathless before he turned and left. Tink stood staring at the closed door, looking lost.

"Come, child. Sit and have some refreshments. He will return as soon as possible," Tresa guided Tink over to the couch gently pushing her down into the soft cushions. She poured some tea for Tink and handed it to her. "I have never seen my son look at a female the way he looks at you."

"What do you mean?" Tink asked distractedly. She took a sip of the tea and let the warmth flow through her. She missed J'kar already, and he had just left. She totally had it bad.

"He loves you," Tresa said with a smile. "I am most pleased."

Tink looked up, startled. "You are?"

"Of course. I always dreamed my sons would find their bond mate. To find her and love her is a blessing of the gods and the goddesses," Tresa said, watching Tink's reaction to her comment.

"I love him. I don't understand how I can feel this way so quickly, but I do," Tink said softly. "I can't believe we are going to have a baby." She rubbed her hand over her stomach in amazement.

"Tink, may I ask you something?" Tresa asked hesitantly. She twisted the material of her long dress between her fingers nervously.

"Of course," Tink responded, suddenly cautious. Was this when the mother-in-law grew claws, she wondered.

"Last night Teriff, J'kar's father and my bond mate, came to me. He—" Tresa took a deep breath and turned her face away from Tink. "—he came to my bed. He did things... things I had never experienced before. He... Oh, dear." Tresa rose and walked over to the windows overlooking the gardens. Straightening her shoulders, she turned and looked at Tink. "He used his mouth on me in ways I never knew were possible," she finished with a nice rosy red to her cheeks.

Tink stared at J'kar's mom for a moment, absorbing what she was saying. "Are you saying he used oral sex on you?"

"Yes," Tresa whispered, twisting her hands together. "He told me he watched a vidcom on you telling the men on the warship about it. He said it was the most amazing thing, and he wanted to try it."

Tink shook her head, trying not to laugh. She was famous for her Sex Ed class. Wow! "So, what is your question?"

"I want to do it again and again, but I want to pleasure him the way he pleasured me. How do I do it?" Tresa asked anxiously.

"Oh boy, I could really use my mom here," Tink said as she leaned back into the cushion of the couch. "Well, for starters, you could…"

Tink and Tresa spent the next hour talking about all the things Tresa could try in the bedroom. Tresa's eyes widened, and she gasped a few times, but she seemed really interested in learning about ways to entice her bond mate to greater pleasure. When the knock on the outer door sounded Tink didn't know whether to be relieved or irritated. She was getting some really good ideas from the discussion they were having.

"Mother, I apologize for taking so long. I had a most rewarding discussion with Tink's RITA," Terra said as she came into the room.

"Hi, Terra," Tink called out in greeting. It turned out she really liked Terra, which turned out to be even better after learning she was J'kar, Borj, and Derik's sister. "How's it going?"

"Very well, thank you. I had a most enjoyable discussion with your RITA. She is very informative," Terra said, pouring herself a cup of tea.

"Hey, why don't you tell me about it while I fix us something to eat. I could eat a horse right now," Tink said as she headed for the small kitchen area. Opening cabinets, she discovered several strange-looking items.

Terra and Tresa laughed at Tink's puzzled look, pushing her gently into a chair as they took over the cooking. The three of them spent the next several hours talking about everything from the weather, to what Earth was like, to family, and finally ending up back on their first topic—sex.

"So, you humans use toys as well during sex?" Terra asked in awe.

"You guys are asking the wrong person. You need to talk to my mom. She can tell you all the really good stuff," Tink said with a laugh. A sudden case of homesickness hit her making her catch her breath. A sob escaped before she could stop it, followed by another, then another.

"Oh, my dear. What is wrong?" Tresa asked anxiously, pulling Tink into her arms.

"I miss my family so much," Tink sobbed.

It took almost half an hour for Tresa and Terra to get Tink calmed down. By then, Tink was totally exhausted. Terra gave Tink a light sedative to help her sleep and tucked her into bed.

"Mother, you must talk to Father about bringing Tink's family here. She needs them. I could not imagine being in her position without you, Father, and my brothers to support me," Terra said anxiously.

Tresa smiled wickedly. "I will talk to your father. I believe I may know a way to convince him."

"How?" Terra asked, confused.

"Didn't Tink say her mother could tell us more ways to pleasure our men?" Terra nodded, suddenly understanding.

"Oh, mother. I never knew you could be so devious," Terra laughed.

She almost felt sorry for her father. If her mother's plan worked, Tink's family would be with her very soon.

Chapter 29

J'kar frowned at the report he was receiving from the trackers. He had flown one of the search vessels to the last location the human had been tracked to. They had lost the human's trail about halfway over the Eastern Mountains.

It was almost like he had disappeared into thin air. J'kar worried it wasn't thin air he had disappeared into, but into one of the Eastern Mountain clans. They were a smaller warrior clan who lived in the thick forest.

The warriors did not tolerate intruders to their region. If the human had just disappeared, there was a good chance he had been captured by them. Kneeling, J'kar looked at the ground, then up at the dense forest covering. Turning, he looked at one of the two trackers who had met him.

"What information do you have?" J'kar asked impatiently.

"He was traveling fast much of the way. His tracks suddenly vanished here. We found evidence of movement in the higher levels of the forest and suspect he was taken up through the higher canopy," one of the trackers said.

J'kar trusted the tracker's judgment. He had been raised in the region and often traded with members of the Eastern Mountain clan.

"Use what contacts you have to locate him. I want him dead," J'kar snarled. The tracker nodded and disappeared into the woods.

Borj moved to stand near him. Putting a hand on his shoulder, he murmured. "Do you think the Eastern Mountain clan will kill him?"

"Not if he gives them something worth keeping him alive," J'kar glared up at the trees. They were so thick not even the light from the sun could penetrate all the way through.

"What could he have to barter with?" Borj asked curiously.

"He took one of the vidcoms from the warship. It had information about Tink. If they know about her they may try to take her." J'kar turned to look at Borj with worried eyes. "If he tells of what human females are like, it could become very dangerous for her. They are known for their hunting abilities."

"Hopefully he will use his charming personality to convince them, and they will kill him as soon as he opens his mouth," Borj suggested.

J'kar shook his head. He could only hope Bachman would be such a fool, but he feared the human was much more cunning than they had given him credit for. J'kar nodded to several of his men and turned to return to the search vessel. He had been away from his bond mate most of the day and needed to see her, touch her, taste her.

* * *

Tresa waited until her bond mate came through the door later in the evening, watching him carefully as he strode through their living area. She had spent the afternoon planning ways to convince him to allow Tink's family to be brought to their world. She knew the council would go along with whatever he suggested. If he said Tink's family needed to be here, it would happen. She would like to meet Tink's mother, Tilly. She had fallen in love with Tink immediately, recognizing the gentle and loving touch of the tiny female.

Teriff looked at Tresa, trying to gauge her feelings as he strode through the room. When he had left his sons last night he had been burning with need. He had always found pleasure with Tresa, and loved her in his own way, but after last night he could not imagine looking anywhere else for pleasure.

He had never known a physical relationship with his bond mate could be so explosive. He had done some of the things his new daughter had talked about to Tresa, and her screams of release last night had haunted him. He had been hard for her all day. He was not sure of what he expected tonight. He had kept the restraints out in case he needed to use them again. He wanted to see if he could bring his bond mate of almost thirty years to pleasure again and again.

Nodding to her, he moved to his bedroom, planning on showering before dining. He had met with the council members to discuss the need to explore methods of bringing more human females to their world. He had also talked with J'kar.

J'kar had expressed the need to bring members of Tink's family to their world to support her during her breeding period. J'kar was fearful the stress would be too much without them and feared for his bond mate's health. The council had reluctantly agreed for Borj to bring one of Tink's family members to her.

They would go from there as to whether they would allow the rest. Talk of the missing human male had also caused a heated discussion. The council members wanted the human male eliminated as soon as possible.

Shrugging out of his clothes, he moved to the bathroom, commanding the water to flow. He stepped under the flow of the water and let his head fall forward. Closing his eyes as he let the water wash away the trials of the day, his thoughts turned to his bond mate, and he could feel his cock stir with desire. He started when he felt soft soapy hands move over his shoulders to wrap around his waist. Twirling around his eyes widened to find his bond mate standing naked under the flow of water, a soft smile curving her lips.

"I thought you could use some help bathing," Tresa said softly, running her soapy hands lower to grip Teriff's suddenly hard length.

"Tresa," Teriff breathed lowering his head to capture her lips. Pulling Tresa against his hard body, he groaned as she ran her hands through his short hair, returning his kiss.

* * *

J'kar let out a satisfied smile. He returned to find Tink in the shower. His sister, Terra, had stayed with her until his return. She assured him Tink had eaten and rested while he had been gone. She had bid him good-bye, promising to return the next day to spend time with his bond mate.

J'kar quietly let himself into the bedroom, not wanting to disturb Tink if she was still sleeping. Instead, he was drawn to the bathroom by the sound of water. Standing in the doorway, he watched as she ran her soapy hands over her body. J'kar was unable to contain the growl that escaped as she cupped her full breasts. Pulling his clothing off, he reached for the glass door, stepping in to join her.

Tink gasped as his hands took over the task of washing her body. Leaning back into his arms, she moved sensuously against him. J'kar turned Tink, pinning her against the wall. Tink moaned softly as she wrapped her legs around him, crying out loudly as J'kar buried himself in her over and over again.

He couldn't seem to get enough of her. J'kar wrapped his arms tightly around Tink, holding her against him as he pulsed deep inside her. Several hours later they lay together with Tink sprawled across J'kar's chest.

"I missed you today," Tink whispered softly, nuzzling her cheek across the light coating of dark hair covering J'kar's chest.

J'kar's arms tightened around Tink's small form. "That is your job," he teased, brushing a kiss across the top of her head.

"I talked to my father. The council has agreed to bring one member of your family here for now with the promise to see about bringing the rest over at a later time. Borj is to go," J'kar said.

Tink pulled herself up so she could look into J'kar's eyes. "Oh, J'kar, thank you!" Tears shimmered in her eyes. "Do you know who he will bring?"

J'kar's eyes twinkled. "I believe he wants to bring your sister, Hannah, first. He is quite taken with her image. I found him and Mak fighting over an image of you and your sisters earlier. Mak had stolen it out of his hand last night, and Borj was furious. Mak had to make a copy. I believe they plan on claiming your sisters."

Tink groaned. "They have no idea what they are getting into! Hannah and Tansy are nothing like me! I'm the baby of the family. I get along with everyone. Hannah is the oldest and is very independent. Tansy is the middle child. They are both as wild and unpredictable as they come. We never know what they are up to."

J'kar laughed. "I have my hands full with the baby of the family. I will let them deal with your sisters. He will also let your friend, Cosmos, know you are well."

"J'kar, I love you so much." Tink felt like she was going to burst she was so happy.

J'kar's eyes softened as he gazed up into Tink's beautiful dark brown eyes. "I love you too, little one. Forever."

Tink leaned down and kissed J'kar. She loved him so much. Tink couldn't help but smile. Her parents always told her everything always worked out for the best even if at first it didn't seem like it.

Now, she realized perhaps it did. She had been transported to the furthest star to the left and found her own Neverland. J'kar's family, including his father, and the council were hopeful about finding a species they could not only bond with but were successful with breeding with, and they were going to let her family visit. Life was not only good, it was great. Who would've thought?

To be continued... **Hannah's Warrior**

Enjoy this adventure? Continue it with **Hannah's Warrior**, book 2 of the Cosmos' Gateway series!

Preview of *Hannah's Warrior*

(Cosmos' Gateway: Book 2)

Synopsis

Hannah Bell, the oldest of the three Bell sisters, spends most of her time in the remotest parts of the world photographing endangered animals. She is also gifted with an extraordinary sixth sense which has saved her life on more than one occasion. When she senses something has happened to her littlest sister, Tink, she will do whatever it takes to protect her. What she doesn't know is her sister's best friend Cosmos' new science experiment has opened a portal to another world. A world she is about to be taken to whether she wants to go or not.

Borj 'Tag Krell Manok is the calmest of his four brothers, or so he always thought. The second oldest, he has been assigned the task by his father and the council to bring the sister of his brother's bond mate to their world. Borj knows deep down that Hannah is destined to be his bond mate, something he has hoped for since his first mating rite ceremony. What he doesn't expect when he meets her is her resistance or her independence.

When she is kidnapped by a rival clan, Borj will do anything to get her back. Hannah and Borj's escape into the vast forest of Prime draw them together in a fight not only for their lives, but for a deeper understanding and trust between two vastly different worlds. Borj discovers Hannah is a fierce and cunning mate while Hannah discovers Borj is the perfect warrior to protect and love her.

If you loved this story by me (S.E. Smith) please leave a review. You can also take a look at additional books and sign up for my newsletter at **http://sesmithfl.com** to hear about my latest releases or keep in touch using the following links:

Website: http://sesmithfl.com
Newsletter: http://sesmithfl.com/?s=newsletter
Facebook: https://www.facebook.com/se.smith.5
Twitter: https://twitter.com/sesmithfl
Pinterest: http://www.pinterest.com/sesmithfl/
Blog: http://sesmithfl.com/blog/
Forum: http://www.sesmithromance.com/forum/

Excerpts of S.E. Smith Books

If you would like to read more S.E. Smith stories, she recommends Hunter's Claim, the first in her Alliance series. Or if you prefer a Paranormal or Western with a twist, you can check out Lily's Cowboys or Indiana Wild...

Additional Books by S.E. Smith

Short Stories and Novellas
For the Love of Tia
(Dragon Lords of Valdier Book 4.1)
A Dragonling's Easter
(Dragonlings of Valdier Book 1.1)
A Dragonling's Haunted Halloween
(Dragonlings of Valdier Book 1.2)

A Dragonling's Magical Christmas
  (Dragonlings of Valdier Book 1.3)
A Warrior's Heart
  (Marastin Dow Warriors Book 1.1)
Rescuing Mattie
  (Lords of Kassis: Book 3.1)
Science Fiction/Paranormal Novels
Cosmos' Gateway Series
Tink's Neverland (Cosmos' Gateway: Book 1)
Hannah's Warrior (Cosmos' Gateway: Book 2)
Tansy's Titan (Cosmos' Gateway: Book 3)
Cosmos' Promise (Cosmos' Gateway: Book 4)
Merrick's Maiden (Cosmos' Gateway Book 5)
Curizan Warrior
Ha'ven's Song (Curizan Warrior: Book 1)
Dragon Lords of Valdier
Abducting Abby (Dragon Lords of Valdier: Book 1)
Capturing Cara (Dragon Lords of Valdier: Book 2)
Tracking Trisha (Dragon Lords of Valdier: Book 3)
Ambushing Ariel (Dragon Lords of Valdier: Book 4)
Cornering Carmen (Dragon Lords of Valdier: Book 5)
Paul's Pursuit (Dragon Lords of Valdier: Book 6)
Twin Dragons (Dragon Lords of Valdier: Book 7)
Lords of Kassis Series
River's Run (Lords of Kassis: Book 1)
Star's Storm (Lords of Kassis: Book 2)
Jo's Journey (Lords of Kassis: Book 3)
Ristéard's Unwilling Empress (Lords of Kassis: Book 4)
Magic, New Mexico Series
Touch of Frost (Magic, New Mexico Book 1)
Taking on Tory (Magic, New Mexico Book 2)
Sarafin Warriors
Choosing Riley (Sarafin Warriors: Book 1)

Viper's Defiant Mate (Sarafin Warriors Book 2)
The Alliance Series
Hunter's Claim (The Alliance: Book 1)
Razor's Traitorous Heart (The Alliance: Book 2)
Dagger's Hope (The Alliance: Book 3)
Zion Warriors Series
Gracie's Touch (Zion Warriors: Book 1)
Krac's Firebrand (Zion Warriors: Book 2)

Paranormal and Time Travel Novels
Spirit Pass Series
Indiana Wild (Spirit Pass: Book 1)
Spirit Warrior (Spirit Pass Book 2)
Second Chance Series
Lily's Cowboys (Second Chance: Book 1)
Touching Rune (Second Chance: Book 2)

Young Adult Novels
Breaking Free Series
Voyage of the Defiance (Breaking Free: Book 1)

Recommended Reading Order Lists:
http://sesmithfl.com/reading-list-by-events/
http://sesmithfl.com/reading-list-by-series/

About S.E. Smith

S.E. Smith is a *New York Times, USA TODAY, International, and Award-Winning* Bestselling author of science fiction, fantasy, paranormal, and contemporary works for adults, young adults, and children. She enjoys writing a wide variety of genres that pull her readers into worlds that take them away.

CPSIA information can be obtained
at www.ICGtesting.com
Printed in the USA
FFHW02n0249011018
48576778-52485FF